WHAT
MEETS
THE EYE

WHAT MEETS THE EYE

A MYSTERY

ALEX KENNA

CROOKED
LANE

NEW YORK

Published in the United States by Crooked Lane Books, an imprint of The Quick Brown Fox & Company LLC.

Crooked Lane Books and its logo are trademarks of The Quick Brown Fox & Company LLC.

Library of Congress Catalog-in-Publication data available upon request.

ISBN (hardcover): 978-1-63910-184-9
ISBN (ebook): 978-1-63910-185-6

Cover design by Kara Klontz

Printed in the United States.

www.crookedlanebooks.com

Crooked Lane Books
34 West 27th St., 10th Floor
New York, NY 10001

First Edition: December 2022

10 9 8 7 6 5 4 3 2 1

To DW, for putting up with so much

PROLOGUE

Six Months Ago—Margot

A LL WEEK LONG, I'd felt a fire in my belly. The spirit passed through me like lightning, brushes flying from wet canvas to wet canvas. Cooking was a waste of time, so I ordered takeout and drank whiskey. Sleep was out of the question. I cranked up the music and worked to the beat. Sometimes I sang along, dripping globs of color onto the floor. The paint went on smooth, like buttery icing. After a while, my brushes stayed in their jar and my fingers danced across the canvas. No bristles between skin and cloth.

Soon the images came alive. I'd been studying the Spanish greats: Velázquez, Goya, Zurbarán, Ribera. For them, it was all about bottomless darks with hints of warm, mellow light. I took a break from bold colors, indulging in white and yellow ochre on burnt sienna. The effect was sinister but mesmerizing. My hands pulled ghostly figures, one after another, out of a dark void.

I finally passed out around dawn on Thursday, just as the birds were starting to chatter. When I woke, it was midafternoon, and the magic was gone. My mouth tasted of bile and I felt like someone had scooped out my eyeballs and punched me in the sockets.

I wandered into the bathroom and looked at myself in the mirror. One of Goya's haggard witches stared back at me. My skin was the color of rice pudding. There were purple half-moons under my eyes and a cadmium streak in my hair. I picked at my nail beds, which were filled with prussian blue. The thought of cleaning them was exhausting, so I didn't bother.

My stomach let out a growl, and I stumbled over to the fridge. Nothing inside was fresh enough to tempt me. I turned to a soggy takeout container on the kitchen table. The waxed cardboard had partially melted, and a puddle of sauce oozed onto the table. A dead fruit fly was trapped inside the congealed orange liquid like a mosquito in amber. I pulled a half-eaten egg roll off last night's dinner plate and popped it in my mouth. At least it was still crispy.

After lunch-breakfast-dinner, I had an edible and downed a pot of coffee. I tried to get back to work, but the electricity was gone. The images that had been so alive last night now looked dull and mannered. A self-portrait smirked at me. I'd given myself a pouty red mouth like an Instagram twat and artificial Jolly Rancher–green eyes. It was pathetic. The last desperate cry of a lonely train wreck nearing forty. I felt worthless. I should go jump off a bridge or wander onto the freeway.

I lay on the couch for what must have been hours, binge-watching some show about British aristocrats and their servants. Thank god I wasn't born in nineteenth-century England. You can't be a British lady if you're a mouthy alcoholic who screws half the landed gentry. I would've done worse as a servant. I can barely fry an egg, and half the time I'm too paralyzed by my own shit to get out of bed. I'd end up as a consumptive whore blowing sailors for my supper in a London tenement.

The curtains were drawn, and eventually light stopped leaking in from the window edges. I usually do better when the sun goes down. But nightfall didn't bring me a second wind. It made me feel worse. I poured myself another drink and lit a cigarette.

My cell kept blowing up with a number I didn't recognize. I'd had this phone for six months and never transferred my contacts over from the last one. Now my caller ID served as a kind of litmus test. If someone hadn't reached out in half a year, they weren't worth my time. I let it go to voice mail and turned back to the aristocrats. The only decent one was dead now. This show was making me tired.

There was a knock on the door. Probably the neighbor coming to tell me her baby couldn't sleep because I make use of my electronics. I ignored it, took a swig of whiskey, and lit another cigarette.

Then whoever it was started pounding. "Margot, open up," said a loud tenor. The voice was familiar, but I couldn't place it. His tone had an edge of desperation. Could it be that cop from last week? A wave of dread flowed through me. My hands started shaking and a clump of ash fell on the couch. If I kept very still, maybe he'd think I wasn't home and go away. No, the TV was too loud. He knew I was in here.

I tiptoed over to the keyhole and gasped. My drink flew from my hand and shattered, coating the floor in alcohol and shards of glass.

CHAPTER

1

Present Day—Kate

S EVEN LETTERS DOWN: a heavenly body. Jupiter, that's an easy one. It even has a double meaning—a planet and a Roman god. Crosswords try to be cute like that. It's one of the many discoveries I've made since the divorce. You pick up a lot when you have long stretches of alone time. Give me another six months and I'll have more hobbies than a Jane Austen heroine.

The appointment alarm on my phone buzzed with a fifteen-minute warning. I looked down at the small screen. A new client meeting with some guy named Starling. The name sounded familiar, but that was about it. In moments like this, I wished I could afford a secretary.

I grabbed the three half-filled legal pads at the end of my desk and started flipping through pages of my barely legible scribble. I make up for my lack of organization by being a pack rat. My drawers are filled with half-used notebooks with tidbits from different investigations. When a case gets complicated, I rip out the scrawl and stick it in a separate folder with the client's name written in Sharpie. It's not exactly the Dewey Decimal System, but after thirty-six years of flaming ADHD, it's the best I've come up with. And frankly, I'm competent despite my shortcomings.

I'm a better-than-average PI. In another life, I was a damn good detective.

The relevant note was buried in the third legal pad, below doodles of a sad-looking older man and a girl in a beret hanging from a rope. I draw during client calls to help me focus. *Milt Starling: artist daughter killed self but father thinks murder.* Now our conversation was starting to come back to me.

A loud knock broke the silence. I looked over at the wood-and-frosted-glass door to my office and saw the outline of a stalky male figure. He was early. My hands grabbed for everything in sight, shoving things in drawers to clear desk space. I picked up a cheap red ukulele—another newfound hobby—and slid it under my desk. Normally I try to clean up before a client meeting, but today had slipped through the cracks. Hopefully it wouldn't cost me a job. The bills were piling up, and I wasn't going to give John more ammunition by missing a child support payment.

I raced toward the shadowy figure on the balls of my feet, trying not to sound like I was running. As I pulled open the door, the man on the other side presented me with a pink, fleshy hand. His skin was warm and coated in a briny sweat.

"Nice to meet you, Mr. Starling," I said. "Right this way." I gestured toward the clunky antique chair across from my desk. It's a ridiculous piece of furniture that I bought for thirty dollars at an estate sale. When I saw it in a Glendale living room sandwiched between floral lamps, it looked respectable. But when I was unloading it from my car, the leather seat cushion flew up to reveal a ceramic basin. That's when I realized I'd purchased a vintage commode. Now prospective clients sit on a nineteenth-century toilet and tell me their woes. I like to think it's symbolic.

Milt Starling held on to each arm of the sturdy seat and low-ered himself down with determination. He was not the youngest sixty-something I'd ever met. Then again, grief had probably taken its toll. I looked him over, trying to get a sense of his finan-cial status. He wore a blue Hawaiian shirt with yellow pineapples tucked neatly into a pair of khakis. His feet were sensibly clad in white socks and sneakers. The clothes were newish, and what was left of his hair had been mowed to within a half centimeter of his pink scalp. This wasn't a rich man, but he didn't seem to be struggling. He most likely wouldn't be one of the clients who skipped town or tried to pay me with their dead mother's wedding ring.

"What can I do for you, Mr. Starling?" I asked.

He glanced over at the graveyard of half-finished Coke bottles on top of my file cabinet. I felt my cheeks turn hot and mumbled an excuse about Wednesday being recycling day.

Milt cleared his throat and brought his eyes around to meet mine. His breathing was heavy and audible—almost like he was day-snoring. "I assume you've read the articles?"

Nope. I'd read nothing. Bupkis. All I had for preparation was my one-line note and my nasty little doodle. "I want to hear it in your words," I said. "Tell me about your daughter and what brought you in today." I really needed to get my act together. This guy was here about his dead child, and I was winging it like a lazy amateur.

He nodded and coughed into a beefy hand. "The police think she killed herself. I keep telling them Margot wouldn't do that. Especially in that horrible way. But they don't listen."

"What do *you* think happened to her?"

Milt looked at me with a touch of impatience. "I told you, someone killed her. They found her hanging from a chain in her bedroom. I keep telling the police she wasn't suicidal. They didn't even find a note." That didn't mean much. Most suicide victims are too distraught to remember the good-bye letter. "The timing doesn't make sense," he continued. "She'd been selected for a big exhibit in Italy. So why would she kill herself now?"

He sounded exasperated, like he'd made this pitch several times before. I had a feeling my door wasn't the first one he'd knocked on. "Hanging is not a very feminine way to kill yourself," I offered. "Women usually try to look pretty for whoever finds them."

Milt nodded. "Exactly. Margot liked to look nice. She cared about clothes, that kind of thing. She was a beautiful girl." With effort, he adjusted his weight onto one haunch and straightened the opposite leg to loosen the fabric around his pocket. This was about the time in an interview when a client shows me a picture of their loved one and I supply a generic *Your husband was so handsome* or *What a great smile* or *She looks happy*.

He flipped open his wallet and pulled out a photo of a stunning young woman. Black hair, big light eyes, and delicate features. She wore an amethyst-colored dress and a matching necklace.

"Wow, Mr. Starling, she looks like a movie star," I said truthfully. She didn't seem like the type of woman who would hang herself. Swallow pills, maybe. But only after doing her hair and makeup. Then again, I knew nothing about Margot, and stereotyping was a great way to wreck an investigation before it got started.

Milt nodded again. "She was beautiful and talented. None of the other artists could paint like her."

"Is there anybody you can think of who might have wanted her dead?"

He shook his head. "I've gone over it in my mind every day for months. I can't think of anyone."

"Did she have a boyfriend?"

Milt grimaced. "She didn't talk much about her love life."

I noticed a Saint Christopher pendant around his neck, like the one my grandfather used to wear. Maybe the Starlings hadn't approved of their daughter's bohemian lifestyle.

He went on. "There were a lot of boyfriends. A serious one in art school. She was seeing her dealer for a while, but I think he was using her, to be honest. Slimy little parasite."

This was interesting. If Margot had a drug habit, she could have been involved with some unsavory characters. "Her dealer?" I asked. "Did she—"

I must have made a face, because he quickly cut me off. "No, not like that. Her *art* dealer. He sold paintings, not drugs." Milt paused for a moment and stared at his hands. "You know, Margot's mother followed her on the gossip websites. She was always pictured with some rich businessman or useless party boy. One of them had bleached hair and wore eyeliner." He let out a bitter chuckle.

"Did anyone have a grudge against her?" I asked. He shook his head. "Even an argument that seemed minor at the time could turn out to be relevant."

"Not that I know of," said Milt. "But we weren't that close anymore. I saw Margot at holidays, and sometimes she called me to chat. When she was younger, we talked about everything. But once she went the art route, she kept it superficial."

I nodded and scribbled on my notepad. He wasn't giving me a lot to work with. Surely there was some ex or former business partner with whom she shared bad blood. "Was Margot unhappy?" I asked.

Milt shrugged. "She always sounded cheerful when we talked, but I know that world took a toll on her. They expected her to be this free spirit, and she put on a show for people. It must have been tiring after a while."

He hadn't really answered the question, and I had a feeling he was holding something back. "Did you get the sense that she was depressed?"

"Margot was diagnosed as bipolar," said Milt. He spoke these words in the dissociated monotone of a long-suffering parent. I'd heard that voice a thousand times when I worked family violence: *It's not Billy's fault, Officer. He's a sweet boy when he takes his clozapine.*

"Do you know if she was on medication?" If Margot went off her meds, it could explain why she decided to end things.

Milt shook his head again. "She tried, but it flattened her out. Margot said it took away her creativity and her painting got— *muddy* was the word she used. She just dealt with it when she got dark. But she's never tried to kill herself. She wouldn't do that."

I had an uneasy feeling. This would be the third case I'd taken from a grieving parent convinced their child wasn't the suicide kind. Each time I confirmed that the victim had taken his own life. Afterward, both clients called me a hack and left nasty Yelp reviews. This case would probably be more of the same: Margot was a troubled woman who "got dark" and refused to take meds. Plus, it sounded like her death was heavily publicized. The LAPD takes media cases very seriously. They would have explored every lead. Reopening the inquiry would just prolong the Starlings' pain without bringing them any closure.

"Mr. Starling, I need to be honest with you," I said. He winced, and I could tell I wasn't the first person to give him this speech. "I've worked suspected suicide cases before, and every time I've confirmed that the police got it right. I'm hesitant to take your money when, in all likelihood, I'd just be duplicating their efforts and wasting your time."

Milt let out an exasperated sigh. "You're the fourth private investigator I've talked to. Everyone says the same thing." He glanced again at the Coke bottle assemblage on my file cabinet. I get it; I'm used to being the fourth choice. "Look," he said. "Money's no issue. My daughter left us a fortune. But we need to know what happened to her. My wife is still in Ohio. I've spent the last six months away from home, trying to get answers. If you won't help me, I'll go through the phone book until I find someone who will. If that doesn't work, I'll start knocking on doors myself."

He was breathing heavily now. His barrel chest heaved up and down and his eyes shone. I can't stand it when older men cry. Men like my dad, from a generation where stuffing your emotions was the name of the game. I'll do just about anything to keep it from happening.

"Okay," I said, regretting it the instant the words left my lips. "I'll do what I can to help you. Give me everything you have on your daughter."

CHAPTER

2

Present Day—Kate

MILT HAD LITTLE to show for his time in Los Angeles. The file he had handed me consisted of obituaries neatly cut out of newspapers and culture magazines. The articles were organized chronologically. As the months passed, focus shifted away from Margot's death toward the rise in prices for her work. Her paintings were selling for fortunes. People couldn't get enough of them.

As I skimmed through the clippings, my phone chimed to life. *Reminder: you're picking up Amelia*, texted John, my ex-husband. Crap, I'd lost track of time. I must have forgotten to set my go-get-the-kid alarm. Or maybe I'd accidentally turned it off somehow. *On my way*, I text-lied.

John has custody, and I'm relegated to every other weekend. When I tell people this, they assume there's something wrong with me. Several parents won't even let their children play at my house. I get it—better safe than sorry. I overheard a group of moms speculating once: I'm an ex-cop, I must have anger problems. Maybe I even hit Amelia. I just grit my teeth and keep my mouth shut so she doesn't lose any more playdates. Besides, after hearing the real story, no one would let their kid within a mile of me.

I stuffed Milt's pile of articles into the giant tote bag I use for a purse and raced out the door. Today I had a rare weekday visit with Amelia so John could take Kelsey, his replacement wife, out for her birthday. And I was not off to a great start. Even with traffic in my favor, I'd get to the school fifteen minutes after the bell. Hopefully Amelia's teacher wouldn't complain to John. I was practically handing him ammunition for court. *Deadbeat mom can't even remember to pick up her kid.*

The teacher recognized me as I drove up to the meeting point. She was holding hands with two stragglers, my daughter and a little redheaded boy with a finger in his belly button. I couldn't help but feel a touch of relief at the sight of the other kid. I was only the second-biggest-loser parent today. Amelia was sucking her thumb. She looked sulky but adorable.

"Mrs. McDaniel?" asked the teacher. She looked like a horny dad's fantasy of an elementary school teacher, complete with caramel curls and a blouse with little blue flowers that matched her eyes. I thought of my own colorless ponytail and drab work sweater. To be twenty-five again . . .

"It's Ms. Myles, but please call me Kate." I gave her my best attempt at a winning smile. "I'm so sorry. I had a work emergency."

"It's fine, Ms. Myles, but in the future, pickup is at three fifteen," she said with restrained annoyance. "We had this issue a few weeks ago."

My cheeks burned as I nodded an apology. She was right. Last month a client melted down in my office after learning that her husband's "business trips" involved shagging the neighbor at a Motel 6. I had walked the poor woman to her car, forgetting my phone on my desk. When I got back, my pick-up-Amelia alarm had been blaring for ten minutes—just enough of a delay for me to hit pre-rush-hour traffic. Of course, none of that was the teacher's problem. "It won't happen again," I mumbled.

I stepped out of the car, leaned down, and gave my daughter a big hug and kiss. The embrace left a lip gloss mark on her cheek. I reached up to wipe it away with my thumb.

"Let's go, sweetie," I said. She lifted her arms in a signal for me to pick her up. "You know, Mommy can't do that anymore," I reminded her. Amelia rolled her eyes and climbed into the back seat. I forced myself to smile as I buckled her in. After the car accident, carrying my fifty-five-pound daughter has become basically impossible. I don't think she really understands why, and that's the hardest part. She doesn't get concepts like sciatica and herniated disks. To her, it's just another thing Mommy used to do and doesn't do anymore. The last time I tried to lift her cost me three days in bed and an epidural. They weren't trusting me with pills anymore by that point.

"Are we going to the tree house?" asked Amelia. The tree house is my daughter's descriptive name for my overpriced 650-square-foot shack in Silver Lake. It's tiny, wood paneled, and you have to climb a half flight of wobbly stairs to get to it, so tree house was the first thing that came to her mind. My little girl is used to living in the comfortable three-bedroom her dad bought in Sherman Oaks. He's been rolling in dough since he left the DA's office and joined a cushy defense firm. It also gave him a wonderful opportunity to meet and marry his summer associate, Kelsey. I would have preferred if he had waited till we were divorced to shag her, but that's another story.

"How about pizza, then ice cream, then bowling?" I suggested. When I was a rookie on the force, my training officer used to complain that her ex got to be "fun dad" while she was stuck holding down the fort. I would nod politely, not really paying attention. Now I get it. When you see your kid only a few days a month, all you can do is show them a good time. Flash forward and I've become "fun dad," struggling to maintain some semblance of a relationship with my kid.

"I want to play pirates," demanded Amelia.

Done. An hour later we were wearing bandannas and eye patches, eating frozen pizza, and watching Johnny Depp cackle at the screen. I even smeared burned cork on our chins for goatees.

Amelia got bored partway through the movie and started picking off her glittery nail polish. She puffed her belly out as far as it would go and balanced a pile of nail polish peelings on top. I'm worried that she's inherited my restlessness and attention problems. *Your family condition*, as John likes to call it. Kelsey suggested that we medicate her. She's already tired of dealing with Amelia's excess energy and constant messes. I told John he could drug her over my dead body. In a few years, if she's struggling in school, I might reconsider. But for now, we're leaving her seven-year-old brain alone.

The glum expression had returned to her face. "Time for dessert?" I asked. Amelia nodded. "Ice cream or shaved ice?"

We didn't bother changing into street clothes. LA is full of weirdos, and our pirate getups barely stood out. There's a vintage tiki bar and grill a few blocks from my house. The midcentury hideaway is festooned with hula girls, beaded curtains, and a hideous carved idol with rhinestone eyes the size of walnuts. The place is run by Charlie, a grizzled septuagenarian, and Otis, a blue-and-yellow macaw perched on his shoulder. Amelia is fascinated by Otis, and Charlie dotes on Amelia. I like to think it's because she's unusually cute. But it may be partly because Charlie knows about my custody situation and feels sorry for me. There was a low point when I lost it and started crying into the dragon punch.

Charlie and Amelia exchanged semitoothless grins. "How's it going, princess?" he said, with a raspy voice born from a half century of cigarettes and hard living. The bird was at its usual perch.

"Can I feed him peanuts?" asked Amelia. Otis cocked his head to the side, recognizing the name of his favorite delicacy. My daughter tilted her face to mirror the parrot's.

"Of course!" said Charlie. He reached a trembly hand into his shirt pocket and pulled out several unshelled nuts. Amelia knew the drill. She cupped her hands together like she was going to scoop up a mouthful of water. Charlie poured the bird food into her outstretched palms. "Remember, princess: hold the nut by one long end and keep your fingers as far away from his beak as you can."

Amelia gave a little gasp followed by a giggle as the bird's forceful beak pried away her offering. "Another?" she asked.

"Sure, sweetheart, go for it," said Charlie. Like clockwork, she gasped again when the beak snapped forward.

As she chuckled, an amazingly handsome bartender left a rainbow concoction in front of Amelia and handed me a Coke. The culinary masterpiece distracting my daughter was a snow cone served in a hollowed-out coconut and topped with condensed milk, an umbrella, and at least five maraschino cherries. It's called the Dreamboat, and Charlie invented it for Amelia. She had a look of pure contentment as she eyed the magnificent macaw and spooned cold bites of mango-flavored ice into her mouth.

I don't want her to have too much sugar, I could hear John saying. He's right—I know it. But Amelia and I have so little time together, I want our visits to feel fun and special, not like a depressing bimonthly obligation in mom's rundown shack. And it's one night. One night of junk food won't hurt her.

She downed her Dreamboat in minutes. I paid, and we held hands on the walk home. Amelia insisted that I sing to her, so together we belted out her favorite Taylor Swift song until we were back at the tree house.

My phone beeped. It was John reminding me to make sure Amelia brushed her teeth. *Really, John?* We did her nighttime rituals, and I sang more off-key tunes until she passed out in the oversized storage closet that my realtor called a second bedroom. It lacks a window, but it's painted princess pink, and the ceiling is covered with glow-in-the-dark stars.

I stroked Amelia's hair as she slept, basking in her presence. She rolled over toward the wall, and I noticed an orange stain on her chin from dessert. Why hadn't I remembered to have her wash her face? After all these years, I was still winging it. I've never been a natural at parenting. Even when Amelia was a baby, I was overwhelmed by the physicality of motherhood—holding her fragile little body, supporting her wobbly head, rocking her for hours when her little body went red and rigid from colic. Then there was the terror of trimming her nails without cutting into a tiny fingertip—little digits wriggling like sea anemones.

Amelia's pink kitty-clock meowed the hour. It was already eleven, and I'd been sitting at her bedside for ages. My back screamed in agony as I slowly stood up and made my way back to the living room. There was a scarf-and-junk-jewelry collection on the floor, dirty plates on the TV table, and a half-eaten pizza on the counter. The whole place smelled like pepperoni. Just thinking about cleaning made me tired. So I lay down on my couch and started cruising the internet for information about Margot Starling.

I scanned her Instagram for angry ex-boyfriends. Instead, I found row after row of artwork. The paintings were mostly realistic, but her colors were enhanced, almost day-glow. Margot drew her subjects from the dark side of life. There were prisoners in what I recognized as Men's Central Jail, wildfire victims driving an aging station wagon away from a burning ranch house, someone's suit-clad legs walking past a junkie collapsed on a downtown street. I was repulsed but at the same time unable to tear my eyes away from the screen.

And then there was Margot herself, just as lovingly painted and staring at the viewer as blood dripped down her nearly naked body. "Yeah, not suicidal at all, Milt," I muttered, shaking my head as I closed the window. This woman clearly had issues. Still, I had to admit, I was intrigued.

Then I clicked on an article about the death investigation and saw a familiar name. And my faith in the police work-up on her death took a nose dive.

3

Fourteen Years Ago—Jason

THERE IS NOTHING on earth I dread more than art school critiques—called *crits* for short. It's a cute little word for an exercise in public humiliation. Each week, a victim is asked to bare his soul in front of the class. This jury-of-your-peers listens, quietly sharpening their knives until it's time to eviscerate the sacrificial lamb. The victim is left holding his brushes and innards. When it's over, he picks up the bleeding carcass of his artistic vision and refashions it into something new. Until it's time to rinse and repeat.

If you think I sound melodramatic, you've never been to art school. And you've certainly never taken a class with Clark Von Heller. I signed up for a painting seminar with the famous critic because everyone says he's a genius. But I soon learned that he's more interested in torturing students than passing on wisdom.

Clark starts every class with a slideshow of works by famous living painters. These minilectures are designed to expose us to *the contemporary visual world*. He accompanies each slideshow with brutal witticisms and an explanation of why each artist is a derivative hack. Clark especially enjoys picking on women and minorities. One day he railed against Elizabeth Peyton, who "makes washed-out paintings of celebrities she wished were her friends." Another time, he treated us to Dana Schutz, who "made it big at twenty" and "never bothered to learn the basics of figure drawing."

After this introduction, we usually separate and return to our respective easels. Then Clark makes the rounds and tells each student that their colors are garish or their foreshortening is off. Last week, my piece was deemed too "art school," whatever that means. The more he likes you, the more he tears you down. Silence from the great man means there's nothing worth commenting on.

Today we were in for what Clark described as a real treat. The treat consisted of a live model: an Eastern European beauty with long, curly hair. The woman entered the room wearing a dingy floral robe, which she quickly removed and placed on a bench in the corner. After years of professional modeling, she had no qualms about baring her body in a roomful of artists.

She strode over to a stool in the middle of the classroom and assumed a modest pose. I started to relax. I've always had a knack for figure drawing, and this spritely beauty had an interesting face, with almond-shaped eyes and a slight gap tooth. So of course, Clark had to ruin it. He walked up to the model and slipped a hideous Halloween clown mask over her head. It was another one of his sick mind games.

"I don't want to draw a fucking clown," I muttered under my breath.

"What was that, Jason?" asked Clark.

"Nothing, Professor," I said meekly.

"Clark, we need some tunes to get us in the mood," cooed Margot. Fucking bitch. Margot Starling is his favorite. She's gorgeous, and she can draw better than any of us. But most of all, she's adaptable. Margot figured out early that you win over Clark by treating his suggestions like manna from heaven. And being extra sadistic in crits. After Clark, she's the meanest one. Worst of all, her comments are always spot-on.

Clark wandered over to me and silently watched me work. I could feel his hot breath on the back of my neck and sense the weight of him. I tried to paint without moving my elbow too far back and poking him in his impressive belly. After what felt like an eternity, he reached past me toward the small dolly that held my pallet and brushes. His charcoal-stained fingers clamped onto the straw of my still-full iced coffee and slowly pulled it out. "Can I borrow this?" he asked. It wasn't really a question.

"Um, sure," I mumbled. I mean, why would I want a straw for my drink that I'm drinking?

He walked away without uttering another word, sauntered over to Margot, and started giving her feedback, using my straw as a pointer. "You've got to be kidding me," I muttered.

Margot responded politically, as always. "You're right," I heard her say. "That line totally situates her. I was concentrating so much on her figure, I didn't realize she was floating in space." Barf.

I kept looking at my painting, but my concentration was off. Maybe it was Clark's rejection. Maybe it was the damn clown mask. I was up for crit today and didn't feel prepared. My work wasn't ready to be shared. I was still trying to figure out a few things, find a way to use formal technique to talk about community and family—things that mattered to me. But right now, my paintings were a hodgepodge of ideas that didn't quite come together.

After two hours of aisle time, Clark told the model to get dressed. The young woman removed her mask, slipped back into her robe, and left the room.

"Sacha, what do you have for us?" asked Clark. At least I wasn't going first. I watched Sacha remove two canvases from the painting racks against the wall and line them up in the front of the classroom. She looked a little seasick. The weakest of our group, Sacha is Clark's favorite target. Today her paintings were even more mediocre than usual. This was going to be a bloodbath. I felt nauseous, like when you're watching a horror movie and you know a torture scene is coming up.

Clark clapped his hands together to get our attention. "Everyone, gather around." He walked over to the boom box and turned off the music. Sacha stood next to her work, and we all sat on the floor in a semicircle around her. "What are we looking at?" asked Clark.

"Um," stammered Sacha. Her face turned red and she stared down at her fidgeting hands.

"Speak up," snapped Clark. "Someday you're going to have to talk about your work with dealers and collectors. Or at least that's the goal." She winced at the obvious dig. "You'll need to sound confident, and you might as well start now."

"The series is about my personal experience with woman-hood," Sacha explained. This was not a good start. She was speaking too fast and her voice was about an octave higher than normal. Sacha turned to the first canvas. It was a painting of her own head on the body of a naked Barbie doll. "This piece addresses my struggle with anorexia. Barbie is a symbol of the unrealistic cultural expectations for women." She'd practiced this spiel, but it came out sounding hesitant and defensive. And feminism was not one of Clark's favorite topics.

"Tell us about the second painting," he ordered. By now Sacha was nervously pulling at her fingers, like she was trying to remove a pair of latex gloves. "Stop fidgeting," he snapped. "You're not competing in the sixth-grade spelling bee. You're an artist talking to a group of professionals."

Sacha looked at the audience. There were an equal number of snickers and sympathetic winces. Her eyes met mine, and I tried to give her an encouraging smile.

"Tell us about the second painting," Clark repeated.

The painting was sepia toned and showed an old woman in a simple dress with a scarf around her hair. Her awkwardly drawn fingers clasped together in her lap. It was clear that Sacha simply lacked the drawing chops to render hands: an unforgivable flaw in such a straightforward composition. "I wanted to contrast my first painting with the idea of femininity from my grandmother's generation," she stammered. "This is painted from a photograph of my grandmother, who died last year. She came over to escape persecution in Romania with her husband, who she married at seventeen. She raised fifteen children. Three of them died in childhood. My grandmother defined femininity in terms of being a wife and a mother and never gave a second thought to things like how she looked, which she viewed as trivial."

"All right, what does everyone think?" asked Clark. His eyes landed on Margot, whose face showed intense concentration. She was crafting her words, preparing for battle.

"I can tell this is a subject you feel really passionate about," I offered.

Clark rolled his eyes. "That's sweet, Jason, but this is a crit, not art therapy. Margot, what do you think? Let's start with the first painting."

Margot sat up a little straighter. "First of all, Barbie as a symbol needs to be permanently retired."

"Thank you," said Clark. "This isn't 1980. Barbie was passé twenty-years ago. I'm banning her from my classroom. It's like trying to be edgy with an ironic Mickey Mouse." Sacha started fidgeting again, trying to maintain her composure. "What else, Margot?" prodded Clark.

"Both of these concepts require a level of drawing mastery that you don't have yet," Margot continued. "Especially the one of your grandmother, since it's obviously from a photo." Clark nodded approvingly. "And the sepia-tone thing is very derivative. It's clearly a reference to a photograph and makes me wonder why I'm not just looking at a photo, which would give me all kinds of visual details that your painting lacks."

"Exactly," agreed Clark. "What about the juxtaposition of these paintings?"

"Honestly," said Margot, "that's the part that bothers me the most. You're kind of exploiting your grandmother. Your work is allegedly about showing women as complex human beings, but you've reduced her to a one-dimensional baby-making machine. I don't believe that she was indifferent to her looks. She was a wife with a husband to keep happy. I want to know what she did to feel feminine when she set about making baby number twelve. This tells me nothing about her other than that she was haggard and wore a headscarf. And frankly, it's a little on the sentimental side, given everything this woman survived. I think you owed her a deeper exploration."

"Well, Sacha," said Clark. "How do you respond to that?"

Sacha's eyes filled with water. "I guess," she began. Her voice started to crack, and it was clear she couldn't hold it together. "Excuse me," she stammered. "I need to use the restroom." Sacha stepped over the crossed legs of one of our classmates and speed-walked toward the door. I could tell she was going to lose it by the time she reached the bathroom. As she grabbed for the handle, Clark let out an exasperated sigh. "Well, painting isn't for everyone. Jason, what do you have for us?"

4

Present Day—Kate

I F YOU POURED pure testosterone into a cookie mold and baked it, you'd get Detective Ron Bennett. He's the type of cop destined to either make captain or blow up his career with a bad shooting.

We worked patrol together in my early years. Bennett was always experimenting with some new fad to enhance his sense of manliness and intrigue. He tried chewing tobacco for a while, until the sergeant told him his breath made her sick. Next it was CrossFit, which was all he talked about until he injured himself lifting a three-hundred-pound barbell without checking his form. Then his obsession shifted to tattoos. Within a four-month period, Bennett went from tattoo-free to fully sleeved. Our sergeant called him "the gangster," since his ink gave him a passing resemblance to some of the guys we were trying to bust.

Bennett could be a good investigator when he wanted to. But he liked big, easy-to-solve cases. Fast glory and no risk of stalling out. If a wife's lover stabbed her husband and left prints at the scene, Bennett was all in. The hanging death of a mentally ill artist was a different animal. It was the kind of case you could spend a year investigating just to confirm what everyone suspected: she killed herself. I had no doubt that he'd put in a cursory amount of work and then dropped it like a hot potato, eager to move on to something more straightforward.

The day after seeing Bennett's name in an LAPD press release, I left three messages on his voice mail, all of which went unreturned. Bennett tends to think he's too important to answer the phone. Too busy serving warrants and knocking down doors to check his voice mail. I've often wondered how many tips disappear because he can't be bothered to pick up the receiver.

On my fourth try, a robotic female voice informed me, "The party you are trying to reach has a mailbox that is full. Good-bye." And then a dial tone.

"Lazy asshole," I muttered, pounding my fist on the table. I winced and rubbed my hand against my thigh until it stopped smarting.

Might as well show up at the station and try my luck in person. I felt a pang of nostalgia as I drove up to the LAPD headquarters on Spring Street. With a price tag topping four hundred mil, the limestone-and-glass structure elicits a mix of pride and controversy. When it was built, critics called it a grotesque waste of money and a symbol of government excess. I never made it to one of the elite units housed inside. But I'd come here often enough for trainings or to brief the higher-ups. The field stations where I spent my career were low-ceilinged, asbestos-ridden shacks with chronic mold infestations. A bit of the headquarters money would have gone a long way to improving a place like that.

I parked in a nearby lot and walked past the station's manicured landscaping toward the front steps. A strung-out young man with dirty-blond hair was rolling around on a grassy patch in front of headquarters, conversing with the voices in his head. He might have wandered over from a homeless encampment a block away. Our eyes met and his expression darkened. "What you looking at, bitch?" he shouted. I lowered my gaze and walked steadily toward the entrance. The young man quickly forgot me and returned to his state of ecstasy.

Inside, I approached the front desk, which was manned by a young rookie with freckles and a bit of softness under the chin. "I'm looking for Detective Ron Bennett," I said. "Can you tell him Kate Myles is here?"

The guy at the counter shot me a dubious glance. "Is he expecting you?"

I looked down at my civilian attire and felt a weird mental disconnect. Two years ago, I could have gone up to the elevator, no questions asked. In my head, I was still the detective who moved easily through these spaces, who followed in her dad's footsteps and dedicated her life to solving murders. But that version of me was dead.

Of course I didn't say any of that. "No, but we worked patrol together at Newton."

He seemed to relax. "Oh, I'll tell him you're here." I winced as he picked up the phone, remembering something else I should mention.

"Also, I have a concealed carry permit, and I do have my gun. I'm sorry, I should have left it at home." The desk officer looked confused—he must have thought I still worked here and was just in plain clothes. "I retired on disability a while back," I explained, feeling my face grow hot. "I'm privately employed now. I'm sorry, I wasn't thinking."

"Um, can you go put it in your trunk?" he suggested.

"Sure thing." This was mortifying. I was glad he hadn't called Ron yet. I knew a civilian couldn't waltz into headquarters with a gun. I must have been acting on muscle memory. My PI work hadn't taken me down here yet, and being at headquarters was like going back in time to when I still felt normal.

I forced myself to snap out of self-pity mode as I walked back to my car. The sun-heated metal of my trunk burned when I touched it. Looking around to make sure no one was watching, I took my Glock out of its holster and placed it inside. As I walked back to HQ, I spotted Bennett coming up the sidewalk. Three forty-five and he was calling it a day. Some things never change.

"Ron!" I called, jogging up to him. I did my best to plaster on a glad-to-see-you smile.

"Is that you, Myles?" he laughed. "I didn't recognize you in your civvies. The hair looks good." I instinctively reached up and touched the back of my head. On the force, I'd always worn my hair in a tight bun so it didn't get in the way. Now I let it hang down to cover the surgical scar on the back of my neck.

"Thanks," I said awkwardly.

"God, we were just talking about you the other day. We were wondering what happened. You were a good officer. Why'd you leave?"

Fucker doesn't beat around the bush. But I needed something from him, and sating his curiosity might put him in a sharing mood. I'd give him the short version.

"Car accident. I went out on medical."

Bennett looked unimpressed. He would add this to his women-don't-have-the-stones-for-police-work file. "Ah, Myles, you shouldn't let that stop you! If you're up and walking, they can find you a job. Think of all the old-timers sticking around and waiting out their pensions."

It's too late now, you patronizing asshole. I contemplated bringing up the time he missed a preliminary hearing to nurse a hangover and the DA had to dismiss the case. "Not much to be done now," I said. "At any rate—I don't know if you heard, I'm doing the PI thing."

"No shit?" he said. Apparently he hadn't heard.

I needed to get down to business. The gun incident had already rattled me. I didn't feel like listening to him Monday-morning-quarterback my life choices. "Milt Starling hired me to look into his daughter's death."

The smile evaporated from Bennett's face. "Yeah, that's a non-starter. She killed herself. The chick was crazy. She used to cut herself and everything."

Milt hadn't shared that little nugget.

"Seriously, you're wasting your time," he continued. "We followed every lead. There's no question about what happened."

"I'm sure you were thorough, but I want to put this guy's mind at ease. Is there any chance I can peek at the file? As a professional courtesy?"

Bennett shook his head. "Myles, professional courtesy is for other agencies. You're not law enforcement anymore. You know I can't be giving out sensitive case materials to any member of the public."

His words were like a slap in the face. "I put in ten years with LAPD. I had the second-highest solve rate in Southside Gangs—"

Bennett cut me off. "All that's in the past, Myles. You quit. You didn't have to. You know I can't cut you any special favors. I'd have a line of private detectives outside my door. And there are rules about giving out active case information."

"So it *is* active?" I pressed. "I thought you guys cleared this one. You're still looking into it?"

Bennett let out a frustrated laugh. He placed his hands on his hips and looked up toward the ceiling, like he was asking God to deliver him from his tormentor. His shirt sleeves rode partly up his forearms, and the tattoos poked out. I thought I could see Tigger from Winnie the Pooh. Manly. "Myles, you're killing me," he said.

"Ron, at least give me a straight answer." Bennett's eyes darkened. He hates it when a woman shows the slightest hint of irritation. "Is the case closed or not?"

"The homicide investigation is closed," he said coolly. "But there's an ongoing forgery case. I guess some rich people bought her paintings and thought they were fake. There's a fraud detective looking into it." He said *fraud detective* dismissively, like he was discussing someone who barely warranted his attention.

"How do you know about the forgery case?" I asked. "I can't imagine you have a lot of interaction with those guys."

Bennett's ego took the bait. "No, it's not exactly my thing. He emailed me for some documents. Said they might be relevant to his investigation."

"What kind of docs?" I asked.

Bennett let out an exasperated sigh. "I don't know, Myles. Why don't you ask him?"

"I will. What's his name?"

"Delgado. I think you know him."

I felt the corners of my mouth turn upward. If Luke Delgado was involved, this case was far from over.

5

Two Years Ago—Kate

I ALWAYS WOKE UP right after the crash. In my dreams I was back in uniform, my car part of a line of police vehicles forming a barricade across the 110 freeway. We were supposed to stop a drug-crazed joyrider who'd carjacked an old lady and taken cops on an hour-long chase across the county. I could hear the Channel 5 News helicopter circling overhead, capturing the scene. For some reason, police chases are always crowd pleasers. I'd watched the news footage later, after the asshole plowed through the barricade and sent my vehicle careening into the sound wall.

Everything looked so antiseptic from a thousand feet in the air. Even when the junkie's ride turned over and burst into flames. You couldn't hear him scream in the video footage. But I hear him in my dreams. Those animal howls still haunted me.

I usually woke to the crunch of metal and the smell of smoke, my body's way of telling me the pain pill had run its course. This time, I was spared the dream's finale. I heard keys turn in the door and my eyes opened. I rolled over on my yoga mat. Our bed was too soft to support my back in its current condition, so lately I'd taken to the floor. Pushing myself up with my right arm, I rose to a sitting position. I could hear the vertebrae in my neck shift as I moved, and pain radiated down my arms.

My husband had walked in and gone into the extra bedroom he uses as a home office. He hadn't bothered to check on me or even acknowledge my presence. "Hi," I said tentatively. I touched the screen of my phone: it was early; John should still be at work. "What are you doing back here?"

"I forgot my flash drive," said John. "It has something I need." His voice sounded strained, like each word was a grudging concession. I watched him walk into the kitchen and pour himself a glass of water. "Have you been lying there all day?" he asked. "You could have picked up at least."

I looked over at the kitchen. Dishes from breakfast and dinner were piled near the sink. It was probably starting to smell. Before the crash, because John's job kept him working late most nights, I'd done the housekeeping. My standards of neatness had never met his expectations under the best of circumstances. And now I'd let everything go. "I was planning to," I said, "but I had a bad movement, and my neck muscle seized up. It kills if I try to look down."

John took a gulp of his water, and I thought I caught him roll his eyes as he turned away from me and set his glass down by the sink. His movements were tense. Even the sound of the glass meeting the counter gave a sharp little bang that seemed to be telling me off. He didn't ask how I was feeling. For heaven's sake, a minute ago I'd been lying on the floor unconscious in the middle of the day. I knew we had problems, but a touch of empathy would go a long way.

"I'm doing the best I can," I said quietly.

"It's been two months, Kate," he replied. "Two months, and all you do is lay there. You don't even bother to pick up. I mean, what do you want me to say? Meanwhile, I'm working twelve hours a day and busting my ass prepping these depos. I don't think I'm asking that much. Did you even put the laundry away?"

No, I hadn't. I'd started the washer. Then I'd tweaked my neck, so I'd taken a pill and fallen asleep. The clean clothes were sitting in the washing machine, where they'd been for six hours, waiting to be transferred into an already full dryer.

"John, I'm in pain," I started to explain. He walked out of the room while I was midsentence. It was like he couldn't stand the sound of my voice. I heard him throw the dry things into a hamper and transfer over the wet ones. He walked back into the room but failed to meet my eye. His face radiated controlled fury.

"What is going on?" I asked. "I know I haven't been the best partner lately, but for god's sake, I need spinal surgery. I don't even know if I'll be able to work again." He had turned and was looking at me, but his face said he was just waiting for me to finish speaking so he could leave. "I feel like I'm barely hanging on here, and I need your support."

"I really don't have time for this, Kate," said John, rubbing the bridge of his nose with his thumb and index finger. "I'm going to be at the office until midnight as it is."

There was silence, and I looked at his face, trying to detect a sign of love or residual warmth. But he just looked through me. I could feel in my bones that I'd already lost him.

"Would you still be here if it wasn't for Amelia?" I asked. The question hung in the air between us. The pregnancy was why we got married in the first place, but I'd spent five years constantly working to please him, doing everything I could to turn the relationship into an alliance. I'd nailed the "for better" part of our vows, but right now we were decidedly living through the "for worse." And we didn't have enough heat to see us through to the other side.

I looked at John, eyes pleading. He broke my gaze. "I don't have time for this, Kate. I have to go." I watched him walk toward the door. Tears streamed down my cheeks, but I said nothing. It was almost time to pick up Amelia from day care, and I was in no state to care for a five-year-old. She needed her mom to be happy and energetic, to play with her and read her stories. I wasn't due to take my next pill for another two hours. But I couldn't move without some pain relief. I popped one in my mouth and swallowed. Then I set an alarm for fifteen minutes, lay back down on the mat, and closed my eyes.

CHAPTER

6

Present Day—Kate

Luke Delgado had been my training partner for six months in Southside Gangs. We were a great team, racking up solve after solve.

Working a homicide in gang territory is more of an art than a science. You have to glean information from people who have every reason to hate cops and who know that snitching could get them killed. Half the battle is building trust, and Luke was great at it. His technique was simple: he showed up, he cared, and he didn't bullshit people.

As the junior member of the duo, I was responsible for the paperwork. Early on in our partnership, Luke taught me a powerful lesson: not everything gets recorded. I don't mean sketchy shit, like if we thought we'd gotten the wrong guy. We weren't psychopaths. I mean that there are witnesses who will tell you stuff, but who'd rather chew off their own tongue than take the stand. People with no realistic ability to relocate and for whom a subpoena would be a death sentence. For those witnesses, you listen, but if you can make your case without them, it stays off the record.

Luke's work ethic and willingness to occasionally bend the rules boded well for me. If he was asking for material from Bennett, he clearly had his doubts about what happened to Margot. But I couldn't help wondering what he was doing in the fraud section. Luke used to say that after working a murder, nothing else mattered. So how did he end up chasing down embezzlers at CarMax?

I glanced at my watch. It was late in the afternoon, and Luke would probably be leaving soon. Since I was already here, maybe I could squeeze in a meeting. I scrolled through my list of contacts until I found his cell number. Luke picked up on the second ring.

"Myles?" he asked, laughing. "Where the hell have you been?"

He was never one to mince words. "Hey, Luke, how's it going?"

"Well, they stuck me down here in the land of paperwork, but other than that, I can't complain. What's up?"

"I'm doing private investigations now. Margot Starling's dad hired me to look into her murder." I paused for a second and waited for a response. Luke was silent. "Bennett just told me to take a hike."

"Sounds like Bennett," he said.

"Pretty much. But he let slip that you were nosing around this too."

"That's not exactly true. I'm looking into a forgery. It's a different case." His tone had cooled considerably. He'd be tougher to crack than I'd hoped.

"Listen, I'm already outside headquarters. Let me buy you a beer. I want to ask you a few questions. At the very least, we can catch up, since it's been about a hundred years."

There was more silence on the other end of the line. "Luke, I'm not contagious, okay? It's not like if you talk to me, you'll end up quitting too."

"I know you're not contagious." He was on the defensive.

"Good. Then meet an old friend for a drink. Like I said, I'm gonna do my due diligence and ask you a few. If you want to stonewall me, we'll move on to other subjects, like my train wreck of a life and whatever's new with you. Capisce?"

He let out a sigh. "I'll come for a drink, but I won't discuss the case."

"Fine," I said. "Cole's in twenty minutes?"

"Sounds good."

Cole's French Dip is a downtown landmark. The low-ceilinged, subterranean dive is decorated like an old-time saloon: dim lighting, blood-red Victorian wallpaper, sepia-toned antique photographs. A small sign directs you to the favorite booth of Mickey Cohen, legendary twentieth-century crime boss. There's a discreet door in the back of the restaurant that leads to a posh speakeasy called Varnish. This setup makes for great people watching. Sloppy-sandwich fans pour themselves into leather booths while trendy, gazelle-like hipsters pass through on their way to the chic joint on the other side of the wall.

I slid into a narrow two-person booth across from the dark-wood, mirrored bar and ordered an iced Irish coffee. It's as good as it sounds. And yes, I'd suggested this ridiculous restaurant because I was craving one and I have no self-control. I sipped my decadent concoction and eavesdropped on a couple at the bar. A lithe Audrey Hepburn lookalike with a pixie cut was explaining her dissertation on Icelandic folk tapestry to a bearded hipster. He was glancing periodically at his phone. I fantasized about putting my arm around her and whispering that she could do better. *Run before you end up raising a kid with a narcissistic man-child who doesn't appreciate you.* She caught my eye and I looked away.

Luke walked into the bar, and I watched him for a moment before waving him over. He had an energy in his step, like a tightly coiled spring. And he looked good, with that same tall, wiry build that I remembered.

There's something about Luke. I've always had a bit of a crush on him. He has an intense face that draws you in, with big dark eyes and a broken nose from a run-in with a so-called sovereign citizen—one of those folks who believe they exist outside the government's authority and tend to get into scuffles with law enforcement. When Luke was on patrol, he stopped the nutjob for speeding and found an arsenal in the back seat. According to a manifesto in the glove box, the driver was en route to the district attorney's personal residence. Luke managed to cuff him, but not before taking a right jab to the nose that permanently changed the topography of his face. Union insurance would have paid to fix it, but he never bothered. Luke said he didn't need to look like a handsome prince to do the job. He might have been prettier before, but I like the busted schnoz, and still find him extremely attractive.

In the six months we were partnered, we developed a slow-moving chemistry—the kind that sneaks up on you. We weren't instantly buddy-buddy, but after a while, we had an ease with one another. One night we grabbed a drink after a difficult solve. We laughed about the day's adventures, and I realized I felt totally natural around him—in stark contrast with my home life, where John had me walking on eggshells. Suddenly, Luke was on my mind all the time. I'm not sure how much of it was him and how much of it was the pleasure of being around a man who enjoyed my company and laughed at my jokes.

After I transferred to another station, I deliberately fell out of touch with Luke. I was trying to fix my marriage, and talking to him didn't exactly engender feelings of matrimonial satisfaction. Besides, he was engaged to a pretty nurse named Martha. They'd probably tied the knot by now.

Luke spotted me and made his way across the bar. He smiled and slid into the other side of my booth. "What is that thing?" he asked, nodding toward my drink.

"Iced Irish coffee. It's like a milk shake with whiskey and caffeine. Want one? Unless you'd prefer something more dignified."

"I'm good. But you got a little . . ." He motioned toward his mouth with an index finger. Great, now I had a whipped-cream mustache. What an auspicious start. I dabbed at my upper lip with a napkin.

"Thanks," I said. "Seriously, what can I get you?" He waved a hand dismissively and walked up to the bar. Martha was a lucky girl.

The bartender, a multi-pierced beauty, quickly met Luke's eye and hurried over to take his order. She giggled at something he said and raced off to mix an old fashioned. Luke was holding on to the bar with his left hand, and I noticed that he wasn't wearing a wedding ring.

Luke smiled again as he set his drink down on the table. "Kate Myles," he said. "What've you been doing? The rumor mill's been spinning out of control, but I never got the full story."

I really didn't want to talk about it, but I had dragged him out here on the pretense of catching up. "I heard a few rumors myself," I said. "Apparently I fell into the tar pits, got indicted, and joined a convent."

"Yeah, I heard those ones. You also got canned for sleeping with a gang leader."

I rolled my eyes. "Nothing so glamorous. It was medical. I got hit by an evading drug DUI and messed up my back." Part of me wanted to tell him the whole story, but shame made me bite my tongue.

Luke winced. "Sorry to hear. Are you okay now?"

I forced myself to smile. "Better. After surgery and a year of physical therapy, I can sit for more than an hour without my back screaming at me."

"Have you thought about rejoining the force?" he asked.

"At least once a week," I said truthfully. "But it's not realistic at this point."

He opened his mouth to say something, but I quickly cut him off, eager to talk about anything else. "What about you?" I asked. "When are you and Martha gonna tie the knot?"

"Actually, we split up," he said. This threw me for a moment. Luke and Martha had seemed like a great couple. And I was used to thinking of him as safely unavailable.

"Sorry to hear." I hoped my face didn't betray anything. "You seeing anyone now? You got that uniform starched?"

He laughed. It was an inside joke. Our former sergeant had a charming little saying about LAPD blues: starch that uniform, hang it in a corner, and a certain type of woman will hump it all night long. Misogyny and offensiveness aside, it's true that some women can't see past the badge and gun.

"Nah, I keep the uniform in the closet these days. Not much need for it in the fraud world." He was dancing around the question, but it wasn't the time or place to pry into his personal life.

"So why are you in fraud, anyway? You should be chasing down murderers, not spoiled grandsons who got creative with nana's checkbook."

Luke looked uncomfortable. Something had happened—it was written all over his face. The empathetic part of me wanted to stop pressing. But if Luke had gotten into a pickle and been transferred to Siberia as punishment, he might be feeling bitter and willing to help me.

"Let's just say I pissed someone off and this is where I landed." I nodded, and there was an awkward silence.

"It could be worse," he added. "I'm still a cop." He looked up at me, trying to gauge whether I'd taken offense. I hate it when people tiptoe around my feelings. "Sorry, I—"

I shook my head. "It's fine," I cut in. "I'm a big girl. You were saying?"

Luke's hands were fidgeting nervously. He had nice hands, actually. Strong.

"You know how the bureaucracy works," he said. "I pissed off the wrong person. On the bright side, I get to leave every day at four thirty. Hell, I'm even thinking of taking up a hobby. Any suggestions?"

"Knitting?" I offered. "Flower arrangement? Dressage?"

He laughed. "All right, dressage it is. Why didn't I think of that?"

"Listen," I said, deciding to turn the conversation back to business. "Milt Starling hired me to look into his daughter's death. He doesn't think it was suicide, and I'm getting the sense that you don't either."

Luke flinched. "Myles, you know I can't talk about an active investigation."

"It's not active," I reminded him. "Bennett wrote it off as a suicide and closed the case. But you're not convinced, which is why you're asking him for documents."

"No," he said. "I'm looking into a claim of art forgery—not murder. I asked for a few things that were relevant to my case."

I rested my elbows on the table and leaned in, locking eyes with him. "You didn't request the coroner's report to solve an art forgery." Bennett never mentioned the coroner's report, but I know Luke. He wouldn't have been able to resist.

He said nothing but looked away from me, letting his eyes wander out toward the bar.

"Luke," I said, "we both know Bennett was eager to drop this and move on to an easy solve. Work with me. Margot probably killed herself, and as soon as I confirm that, I'll be out of your hair. But what if she didn't? If I find anything, I'll come to you. I can be an anonymous source. If you solve the murder, it could be your ticket out of purgatory."

He glared at me. "I don't need your pity."

I let out a self-deprecating laugh. "Have you been listening? I'm a low-end private eye with chronic back problems. Believe me, I don't pity you. I do think your talents are being wasted, and I'd bet my right arm that you're gonna work this case behind the scenes—with or without me. Why not team up? They've already screwed you over, so let's do this. Off the record."

He bit his lip but continued to glare at me. The silence felt like an eternity. "I'll send you the coroner's report," he said finally. "That's something you could have gotten without my help."

"Excellent!" Luke shot me a dirty look, and I reminded myself not to gloat. "Sorry, I know, I'm a jerk. Can you give me a preview? Anything stand out?"

He hesitated for a moment before giving in. "The death was ruled inconclusive."

I could feel myself grinning. "I knew you had your doubts."

Luke shot me a warning glance, and I simmered down. "Margot had nail marks on her neck, which could be consistent with suicide or strangulation," he continued. "She could have been clawing at the chain or at someone's hands. One of her nails had male DNA underneath. Just a tiny bit. They could have been scraped clean."

"Do we know who it came from?"

He shrugged. "It was analyzed—Bennett had that done at least—but there wasn't enough for a conclusive match. It could be from an attacker, a boyfriend. Hell, she could have bumped into someone in the street and accidentally scratched him."

"What about DNA in the rest of the apartment?

He shook his head. "There was a used condom in her bathroom trash, but it didn't come back to anyone in the system."

I nodded, making a mental note to dig into Margot's social life.

Luke glanced at his watch. "I gotta go," he said. "I'm going to my sister's for dinner." As he spoke, he took a small spiral notebook out of his pocket and slid it across the table.

I looked up in surprise. He shot me a meaningful look, and I nodded gratefully. "Thanks, Luke. I'll be in touch if I find anything."

"Do that," he said. "Honestly, she probably did kill herself, but she deserves a proper investigation." I pocketed the tiny notebook.

After he left, I ordered a roast beef sandwich with atomic pickles and garlic fries. A celebration of my first real lead—and the chance to reconnect with Luke. Seeing him again had really lifted my spirits. But the ease of our friendship had always depended on our mutual romantic unavailability. Now that we were both single, I wasn't quite sure how to act around him.

7

Thirteen Years Ago—Peter

S HE PULLED UP to the gallery in a forest-green Ferrari, which
was probably rented for the occasion. A starving student spending borrowed money on a luxury car—just to make an impression
on me. I hadn't seen ambition like this since Damian Hirst in the
nineties. So far, I was impressed.

I watched her walk in—straight-backed and confident. She
wore a matching dark-green evening gown, long sleeved and
ankle length, but with a neckline that plunged nearly to her navel.
The satin material clung appealingly to her pert little breasts. She
strode right up to me, stretched out her hand for a firm shake,
and asked if I was ready to go.

Margot Starling first came to my attention when I was checking
out the UCLA thesis show. I try to go to the graduate student exhi-
bitions at the top art schools to scope out fresh talent. Some classes
are better than others. This year Yale and Columbia were duds.
Good technicians but nothing special. One future high school art
teacher was actually making stripe paintings. I complimented him
on his originality. I think the poor sap thought I was serious.

I almost never offer to represent a new artist right after grad
school. But I like to know who's up-and-coming. If someone

makes an impression on me, I let a lesser gallery develop his talent for a few years. Once he's ready to peak, I scoop him up and turn him into a blue-chip artist. I rarely take someone on without seeing several years of consistent work and at least one good solo show. But there are exceptions to every rule.

UCLA's class was strong that year, but Margot was the clear standout—a photorealist who knew how to handle paint. And her subjects were provocative. Seeing her paintings on the wall, I put her in the category of someone to watch for a few years. If she continued to grow, I might revisit her work and think about adding her to my stable.

Then I met her in person, and everything changed.

You could tell she had a fire in her belly. And she had a face made for the cover of *Artforum*, green eyed and raven haired. Her beauty was almost obscene. That kind of thing matters when you're selling art. Especially a woman's art. You don't believe me? Pick any top-selling woman artist and check out the pictures from her youth. Chances are she's at least a seven. Yayoi Kusama, Eva Hesse, Cindy Sherman—all lookers in their day. Even Georgia O'Keeffe had a killer body. That doesn't mean they're not supremely talented. But it does mean that their homely sisters of the brush got swept into the dustbin of history. It's not fair, but this is a business—an aesthetically driven one at that.

Margot told me in that first meeting that she was curating her own alternative MFA show in a downtown warehouse. It was called *The Body Mortified*, and it included several student pieces that the school refused to exhibit. With the confidence of an old pro, she asked me if I'd I like to attend. She even offered to pick me up at my gallery.

I had turned down similar invitations over the years, but something told me Margot was the real deal. At the very least, she'd make for pleasant company. An appealing diversion. I could invite her for dinner, order a bottle of Dom Pérignon, and give her some stock career advice. One thing would lead to another. She had worn a slinky dress at the MFA show, and I could see those hard nipples poking through the thin fabric. Just enough to whet my appetite.

So, intrigued, I agreed to come. And true to her word, Margot picked me up in a beautiful car and whisked me off to the Arts District in downtown LA—a rose-colored name for a neighborhood next to Skid Row with low foot traffic and a strong scent of urine.

She'd rented a run-down warehouse as a backdrop for the show. The place was a dive, and there were holes in several of the small-paned industrial windows. But it had atmosphere. As a curating choice for a show of tortured art, it was spot-on. A handful of picketers shouted at us—something about killing babies. I turned to Margot in confusion. She smiled, and her eyes lit up mischievously. "One of our artists, Sacha Warren, makes art about abortion. A few of the locals aren't happy about it. She claims to have killed her fetus in the tub as performance art, but no one knows if it's true. I suspect it isn't."

The melodramatic Miss Warren was one of the first exhibits. She was plain, pimply, and angry looking—the type of face you couldn't sell even if she had talent. Her contribution consisted of a badly drawn acrylic painting of a fetus, predictably titled *My Child*. Margot paused and waited for me to take in the underwhelming work. I realized that she was planning to walk me through the entire show. Normally, the presumption would annoy me, but Margot was the only asset I was potentially interested in acquiring, and I wanted to see how she thought.

"Why did you include her?" I asked after we moved on. "You can actually paint, and I think you know that was amateur hour." I stared at her point-blank. She didn't wilt. Instead, a broad smile stretched across her face. "I thought the protesters would add atmosphere. A picture of Sacha's work is on all the flyers."

We passed a well-built young man doing what I suppose he thought was a performance. He wore a severed bull's head like a mask, and his naked body was drenched in animal blood. His enormous phallus was pierced and attached to a small chain that was connected to a car engine. Next to him sat a small record player. The spinning disc softly played "La Vie en Rose." Visually, it had some allure—Chris Burden crucifying himself to a Volkswagen meets Picasso's minotaur. The Piaf was a bit contrived, but in this setting, it had an appealing, eerie quality. Back in the nineties, I might have been interested, but the piece was already dated—a fatal flaw for the avant-garde. I wondered if Margot knew that. It suddenly dawned on me that this entire show might be curated with the sole aim of setting the scene for her own work. She was like a stage manager, and her less talented comrades were props. It was a cynical move, and I was intrigued.

Margot's casual demeanor suddenly changed when we passed the station of a young realist. He was a tall, Scandinavian man with high cheekbones and blue eyes so light they were almost translucent. The work was technically good—beautiful nudes, many of them depicting Margot. But subjectwise, the pieces were boring and unsellable as contemporary art. They belonged in some boutique gallery in a seaside town next to frosted glass sculptures of women and horses.

Margot probably knew this, but she spent five minutes singing his praises. She dropped references to Ingres and other neoclassicists. It was a hell of a sales job—not that I was buying. I caught her exchanging a glance with the strapping young Viking. They were lovers, you could tell. There was a certain charge between them. His work didn't go with the rest of the show, and she'd clearly included him out of a sense of obligation. I wondered if they were serious. No matter; she'd betray him if the stakes were high enough.

"How long have you been together?" I asked as we walked on to the next exhibit.

Margot blushed. Her porcelain cheeks turned a dusky rose, and she looked impossibly beautiful. I wondered how long it would last. Skin like that tends to crack after a while, like fine china. "Two years. Is it that obvious?"

"Yes," I said. "Are you in love?" It was a completely inappropriate question, but we both knew I had all the power.

Margot hesitated. "Yes, although as an artist, I believe I have a responsibility to keep myself open to all of life's experiences."

Good girl. We were approaching the end of the warehouse. Along the back wall, I saw an enormous green velvet curtain. Instinctively, I knew this was Margot's. I wondered if it was a reference to Courbet's *L'Origine du Monde*, which depicts the vagina of a reclining woman. In the nineteenth century, it was considered so shocking that the owner kept it behind a little green curtain, a thin membrane that only heightened the scandal and titillation of its subject matter.

"I'm guessing this is you?" I asked.

Margot smiled and pulled on a green-and-gold braided rope with a tassel at the end. The emerald curtain slid back to reveal the shock of my life. The subject of the painting was unmistakable—and there I was, front and center. In the picture, Margot wore the same green dress she had on now. She and a female assistant had rolled up their long sleeves. Her brow was creased with concentration lines. Her right hand held a long dagger and her forearms strained as she worked hard to cut through the muscle and tissue in my neck. I lay before her on bloodstained white sheets. My eyes had gone dull and my mouth hung open.

I stared at her in excitement and horror.

"It's based on Artemesia Gentileschi's painting *Judith Slaying Holofernes*," she explained. I knew this, of course. She'd faithfully copied the composition of the Renaissance painting.

"Gentileschi was a Renaissance painter who was raped by her father's assistant," Margot continued. "She testified against him in court, undergoing torture to prove her veracity. He was convicted and ordered to toil as a galley slave. But the pope fancied his work, so the rapist served no time. And all Artemesia could do was seek solace among her brushes."

"Tell me about your painting," I stammered.

"Well," she said. "You're the most powerful dealer in the world, and you can make or destroy a career with the snap of your fingers."

I felt my attraction grow more intense.

"You're also a collector in your own right and a very wealthy man. So naturally, I cast you as an allegory of the art world—its pressures and its crushing barriers to entry."

I had to have her.

"And if the art world can be Holofernes," she continued, "I cast myself as Judith. The artist. A connectionless girl from a middle-class family. All I can do is express myself by making paintings. But of course, the irony is that I can't say anything, can I? I'm powerless, and you can destroy me in the blink of an eye. If I've offended you, which I hope I haven't, you can blackball me for the rest of my career."

I stared at her. She still projected the same confidence. But I noticed that she was breathing a little heavily. The exposed tops of her breasts quivered and blushed a bit pinker. She was terrified and doing her best to keep it together. This was the make-or-break moment of her life. I realized that her painting and the entire show was an elaborate audition she'd conceived of to impress me. It was brilliant. She was playing the odds. If I didn't like her, I could discard her or even blacklist her. But statistically, she'd be waiting tables by this time next year anyway. On the other hand, if I took the bait, I could make her career. And the truth was, she wasn't as powerless as she made out. The work and the setup were sensational. It was the stuff of legend. Rumors of this night would get out, and if I rejected her, I'd look petty and shortsighted. Or I could discover her and be seen as a visionary.

Margot was looking directly into my eyes. Desperately waiting for me to say something. So I obliged. "Margot. I'm going to represent you, and you're going to be a phenomenon."

8

Present Day—Kate

THE DAY AFTER our conversation at Cole's, I pulled out Luke's notebook and reacquainted myself with his chicken scratch. Most of the notes didn't mean much to me, but one name leapt off the page: Clay Banks. Even I had heard of the famous music producer. He was married to a talented soul singer named Babette, whose mournful ballads had been a staple of my mid-divorce men-are-scum phase. There was a memorable night where I drank whiskey and smashed framed photos to her debut album. Not my proudest moment.

Underneath Banks's name, Luke had scrawled *Renate Rossi— advisor* and a phone number. I left a message without expecting a response, but Renate called me back within minutes. She sounded genuinely glad to hear from me, and we set up a meeting for later that morning at the Banks residence. I did a happy dance as I hung up the phone. What can I say? The idea of ambling through the private digs of music royalty had its appeal.

The mansion was situated in the hills north of Sunset. I followed Renate's directions until I came to the entrance of a narrow lane with a sign reading *Private Road*. Long driveways extended from either side and I wondered what celebrity hideaways I was passing. The Bankses' property began at the fourth driveway on the left, which wound its way up the hillside. I pulled up to a wrought iron gate, pressed the button on the intercom, and announced my presence. The gate opened inward with a low electric hum.

Giant palm trees lined the long stone driveway, creating purple stripes of shade. When I reached the top of the hill, a magnificent Spanish-style home came into view. A small-boned woman in all black stood on the colonnaded veranda. One hand rested on her hip, and the other shaded her eyes from the sun. As I drove up, she motioned toward a guest parking area off to the side.

I pulled into the designated spot and glanced down at my blue jeans, which had a tiny hole forming at one knee. Maybe I should have dressed up for this. My default is casual verging on sloppy. As a cop, I hadn't often crossed paths with the wealthy elite, and that hasn't changed much in my new life as a low-rent PI. But as I sized up the beautiful house and the elegant woman, I felt sorely out of place. Between my clothes and my ten-year-old Ford Fiesta, I was probably not what she'd been expecting.

The woman in black nodded as I approached. Her chestnut hair was cropped in a chic bob and her small, birdlike face was punctuated with a shock of coral lipstick. Her only decoration was a gold pendant that looked like an ancient coin. "Hi, Kate, I'm Renate," she said.

I shook her extended hand. "Thanks for making time to meet me."

"Of course! As you can imagine, this whole business has been embarrassing and stressful for my clients. They're eager to get this sorted out. Remind me again, how you're connected to the investigation? Do you work with Detective Delgado?"

I felt myself blush. "Not exactly. I'm a private detective working for the Starling family."

A look of annoyance flashed across Renate's face, but she quickly recovered. I'd been deliberately vague on the phone, hoping that dropping Luke's name would get me a meeting. "I can certainly understand their frustration," she said. "It's a valuable

WHAT MEETS THE EYE

estate, and they need to maintain its integrity. You know, I reached out to your clients a few months ago but never heard back."

Not exactly surprising. Their daughter had just died, and they were in mourning. "I'll let them know we spoke," I assured her. Renate's agenda was to prove a forgery, and she'd be more forthcoming if she thought of the Starlings as allies. I decided to stay away from the death angle for now and focus on the potential fraud.

"Have you spoken to Peter yet?" she asked.

"Who?"

"Peter Garlington? Margot Starling's dealer—"

"Of course, *that* Peter," I said quickly. "He's next on my list."

Renate gave a tight-lipped smile. She was not impressed. "Well, why don't you come in. I'll show you the painting." She led me into a spacious foyer with vaulted ceilings supported by wide oak beams. A portrait of the glamorous couple hung in the entryway. Babette wore an ice-blue Grecian-style dress. Her smiling husband rested a proprietary hand on her pregnant stomach. They looked happy and impossibly gorgeous.

"The painting is in the library," said Renate. "Please follow me." She led me through a keyhole-shaped doorway into a large room with built-in bookcases extending up to the ceiling. Every inch of wall space was taken up by books or works of modern art. Countless frames tugged at my retinas, and I willed myself not to gawk at the luxury.

My host walked over to a table where she'd laid two oil paintings of a naked woman side by side. In one, the subject stood on the edge of a subway platform as a train raced down the tunnel. She looked confidently at the viewer, her hair blowing in the wind as the machine hurtled toward her. The other piece was a more traditional portrait, but the style was similar, and the sitter was clearly the same person. "What am I looking at?" I asked.

Renate pointed to the subway painting. "This is a genuine Margot Starling." She moved her finger over to the other work. "This is what my client bought a few months ago at auction."

"How do you know it isn't real?" I asked. "They're both very good."

Renate sighed. "Maybe I should start at the beginning. My client is arguably the most important contemporary art collector under forty. He bought the genuine Starling years ago from her real dealer, Peter Garlington. It was early in Starling's career, and my client showed incredible foresight in making that investment. His wife, a serious collector in her own right, has a passion for Starling, and an interest in contemporary female artists."

I nodded to show I was listening, but my mind was distracted by a more immediate concern. The venti latte I'd consumed on my drive had worked its way to my bladder. I wondered what the chances were that Renate would let me use her client's bathroom. Maybe there was one for the servants.

"Anyway," said Renate. "Before she killed herself, Margot Starling was one of the most sought-after living female artists. To buy an original, you had to go through Peter, or wait until something was put on auction at Sotheby's or Christie's. But after Starling died, a mainstream art dealer in Venice Beach claimed to have discovered a cache of her early works. This guy has no business going *near* a Starling."

I was amused by the level of contempt in her voice. Apparently she outranked this guy on the food chain. "What's his name?" I asked. "The mainstream dealer?"

"Aksel Berkland. He specializes in second-rate abstract expressionists, or at least that's how he represents himself. The truth is, Berkland never recovered from the 2008 recession. He makes his living hawking acrylic monstrosities—the kind of thing you'd see in a Florida hotel room."

I had to suppress a smile.

"Anyway, the Starlings seemed like a windfall for Berkland," she went on. "He claimed to be selling the work on consignment for a person close to Starling who wanted to remain anonymous."

"Is that common?" I asked. "For a seller to stay anonymous?"

Renate moved her head from side to side, thinking. "It's not uncommon. You see it a lot at auctions. They'll describe a piece as 'from the collection of a prominent European family,' that kind of thing. People have all kinds of embarrassing reasons for liquidating assets, and some collectors just want to maintain their privacy." Her cell phone rang, and she looked down at it anxiously. "Excuse me, I need to take this."

This was my chance. "Wait!" I called, a note of desperation in my voice. "I'm sorry—could I use the bathroom?"

My host was visibly shocked. Apparently art princesses don't have bladders. "If you really need to. The hall bathroom is broken, but there's a guest bedroom down the corridor with an attached bath—you can use that."

Renate answered the call with a brusque greeting and nodded for me to follow her, speaking into the phone as she went. "Richard, the client has given permission to go up to thirty. I need you to get him to raise it to fifty. This is the best Richter that's come on the market in years."

She pointed toward a door and then stepped away. I walked through the bedroom into a giant bathroom that reminded me of a Romanesque chapel I'd seen on my honeymoon in France. There was even a pair of stained-glass windows. Instead of an altar, the room was endowed with an enormous Jacuzzi. I stared at the tub as I relieved myself, thinking of my moldy, shower-only bathroom. What would it be like to take a bath in this thing?

I fixed my lipstick and then started back toward the library. Hearing my footsteps, Renate hung up and sped over to me. She didn't want to leave me alone, I realized. I might try to run off with the painting. Tempting.

"Where was I?" asked a breathless Renate.

"The mainstream art dealer got his grubby mitts on a Starling," I said. Renate flinched, and I regretted my snark. Insulting a witness is not exactly a great investigative move.

"Anyway," she continued, "Berkland did what he could to create a veneer of legitimacy. His pieces lacked provenance, so he donated a couple to museums."

"Provenance?" I asked, raising an eyebrow.

She sighed, growing impatient with my ignorance. "Documentation of prior sales and ownership. It's how collectors know they're getting the real thing. But Berkland's pieces supposedly came from an intimate of Margot's. According to him, no prior bill of sale was ever generated."

"Why is that suspicious?" I asked. "I'm sure artists give away paintings all the time."

"The art world is riddled with fakes," she explained. "A lack of provenance is a red flag for a discerning buyer. Berkland tried to fix that by donating paintings to MOCA and the Cleveland Contemporary."

"Did the museums think they were fake?" I asked.

"No," she admitted. "But smaller museums don't do the same level of diligence when accepting a gift. They don't want to risk offending a donor by questioning authenticity. Have you heard of Mark Landis?"

I shook my head.

"He's a forger who amuses himself by donating fake paintings to museums. A curator friend of mine accepted a work from him. It was terribly embarrassing."

"You think Berkland donated a forgery to MOCA so he could turn around and tell buyers, 'If *they* thought it was real, it must be'?"

Renate nodded. "Yes, that's exactly what I think."

Now this was interesting. If she was right, we were dealing with a very sophisticated criminal. Someone capable of manipulating people at every level of the art world. And someone bold enough to try. "How did your client get involved with Berkland?" I asked.

"A few months after Berkland sold his so-called Starlings, a couple of the paintings showed up at a local auction house called Hughes. You've heard of it?"

I hadn't, but I nodded anyway.

"They do a lot of California-interest shows, you know, Remington cowboy figurines, western landscapes, that kind of thing. Starling would normally be out of their reach. Another serious red flag. Anyway, my client wanted to buy a Starling for his wife's birthday, so he sent his former art adviser to the Hughes preshow to check it out. She assured my client that it was genuine without doing any due diligence. Sadly, it appears his trust was misplaced."

"What made your client suspicious?" I asked. So far, two museums and another expert thought the painting was real. I couldn't help but wonder if Renate had ginned up the controversy to poach a major client. On the other hand, being a snob with good business instincts didn't make her a con artist.

"He brought the piece home and gave it to Babette, and she could instantly tell it was fake."

"And you agree?"

Renate nodded. "There's no doubt in my mind."

"How can you be so sure?" I pressed.

"Starling painted a lot of self-portraits, but they always had a dark, psychological twist. The body was just a vehicle for her to explore deeper ideas about society or the mind." She pointed to the picture on the left. "This one is well crafted. But it doesn't have her edge."

"Maybe she hadn't found her voice yet?" I suggested. "You said these were early works."

Renate shook her head. "No. The hand isn't right. Or the signature." She turned back to the subway piece. "Margot painted quickly and energetically. She used thick paint and hardly any medium. This one"—she gestured toward the supposed forgery—"is more cautious and doesn't have her vigor."

"What's wrong with the signature?" I asked. The penmanship on the two pieces seemed nearly identical.

"It's not a bad effort," conceded Renate, "but the color is wrong. Margot signed her canvases in whatever color her brush happened to be dipped in. Whoever made this painting had obviously studied her writing. But they signed in white—against a dark background. It's almost garish. Margot wouldn't do that."

Maybe. Or maybe Renate had seen an opportunity when a music mogul showed up at her door with complaints about his picture. I mentally checked myself. Something about Renate rubbed me the wrong way, and I couldn't let that cloud my judgment. She was an expert in this stuff, and I didn't know the first thing about painting. "So how do you prove it's fake?" I asked.

Renate smiled sadly. "With older paintings, there are scientific techniques we can use. Last year, a client wanted to buy a Turner, but it didn't look right to me. We tested the pigments and found phthalo blue, which didn't exist until the twentieth century. But forensics won't work for artists using contemporary methods. Disproving authenticity is nearly impossible."

"Can't you talk to experts?" I pressed.

"In the past, you could ask an artist's foundation to weigh in. For example, if you thought you had a Warhol, you'd send it to the Andy Warhol Foundation, and they'd either certify it as real or stamp *Denied* on the back. But that little word destroyed fortunes in an instant. After an avalanche of lawsuits, the foundations got out of the business of authentication."

"Surely there are scholars you can turn to? Like art history professors or something?" I asked.

She shook her head. "For an artist as new as Starling, no one's had time to study her work. The market really heated up in the past few decades. Everyone wanted to discover the next big thing. But who's to say that a brand-new artist never varies the type of white paint she uses, or that her college drawings weren't a little shaky? If she's alive, she can disclaim ownership. But if she's dead, there's no one to speak for her."

"In other words," I said, "either the picture is real, or we're talking about the perfect crime."

From the look on Renate's face, I could tell she agreed.

9

Present Day—Kate

A s I was leaving the Banks residence, my phone chimed, alerting me to a new email from Luke. The body of the message contained one word: *Enjoy*. I clicked on the single attachment and smiled as the coroner's report popped up.

My eyes dropped to a familiar name at the bottom of the screen. I had known Dr. Greco well in my homicide days. Most coroners like talking shop with police officers. Few people in their personal lives want to hear their war stories. You can't chat someone up on a date or at a PTA meeting about your rough day sifting through bone fragments. By contrast, homicide detectives ask about every grisly detail. Cops and coroners tend to have a good working relationship, but Greco takes it to a new level—especially with female officers. He seems to relish the process of describing each death, talking with his long, bony hands as he pantomimes a stabbing. Other female detectives I know have had similar experiences with him. It's a little creepy, but I always took it in stride and was grateful for the detailed explanations.

As a civilian, scheduling a meeting with a coroner can involve weeks of bureaucratic hurdles. But I'd known Greco for years, and he'd probably let me jump the line. I wondered if he even knew I'd left the LAPD. A bit of confusion could work to my advantage.

I glanced at my watch. It was already after one o'clock. Autopsies are done in the morning to free up the afternoon for testimony or other meetings. With any luck, Greco was just twiddling his thumbs or catching up on paperwork. I scrolled through my contacts and selected his number. He picked up right away. "How are you, Detective?" he asked. "Long time no see!"

"Hi, Doctor. I'm doing an investigation involving a young woman you examined. I know I'm supposed to schedule things through the front office, but I was hoping you'd have time to chat this afternoon?" I held my breath. Arguably, I was still a detective. No obligation to correct him over the phone. I could tell him in person about my new job—after he penciled me into his busy calendar.

"Sure!" he said eagerly. "I'm just finishing up lunch here. How's three o'clock?"

"Perfect. See you then."

The Department of the Medical Examiner consists of two buildings. The main structure is a lovely redbrick Victorian. In the early days, this was where all the action happened. Today, it's reserved for offices and meeting rooms. Autopsies are performed next door in a grim utilitarian building with the temperature and meat-and-antiseptic smell of a budget grocery store.

Here, I texted Greco as I walked into the lobby. I sat down on a mission-style chair next to a young man with bad acne who was bouncing a baby on his lap. The man barely seemed old enough to be a father, and I wondered what tragedy had brought him in today. Our eyes met, and I shot him a sympathetic smile.

A few minutes later, Greco waltzed in through the front door in a clean set of scrubs. His eyes lit up when he saw me. "How are you, Detective?"

"Please—call me Kate," I said, feeling a pang of guilt at my earlier omission. "And I should probably mention that I'm no longer with LAPD. I'm working as a private detective for the Starling family."

Greco nodded, but he didn't seem troubled by this information.

I followed him up the central stairway. He looked even more spectral than I remembered: tall and bald with sloping shoulders and the boyish frame of a cycling fanatic. I'd seen him leaving work once in an orange exercise onesie. My brain has yet to recover.

"I'm not surprised that the Starlings have questions," said Greco.

My ears perked up. "Why's that?"

He opened the door to the conference room and held it for me as I entered. I took a seat at the scruffy wooden table. Greco sat down right next to me and placed his report and a manila envelope of photographs in front of him. "I was surprised to read in the paper that LAPD had settled on suicide."

This I wasn't expecting. "You don't think she killed herself?"

He let out a sigh. "Honestly, it's a weird case. Like I told the detective, it could be a suicide, but I have serious concerns."

Fucking Bennett. It was just like him to gloss over the coroner's doubts if they inconveniently delayed an easy solve. "Why? What do you think happened?"

"Well, according to our investigators, the decedent was found hanging by her neck from a chain," he said. "Typically, with a hanging, a rope goes under the chin and then extends upwards, past the ears."

As he spoke, Greco brought his thumb and forefinger together and made a U-shaped motion under my chin. The pantomiming was unnecessary but par for the course with him. "A strangulation happens lower—towards the middle of the neck." To illustrate, he made a sort of claw with his fingers, which he positioned near the middle of my throat.

"Okay," I said, with a strained smile.

"In a hanging," he continued, "I wouldn't normally expect to see a broken hyoid bone."

This caught my attention. "But according to your report, her hyoid had snapped. So was she strangled?"

Greco shrugged. "Possible, but not necessarily. You do occasionally see broken neck bones with a heavy rope, and here you have a metal chain. It's an unusual implement, so I don't have much of a basis of comparison."

I nodded, trying not to show my growing frustration. Basically, he was telling me that from a scientific standpoint, Margot's cause of death was still a mystery. It was the worst of both worlds. I couldn't tell Milt that the police had gotten it right. But Greco hadn't given me anything solid to challenge their conclusion either.

"I also relied on the investigation report," said Greco. "Our investigator spoke to a neighbor of the decedent." He paused and flipped through the documents in front of him. I leaned in to look at the paragraph he was pointing to. This page wasn't included in the PDF that Luke had sent me. I wondered if he was deliberately keeping me in the dark or if Bennett hadn't shared it with him. "The neighbor heard arguing a day or two before the body was discovered," continued Greco. "A week before that, the same neighbor heard a man's voice and a slap coming from her apartment and saw the police arrive."

"Sounds like domestic violence," I said. "Doesn't that support strangulation?" Now *this* was a game changer. If Margot was murdered, whoever had shown up at her place and hit her the week before was probably the killer. It was a crucial piece of information, and the fact that Bennett had potentially kept it from Luke bothered me. It suggested that he had his own doubts about the quality of his investigation and didn't want another detective judging his shoddy work.

"It certainly could mean strangulation," agreed Greco. "It could mean she was being abused and that someone put pressure on her neck. But it could also mean that the bones in her neck were broken on a different occasion, which doesn't rule out suicide."

There was probably a domestic violence report from the week before, or at least something about a disturbance of the peace. In fact, there was probably a 911 call, since something had to have generated the police response. I wondered if Bennett had bothered to check. But I could follow up on that later. Right now, I needed to finish interviewing Greco about his medical conclusions. "Did anything else about the autopsy make you think of strangulation?" I asked.

He turned his body toward me. I thought I noticed a slight upturn at the corners of his mouth. He had spread his legs wide so that his skinny thighs were on either side of my own tightly closed legs. Here we go, I thought. It's mime time.

"Yes," he said. "With strangulation, you tend to see a lot of claw marks. If my hand is around your throat—" He moved his curled fingers toward the middle of my neck, inches away from my skin. Any closer and I might have said something. I flinched, and my back pressed against the chair. "You'll try to grab my hand and pull it away," he continued, dramatically moving his fingers downward from my neck area. "In the process, you might inadvertently scratch yourself, causing injuries to the neck."

"Did you see that here?" I asked.

Greco nodded. "Yes, to some degree."

"Would you see that from a hanging?"

"You could," said Greco. "If the person's neck didn't snap right away and they changed their mind about wanting to die."

"And here the neck didn't snap?"

Greco shook his head. "No, it didn't. I also saw a fair amount of bruising to the throat. Women's necks tend to bruise easily, but I don't see that a lot in hangings. Of course, that could be attributed to the chain, which is hard and heavy."

"Anything else?" I asked. This autopsy was raising more questions than answers.

He nodded. "I saw signs of petechial hemorrhage in her eyes, which is more common in strangulation. I don't usually see much hemorrhaging in hangings. But that could be left over from an earlier incident. And there's always the possibility that both occurred."

"What do you mean?" I asked.

"Strangulation takes about eight to ten minutes," explained Greco. "Let's say it's my first strangulation. I might assume she's dead when she's really just unconscious. I wouldn't know that permanent brain damage takes eight minutes and that I have to keep squeezing." He extended his right hand toward me in a grasping motion. "It's a learning curve. I could strangle someone until they're passed out, think they're dead, and then set it up to look like a hanging."

"So, you might choke someone, but not kill her, and then hang her to cover your tracks?" I offered.

"Exactly," said Greco. "Like I said, there are too many factors here for me to reach a conclusion."

"What would you say the odds were of homicide versus suicide?" I asked.

He scrunched up his eyes and moved his head toward one shoulder, then the other. "I really don't know—let's go with sixty-forty."

10

Present Day—Kate

I CALLED LUKE FROM the steps of the coroner's office. He sounded a bit weary when he picked up. "Myles, I just gave you something to chew on. I thought that'd buy me a day or two of peace—"

"Bennett didn't include the coroner investigator's report," I cut in. I didn't actually know if Bennett was keeping the report from Luke or if Luke had edited it out before sending it to me. Hopefully his reaction would help me clear that up.

"Yeah, I thought that was weird," said Luke.

"Apparently, a neighbor heard arguing and a slap a week before Margot died," I told him. "The police were called out."

"Son of a bitch." Luke sounded genuinely shocked.

It seemed Bennett hadn't shared the document. Normally the coroner investigator's report is included with the other autopsy paperwork. Leaving it out had been a choice. "He probably half-assed the investigation and didn't want you judging him for ignoring leads. Did he even interview the neighbor?"

"The report says he knocked on the door but no one answered," said Luke. "I guess he didn't bother going back a second time. How did you find out about this anyway?"

"I just met with Greco," I said. Luke inhaled sharply. It's illegal to impersonate a police officer, and I could tell he was wondering about the terms of my meeting. "Before you lecture me, I told him what I do for a living. Anyway, the angry male in Margot's apartment really bothers me. Do you know if Starling was dating anyone? Is there a 415 report from before her death? You think you can pull it?"

There was a long silence. I knew I was pushing it.

"Myles, I don't know if there's a report. I'll certainly check. If I find something, I can maybe confirm a name, but I can't give you a police report. You know that."

"Look, I'll keep it on the down low," I pressed. "And if it leads me to anything, I'll bring it to you."

"It's not a fair ask, and you know it. You're taking advantage of our past working relationship."

Luke's voice was stern, like he was scolding a child. He usually saved that tone for civilians dodging service or a neighborhood kid starting to hang with the wrong crowd. Hearing the familiar note of disapproval set my teeth on edge.

"Okay, I get it. Message received." I'd been aiming for neutral, but it came out sounding edgy and aggressive.

"Myles . . ." he said.

"It's fine, Luke. Anyway, I gotta go, I'll talk to you later." I hung up before things got even more awkward. He was right, of course. What I was asking wasn't fair. But his words stung, and I didn't feel a need to prolong the conversation.

Luke and I had always interacted as equals—partners working toward a common goal. But now he saw me as a pesky outsider buzzing around him for crumbs of information. *And in a way, that's just what I am.* The change in our dynamic hurt, because talking to Luke brought me back to a time when I was crushing it at work and still had a family. Sure, my marriage was never a fairy tale, but at least I could tuck my daughter in every night. Now, hearing Luke's voice, I could almost pretend the years of trauma and horrible mistakes had melted away. I could almost feel like me again and not like a shell of a person. Getting shut down by him was like plunging into a vat of ice water. But this was my current reality, and I'd better get used to it.

I walked back to my car and sat there for a minute, waiting for my heart rate to slow down. I knew I'd have to swallow my pride and apologize. I couldn't afford to push him away. And I didn't want Luke to think of me as a mooch who was just using him. We'd lost touch for a few years, but I never stopped caring about him. Maybe more than I wanted to admit.

Back at my house, I typed up my notes from my visit to the coroner's office. Domestic violence seemed like a plausible scenario. Margot's volatile boyfriend could have strangled her and set it up to look like suicide. Luke wouldn't tell me if LAPD had any previous incident reports. But maybe Margot's art dealer would know something about her love life. I'd left three messages at the gallery, but no one had returned my calls. I dialed their number a fourth time, and a perky-sounding receptionist picked up. "Garlington gallery. How can I help you?" she asked.

"Hi there, this is Kate Myles—I think we spoke earlier. I'm investigating the death of Margot Starling. Is Peter Garlington in? I left several messages."

"I'm afraid he can't talk right now. We're having an opening tonight, and he's busy with preparations. Would you like to leave a message?"

No, I would not like to leave another message. "Is the reception open to the public?"

"Yes it is, but—"

"Thanks for your help. I'll try again later." I hung up the phone and pulled up the gallery website. Maybe if I came to his party, Garlington would answer a few questions before ejecting me. Plus, I could tell Luke about the event as an olive branch.

FYI, there's a shindig tonight at Garlington, I texted. *Might be an opportunity to ask about Margot's dating life.* He wrote back a minute later: *Thx—see you there.* I smiled, feeling relieved to bury the hatchet without having to prostrate myself or suffer through a horrible touchy-feely conversation.

I started thinking about what to wear to a fancy art opening. Most of my dressy outfits were too small. In the back of the closet, I had a few sexy numbers from one pregnancy and fifteen pounds ago. I don't know why I keep them. Even if they fit, I'm ten years too old for a strapless minidress.

I slipped on my wedding-guest dress. Every woman needs a someone's-getting-married outfit. You never know when your second cousin or high school bestie's gonna tie the knot. The cut emphasized my waist, which was still good, and minimized my hips, which I don't love. I wriggled into a pair of nude heels and looked at myself in the mirror. My reflection looked tired but passively attractive.

As I headed toward the bathroom to do my makeup, my phone rang again. I slipped off the pumps and ran to catch it. Maybe it was Luke calling to coordinate. I looked down at the screen. It was John.

"What's up?" I asked. "Is Amelia okay?"

"She's fine. But our babysitter fell through, and we have an event tonight. Can you watch her?"

My heart sank. I was supposed to be the first call for babysitting. We'd been over this a million times. "What babysitter? You're supposed to ask me first."

"Don't start, Kate. The girl next door needed pocket money and we were trying to help her out."

"John, we have an arrangement. How old is this babysitter anyway?"

He let out an exasperated sigh. "This is exactly why I *don't* call you. Sometimes it's nice to get a sitter without the histrionics."

I opened my mouth but snapped it closed again. I needed to play nice for my daughter's sake, and John had the upper hand. "I'm not a sitter, I'm her mother," I said.

He gave a nasty little laugh that I'd heard a million times before. "This is ridiculous. We need you here by five."

"I can't. I'm working." My stomach churned. I hated missing an opportunity to see my daughter. Even one sprung on me at the last second.

"No, you're not," sneered John. "What could you possibly be doing? You're not going on patrol."

"I wouldn't turn down a chance to see her if I was free. I told you I'm working," I could hear the anger in my voice. John was trying to get a rise out of me. It helped him maintain the narrative that I was unstable and needed to be kept at arm's length from Amelia.

"You're getting hysterical, Kate. What's really going on? Are you on something? You're not in a condition to drive; is that it?"

I waited several beats before replying. "You know I'm clean, John. I'm just not available. Next time call me first, not an hour before you need me. Have a good night." I hung up the phone and stormed into my kitchen, or rather, the strip of tile and plumbing at the far end of my living room. I hadn't taken anything stronger than a Tylenol in over a year, but he talked to me like I was a junkie. He probably always would. I thought about the bottle of gin in my freezer but pushed it from my mind.

John would punish me for blowing him off tonight. It'd be little things. Dropping Amelia off late, scheduling playdates on my weekends. Small things so he could accuse me of being irrational if I complained. I was sick of being at his mercy. But of course, I had put myself in this position. John hadn't gotten me hooked on painkillers after I was T-boned by an evading junkie. That was on me. As a cop, I'd known the risks and should have been more careful.

I grabbed my iPhone to check the time. The screen lit up with a picture of Amelia in her pirate getup, which made me smile. I change the background image every few days. It helps me feel connected to her during the long weekday stretches. Now I opened my photo app and scrolled through snapshots of her. I selected a picture from a day at the beach. Amelia had one arm in front of her brow to block the sun and was grinning, proud to show off her pink swimsuit with lime-green polka dots.

I sighed and put down the phone. The event started in an hour. I dug through the pile of shoes and laundry at the bottom of my closet in search of my nicer purse. I found my bag and unzipped it to throw in my keys and wallet. Inside, staring at me, was a small orange pill bottle containing two little white tablets. The last time I'd worn this bag was a year and a half ago at my father's funeral. I'd completely forgotten what was inside.

At my dad's funeral, I'd locked myself in a church bathroom stall, in agony from sitting on the tiny wooden benches, missing my dad so badly I vomited. I don't know how much oxy I took then, but enough to make me feel giddy at the reception. I was smiling and greeting people like it was a family reunion.

Uncapping the bottle, I picked up a tablet with my middle and index fingers. I knew it would soften the pain. I'd forget about my six herniated disks. My failed marriage wouldn't seem so bad, and I'd even stop hating myself for a little while. I closed my eyes and willed myself to drop the pill. But then, almost by reflex, I brought my fingers to my mouth and licked off the chalky white dust.

How pathetic. I recapped the bottle and threw it across the room as tears welled in my eyes.

I forced myself to snap back to the present. *Get it together, Kate.* I grabbed my purse and ran out the door before I could change my mind—I'd have to flush the pills when I got home.

In the car, I turned the music up loud and tried to calm down. I needed to get in a calmer headspace if I was going to interview some uptight art mogul.

The gallery was a white, one-story building that spanned half a block. Its front was covered in glass panels. All the windows were frosted, with the exception of a single clear strip at eye level. You could see the art through this peephole, but only if you got close enough to feel like a voyeur. Above the door hung a discreet sign with a single word in sleek uppercase letters: GARLINGTON.

I pulled open the front door and saw a pretty young woman in a one-shoulder dress perched next to a desk. She smiled and offered me a glass of champagne; I stared at it longingly but shook my head. The small entryway fed into a narrow corridor that led to the gallery. An older woman in a kimono-inspired gown floated past the mouth of the hallway. I walked through the cramped passage into a giant room with no furnishings save a table of refreshments and a handful of brightly colored paintings on the wall. Two boulders sat in the middle of the concrete floor. One was spray-painted pink with gold flecks and the other was blue with silver flecks.

As I glanced around the room, my thoughts were broken by a small, excited voice. A little girl in a plaid jumper was galloping toward me. "Mommy!" squealed Amelia.

"Hi, sweetie," I managed. I looked up and saw John and Kelsey talking to a stunning young blond. Kelsey's mouth hung open, and John's eyebrows were pinched into a scowl. He took two giant steps toward me and grabbed my wrist.

"Kate," he hissed through gritted teeth. "What are you doing here?"

I wrenched my arm free. "I told you, I'm working." I looked down at my daughter, who was holding on to the skirt of my dress. Her face registered alarm and confusion. I knelt down and smoothed her hair. "It's okay, baby. Mommy just needs to talk to Daddy. Why don't you go check out those pretty rocks?"

John heaved an exasperated sigh. "No, I don't want her running amok in the gallery, obviously. Amelia—go see Kelsey."

My daughter looked back and forth, sensing the tension. I winced as I watched her slink back to her stepmother. *Do you always have to be such an asshole?* I thought. "Can you not do this in front of Amelia?" I whispered. My daughter was still watching us. I smiled at her before turning back to John, willing myself to stay calm.

John ignored me and continued his interrogation. "Kate—what are you doing here? Are you mentally ill? You refuse to babysit, so now you're following me?" Several people were staring now. We were becoming a spectacle.

"Keep your voice down," I hissed. "I'm here on a job. Not everything is about you. What are *you* doing here?"

"Kelsey's sister, Anya, is the gallery assistant," he told me. "We're here to support her."

I looked over at the two gazelles in little black dresses and then back at John. "How special," I said. "You've always had such wonderful family values."

John sneered. My sarcasm would only wind him up and make things worse, but sometimes I just couldn't bite my tongue.

"Seriously, Kate, are you on something? It's called normal social behavior. What kind of *job*?" he demanded, endowing the last word with extra contempt. "Chasing another philandering husband?"

"No, I believe you were the last," said a deep baritone. I looked over my shoulder and saw Luke. Perfect timing. He was wearing his court suit, which fit beautifully over his broad shoulders. I'd never been happier to see anyone.

"Oh," said John, "you're—Matt, right?"

"Luke," said my former partner. He turned back to me, ignoring John's outstretched hand. "Shall we?" he asked, offering me his arm.

"Just a second," I said. "I need to say good-bye to my kid."

I walked over and crouched down next to Amelia. She had wrapped her arms around her chest and was staring at her feet. I hugged her tightly and then put a hand on each of her shoulders, stroking them lightly with my thumbs. I wondered how much she'd heard of our exchange. Kelsey should have walked her to a different section of the gallery. "Have fun tonight, sweetie. Mommy has to work. On Friday I'm going to take you bowling; what do you say?"

She nodded glumly and I kissed her cheek. I took a deep breath and headed back to Luke. We silently walked to the other side of the gallery, out of earshot.

"Thanks," I managed. "I'm not sure how much of that you heard."

"Enough. I remember you said he was high-strung. You never said he was a world-class douchebag. Is he dating the gallery chick?"

I shook my head. "Her sister. The one who's at least finished puberty. I didn't even know she had a sister, but I guess it's my lucky night." The girl with the champagne tray walked by again. This time I grabbed one and took an emergency gulp.

Luke eyed my drink. "I completely support the impulse," he said, "but first let's see if we can get any intel. I think that's Garlington in the corner." He nodded toward a white-haired man in a sport coat who was talking to an older couple and gesturing at one of the paintings. I reluctantly set my glass down and watched Garlington's dog and pony show from across the room. As their conversation ended, we swooped in.

"Mr. Garlington, Luke Delgado, LAPD. We spoke on the phone."

The gallery master was less than pleased at the sight of us. "Detective, this really isn't a good time," he said. "As you can see, I'm a little busy."

"Don't worry, I'm not going to ask you any questions about the forgery," said Luke with an amused smile. He spoke a little louder than necessary and Garlington's eyes widened.

"Can you not use that word in here?" he demanded. His head swiveled from side to side as he looked to see if anyone was within earshot.

"No problem," said Luke. "We just have a couple of questions about Margot Starling. How about we step into your office, you give us five minutes, and then we get out of your hair?"

"Fine," agreed Garlington, "but this is extremely unfair. Five minutes and that's it. Follow me." He led us back through the narrow hallway to a windowless office behind the front desk. It was surrounded by shelves of art books and glossy show catalogs. "What do you want?" he asked, crossing his arms defiantly.

"Were you ever romantically involved with Margot Starling?" I asked.

He nodded without hesitation. "Yes, years ago, before she became a total basket case. What else?"

I was taken aback by his indifferent tone. He'd known this woman for years, and she had died violently. But his voice registered only annoyance at our intrusion on his evening. "Do you know if she was seeing anyone when she died? Or are you aware of any significant past relationships?"

Garlington let out a chuckle. "Define significant. Margot was a tortured soul. I'm assuming you've heard of her work *Homage to Tracy Emin*?" Luke nodded, and I looked at him blankly.

"In one of her depressive phases, she carved the names of just about everyone she'd ever slept with into her torso with an X-Acto knife—including some very powerful and very married individuals—and then photographed herself. She made paintings of the photo using her own blood. It was a huge scandal, and my phone was ringing for days with angry husbands threatening to sue me for libel."

"How many names?" I asked.

Garlington shrugged. "A couple dozen."

"And they all fit on her torso?"

Luke shot me a look that said *Stay on point*. He was right. Margot was a weird woman with weird art projects, but I shouldn't let that be a distraction.

"Yeah, they did," said Garlington. "An X-Acto knife is small, like a scalpel. And Margot had great technical skills; she was used to painting with tiny brushes. Anyway, I'm not sure how any of this is relevant—"

"Did you sell the work?" asked Luke.

"Of course. She released the photograph on social media, so the names were already out there. Plus, it generated a storm of publicity and practically doubled her market value."

Garlington pulled a catalog off one of his bookshelves and handed it to me. Margot's name was emblazoned on the front. "The piece is in here," he told me. "Knock yourself out."

"Thank you, I will," I said. "Of the angry husbands—did anyone stand out?"

"Yes, one. Barton Grigsby. He's an executive in Bank of America's LA office. Grigsby was involved in their art investment team, which is how he met Margot. Her X-Acto project led to a nasty article about him in *Forbes*, which was the catalyst for his divorce. At any rate, several people threatened to sue me, but he's the only one who physically threatened me."

"When was this?" I asked.

Garlington's unnaturally smooth brow creased the tiniest bit as he thought about his answer. This guy was definitely getting regular Botox hits. "A few months before she died."

If Grigsby had been angry enough to threaten Margot's gallerist, maybe he'd gotten violent with her—or even killed her. He certainly had a motive.

"Listen," Garlington went on, "I have no doubt that Margot killed herself. But she was quite the bridge burner. If you're looking for people she pissed off over the years, it'll be a long list."

I thought of the slap Margot's neighbor had heard a week before her death. "Any chance she rekindled things with Grigsby?" I asked.

Garlington snorted. "Not a chance in hell. He hated her guts."

"Then do you know if she was seeing anyone when she died?" I pressed.

"Yes, some no-talent DJ—he went by Blaze. They were on and off for a while. I think it was pretty turbulent. She came into the gallery with a fair amount of concealer under her eyes about a week before her death, and I wondered if things had gotten violent. Like I said, Margot was a basket case. But if you're looking into her death, I'd start with him."

"Thank you," said Luke.

"Now are we done here? I'd like to return to my opening. You've probably cost me a six-figure sale."

"One more thing," I said. "I'll make it quick." Garlington's eyes narrowed. "When I called your office to try and set up an appointment, someone mentioned that Margot had associated with art forgers before. Do you know what they meant?"

"First of all, Detective, I already told your partner about this over the phone."

"He's not my partner—" I started to correct him.

"Whatever," snapped Garlington. "I don't really care. At any rate, Margot did a show early in her career with an art forger named Arno Winkler. You can read about it in the catalog. Now, if you'll excuse me, I need to get back to my clients."

11

Eleven Years Ago—Peter

I HAD HOPED THE press would take an interest in Margot's first show. But I never imagined anything like what happened. She managed to land write-ups in the *New York Times*, the *L.A. Times*, and *Art in America*. I didn't learn until months later that she'd sent hand-painted invitations to editors at each publication—giving them a direct financial stake in her success. Recently, one of those invites reached a cool seventy-five grand at auction. She'd also been slammed in the conservative press, picketed by street protesters, and hailed as the next great feminist.

After such a stellar debut, I worried she might flame out. A lot of young artists let early success go to their heads. They lose that fire in their belly and get complacent. But as we prepared to open the doors for her second solo show, Margot was generating more controversy than ever. For today's exhibition, *Uncanny Eve*, she'd fed pictures of magazine beauties into a computer algorithm and asked it to draw women based on the source material. The resulting creatures were gorgeously proportioned, but otherworldly, not quite human. And Margot wasn't done yet. She faithfully painted half of the digital beauties. For the other half, she invited notorious art forger Arno Winkler, fresh off a thirty-month stint in a

German prison for producing fake Picassos, to paint the spectral figures and forge her signature. Margot had visited him twice in captivity and then put him to work upon his release.

The forgery twist had been a surprise to me. And no matter how much I begged, pleaded, and threatened, she refused to say which pieces she had painted. The little bitch wouldn't even hint at it. Then, as the cherry on top, she invited Winkler to the opening as her date. She hadn't cleared this with me either; I had learned about it from her interview with *LA Weekly*. I couldn't send him away now—the optics would be terrible. So tonight a famous forger would cavort around my gallery, waxing poetic about the nature of authenticity. It made me want to vomit.

They strolled in together minutes before the show opened. Margot wore a backless evening dress. Her long, pale arms were draped around Winkler, who wore a tweed sport coat open over a wrinkled T-shirt. His long, greasy hair brushed against his shoulders and gave off a disgusting odor of perspiration and scalp. Margot was clearly doing her best to make it look like they were a couple. I knew from a colleague that Winkler preferred men, but the faker was having a lovely time playing his part in her little performance.

It wasn't long before the gallery was packed. My eyes kept wandering back to Margot and Winkler. What was that creep saying to my clients? I tried to work the room, but my game was off. My blood boiled as I was forced to explain over and over that I couldn't reveal who'd painted what, since Margot had kept me in the dark. In truth, I had a pretty good idea. Winkler's brushwork was less varied, more careful. Margot's painting had a reckless intensity.

I looked over at her again. She was laughing hysterically at something Winkler had said. As her body shook, she spilled a bit of red wine down the front of his shirt, which gave them both a case of the giggles. Then I realized who they were talking to: Ryan Goldschmidt from *Artforum*. I felt a wave of nausea. Winkler was gesticulating and talking with great animation. I couldn't risk letting him run his mouth to a journalist without supervision.

"Would you excuse me for just a moment?" I said to a client and made a beeline for them. Margot was going to get an earful when this was over.

She smiled as I approached. Margot looked manic as ever, and she'd clearly been drinking. I'd told her repeatedly to stay sober—she could indulge on her own time. Yet somehow, as sloppy as she got, her marketing instincts never faltered. She was now lecturing the riveted young reporter about how nothing was original. That we'd been telling the same stories and painting the same pictures since the Stone Age.

"Peter!" cried Margot. She abandoned her date and draped herself around me. I could smell the wine on her breath. I forced myself to smile and accept her embrace. Outside of sex, I don't like to be touched. Margot knows this, and we haven't shared a bed in a year. But she was past caring what I thought. "This is Ryan Goldschmidt from *Artforum*," she told me. Like I didn't already know that. "I was just telling him that if Richard Prince can be considered original for photographing other people's pictures, then everything Arno has ever made is original. Arno might sign another name, but that's part of the statement. The draftsmanship and composition are his own."

Hot blood rushed to my face. I had just entered negotiations with Prince to join my stable of artists. Did Margot know that? Was this a power play? Now she was asking me to pan him and praise a convicted forger in fucking *Artforum*. "No, Margot. It's more complicated than that."

"Not to mention," she interrupted. "Nothing Arno ever made could be confused for child pornography."

I could have killed her then and there. It was a reference to Prince's copy of a photo of ten-year-old Brooke Shields in a bathtub. Sure, it wasn't my favorite work, but child pornography? I pinched her side—hoping she'd take the hint.

"Ow!" cried Margot.

I was going to murder her. "I don't agree, Margot," I said. "There's a difference between openly appropriating an image to make a statement, like Barbara Kruger or Richard Prince, and conning people into buying something different from what they expected at an inflated price. That's fraud."

"Which one are you doing?" asked Goldschmidt. "You're valuing all of the works as if they were painted by Margot Starling, when you know that Winkler made half of them."

"And if we're being honest," added Winkler, "all of them were originally conceived by a computer."

This was exactly what I wanted to avoid. "The difference is that we're open about that ambiguity. We're playing with the notion of originality, but we're being transparent about our methods. If I represented to a buyer that a work was by Margot's hand and it wasn't, that would be fraud. And I couldn't make any such representations even if I wanted to, because Margot refuses to tell me which paintings were done by her. But the concept is Margot's, which is why every piece bears her name."

"Actually, that's not true," she said with a mischievous grin. "It's more of Arno's brainchild, isn't it, darling?" She untangled herself from me, much to my relief, and returned to her original perch.

Winkler nodded enthusiastically. "I was so startled when she visited me in prison," he boasted. "She was so beautiful, like an angel. And we discussed the possibility of working together on a collaboration. We conceived of it together."

Margot beamed at him. "Really, the gallery should have billed the show under both of our names. Maybe for the next series."

CHAPTER

12

Present Day—Kate

M Y ALARM CLOCK blared, and I opened my eyes to a spinning
room. I slammed my lids shut to regain stillness. It didn't
work. This was gonna be a bad one.

I ran for the bathroom and jammed my big toe against the
dresser. Pain rocketed through my foot. I cursed and clutched at
the throbbing toe, rubbing it between my thumb and forefinger.
Then another wave of nausea rolled over me. Somehow I made it
to the toilet in time to be sick. That helped a little. Afterward, I
leaned against the bowl and studied my toe.

The night before came back to me in snippets: the gallery,
my argument with John. I flashed on Amelia's face after John had
grabbed my wrist. Her shock and confusion, eyes wide, mouth
hanging open.

And then there were post-gallery drinks with Luke. Probably
too many. I shouldn't have let myself get out of control—but dealing with John always brings out the worst in me. Plus my tolerance
has gone to shit in my thirties. Wait—did I do anything humiliating? I had a vague memory of calling Luke the perfect man and
saying they should clone him as a public service. God, if I could

get through a week without making an ass out of myself, it would be a small miracle.

I forced myself off the floor, brushed my teeth, and made a large pot of coffee. It was already ten thirty. I must have been pressing snooze for at least an hour. Now half the morning was gone, and I'd accomplished nothing. I guzzled my coffee and fished my almost-dead phone out of my purse. One missed call from Milt Starling. I dialed his number and reminded myself to sound professional.

"Hi, Mr. Starling, how are you?"

"Fine," he said. "I'm just checking in to see if you found anything."

"I don't have that much to report yet, I'm afraid," I told him. "However, I did have a meeting with the coroner."

"Oh?" He sounded a bit surprised. "What did he say?"

I contemplated how much to share at this point. There was still a solid chance Margot had killed herself, and I didn't want to create false hope. "Actually, he told me the cause of death was undetermined." I held my breath and waited for Milt's reaction.

"I don't understand," he stammered. "The detective told me it was ruled a suicide."

I exhaled slowly, wondering how to convey the information in the gentlest way possible. I also didn't need him calling Bennett and making trouble.

"That was the detective's conclusion. He based his opinion on a lot of factors, not just the autopsy. The coroner thought it was about equally likely that she hung herself or that she was strangled."

"I knew it," he said. "How can they call it a suicide when even the coroner doesn't believe it?"

"Mr. Starling, I said *equally* likely. We can't jump to conclusions. And it's probably better that you don't mention this conversation to LAPD. I need to have a good working relationship with them while I look into the case. Putting them on the defensive won't help."

"Fine," he said after a moment. "I understand." Milt was working hard to contain his emotions. He had suffered the worst loss imaginable, and now I was telling him that the police had rushed the investigation and he couldn't call them to complain. It was a lot to ask, and I was grateful that, for now at least, he was willing to cooperate.

"Now I know you said Margot didn't talk much about her love life, but did anything come to mind since we last spoke?" I asked. "Did she ever mention a banker or a DJ?"

There was a long pause. "A DJ? No. Why do you ask?"

"It's a tip I'm following up on. I'll give you more information when I have something solid. How about a banker?"

He went silent again. I gave him a moment to reflect, hoping a memory would come back to him. "Possibly," he said. "A while back. Nothing specific. I'll ask my wife if she remembers anything."

Okay, we were getting somewhere. "Please do. I'd actually love to talk to your wife. Would that be all right?"

"Sure," he said. "Do you want her number?"

"Yes, would you text it to me?" I asked, realizing I didn't have a pen handy.

"Okay."

"And one more thing. It would really help if I could look at Margot's phone and computer. Do you have those?"

"Yes," he said. "The police gave them back to us, but there's a password. We don't know it."

"I'd like to at least try to figure it out," I said. "Can I pick them up from you? Maybe later this afternoon?"

"I'll drop them off at your office. I can be there in twenty minutes."

I winced. "I'm actually out in the field," I lied. It was better than telling him I was sitting at my kitchen table in a bra and panties. "But there's an accountant in the office next door, Erin Lopez. She's a friend of mine. Can you leave them with her? She has a key to my office. I'll text her so she knows you're coming." Erin and

I had worked out this arrangement, since she's in the office daily. She occasionally receives a drop-off for me, and when I pick it up, I bring her a venti caramel macchiato with extra whipped cream.

"Okay," said Milt. "I'll do that."

"Thank you, Mr. Starling. And if you can think of any words Margot might have used for her password—dates that meant something to her, names of childhood pets, that kind of thing— that would be really helpful."

"I'll check with my wife and email you anything we think of."

"Perfect. Talk to you soon."

I hung up the phone, popped three Tylenol, and headed for the shower. The hot water reactivated the pain in my toe. As I lathered my hair, I contemplated the day's agenda. First up was a visit to Aksel Berkland's gallery.

Berkland was going to shut down the moment I introduced myself. But if I posed as a potential buyer, I'd have a chance to see him in action. Maybe I could even get him talking about how his gallery had managed to get hold of Margot Starling originals.

I doubted that I could pull off West Side ice princess, but I threw on my nicest pair of jeans, a white button-down shirt, and a strand of pearls that John's mother had given me as a wedding present. They'd been in his family for three generations. The last time I wore them, we were still together. I'd sell the damn things if I didn't feel obliged to keep them for Amelia.

As I looked in the mirror, I remembered I'd worn them the day we got married, in an off-the-rack dress I'd bought to conceal my second-trimester bump. Even then I'd felt deeply ambivalent. So much for trying to do the right thing.

I shook my head violently to snap out of my trip down memory lane. After today, the pearls would go back in my tiny safe, ever so cunningly disguised as a book on my shelf, and stay there until Amelia needed a prom accessory.

Outside, I scanned the street for my car, which was nowhere in sight. Then another flash came back to me from the night before. *Luke drove me home.* I must have looked as drunk as I felt. How mortifying. My car was still parked on the street in Beverly Hills by the Garlington gallery, if they hadn't towed it. I called an Uber, and five minutes later an older gentleman drove up in a white Prius. Thankfully, he wasn't a talker. I had no interest in explaining why I needed a ride to pick up my car.

By some miracle, my Ford Fiesta was in the same place I had left it. There wasn't even a ticket on the windshield. Maybe it was a sign that my luck was changing. I hopped in, turned on the AC, and cruised down Olympic.

The Berkland gallery had little in common with Garlington. Most of the art consisted of abstract paintings in neon colors: lots of turquoise, lime, and hot pink. I studied one called *Boardwalk Dreams* that had the flat, blurry quality of graffiti. It might not be a staggering work of genius, but I liked it. I glanced at the label underneath. Fifteen hundred dollars. Too bad.

Off to the side was a collection of paintings that looked completely different from the rest of the work. The pieces were lovingly rendered and very realistic, with an exception. Instead of painting the sky blue, the artist had applied what looked like real gold. Despite the fancy materials, the scenes he depicted were pulled from everyday life. There were taco trucks, homeless encampments, an old man carrying a giant bag full of empty cans. I looked at the name on the label: Jason Martinez. Unlike the other paintings, these works didn't include a price tag.

"Stunning, aren't they?" said a voice behind me. I spun around and saw a tall, fit man in his early fifties, wearing white linen slacks and a navy sweater. His beard was trimmed into a neat goatee and his skin had the orange glow of a tanning bed fanatic. "Aksel Berkland," he said.

I took his outstretched hand and gave it a quick shake. "They're amazing."

"The more you look, the more you see," he continued. "The artist was interested in exploring wealth disparities in Los Angeles, and the politics of who we choose to look at. Traditionally, it's society's elite who are deemed worthy of depiction—whether it be in Renaissance portraiture or fashion photography. But Martinez inverted that expectation. He used techniques from Byzantine icon painting and medieval illuminations to depict people on the margins of society, hence the use of gold leaf."

"You said he *was* interested in wealth disparities," I pointed out. "Is the artist not still making these?"

Berkland smiled sadly. "I'm afraid not. Martinez died in a tragic accident a few months ago. He went hiking in the San Gabriel Mountains. Somehow he lost his footing and fell off a cliff."

I tried to keep my face neutral, but my internal alarm was blaring. Another dead artist, and even I could tell his work was too good for this gallery. "That's terrible," I said. "Did anyone see what happened?"

Berkland shook his head. "No, he went by himself. That's part of the tragedy. He didn't die right away; if he'd been found earlier, he might have been saved. He was only thirty-nine years old and at the peak of his career. You know, his work has already been collected by several museums. In another ten years, I wouldn't be surprised if an original Martinez would set you back eight figures."

"Let's say I was interested in buying one today. How much would that cost? Say, this little one?" I pointed to the smallest of the paintings, about the size of a spiral notebook.

"Fifty thousand for that one. It's small, but it doesn't lose any power from its lack of scale. Take a step back." I did as I was told. "Up close, it's almost jewel-like, but from a distance, it still holds its own."

He was right. Even from far away, my eyes went right to the little painting. "How about that one?" I asked, pointing to the largest of the group. "How much is that one?"

"That one is more. It's a phenomenal piece. There's so much detail that every time I look at it, I discover something new. That one we're pricing at three-fifty, way below market."

"Why the discount?" I asked.

"I'm selling these for a friend of the artist," said Berkland. "The current owner was an intimate of Martinez."

I could feel the hairs on the back of my neck stand up. That was exactly the story he'd used when selling the so-called Starlings. "Of course," I said. "How did your client know the artist?"

Berkland's lips formed a tight smile. "The owner is an extremely private person and has asked to remain anonymous. Jason's death was very traumatic for my client, as I'm sure you can imagine. My client doesn't want any added attention or publicity."

"But doesn't your client want to keep them as a memento of their relationship?" I pressed.

Berkland was starting to tense up. A minute ago, he'd been talking with his hands. Now they were jammed into his pockets. "That's really the owner's business. I try not to pry. But I can tell you that the owner is very motivated, which is why I'm offering the paintings at these incredible rates. That larger piece"—he pointed toward the biggest work—"could easily fetch three-quarters of a million at auction."

This was the same scenario Renate had described. It couldn't be a coincidence. Was he combing the obituaries for artists to forge? Or was there something even more sinister at play?

"I'm interested in these paintings, but I feel uncomfortable with that level of expenditure without knowing more about the provenance," I said, mentally patting myself on the back for remembering the buzzword. "Is there any kind of certificate of authenticity or something that comes with it?"

Berkland smiled again, warmly this time. "I see that you're a discerning buyer. These are exactly the type of questions you should be asking. Unfortunately, since the works were given to the current owner as gifts, there was never a bill of sale. If it puts your mind at ease, the owner donated one canvas to the Long Beach Museum of Art." Berkland took out his phone and started flipping through photographs. He held up his screen and showed a picture of himself and another man smiling next to a framed painting of a fruit vender. "This is me with the curator on the day of the

unveiling. As you can imagine, they undergo a thorough evalua-
tion of every piece before accepting a gift."

"Why Long Beach?" I asked. But it made perfect sense. Berkland couldn't bring a second questionable painting by a different
artist to MOCA without raising red flags. And Renate had said
smaller museums don't do the same level of diligence when they
accept a donation.

"The artist was born in Long Beach," he explained, without
missing a beat. "It was meant as a tribute to his hometown."

He had certainly perfected his pitch. I had a feeling I could
ask questions all day as a potential buyer and Berkland would keep
supplying me with plausible answers. But I wondered how he'd
react when cornered—his face might tell me if there was an innocent explanation. "There's still one thing that's bothering me," I
said. "Is this the same anonymous owner who sold off a trove of
Starlings?"

Berkland turned pale, and his eyes narrowed. "No," he said
coolly. There was a long silence. "Are you really looking to buy a
painting?"

I took out my business card and handed it to him. "Kate Myles.
I'm a private detective working for the Starling family. I'm investigating her death, and I have some questions about the paintings
you sold recently. Can you tell me who brought them to you?"

Berkland stared at my card. I could see the muscles in the side
of his face flex as his jaw clenched. "That individual also wished
to remain anonymous." He walked over to his desk and threw
my card in a small metal trash can. "Since you're not here to buy
a painting, I'd like you to leave. I'm very busy, and you've wasted
enough of my time."

I looked around the empty gallery as if searching for customers. "Really? It seems like you're having a slow day." His hands
balled into fists at his sides. "Who gave you the Starlings?" I prodded. "Is it the same 'intimate' who brought the Martinez paintings?" I was laying it on thick, but this was my chance to confront
him. Berkland wasn't going to cooperate with me, but the more

I talked, the closer he'd get to losing control. His anxiety could work to my advantage: a sloppy, unplanned lie could be as revealing as an admission.

Berkland was starting to sweat. "I want you to leave."

"What was this person's relationship to Margot? Can you at least tell me that?"

"I don't know what you're insinuating, and I don't appreciate your tone." Berkland was almost shouting now. "Get the fuck out of my gallery."

"I guess that's my cue," I said. "You have my card if you want to talk."

My heart pounded as I pushed open the front door. Two healthy young artists had died suddenly—and within months, their paintings, or at least paintings bearing their names, had ended up in this second-rate gallery.

What is going on?

CHAPTER

13

Seven Years Ago—Margot

THE FIRST TIME I saw Sophie Calle's *Take Care of Yourself,* the installation blew me away. It was a freezing February in New York. Not like the white Ohio Winters of my childhood, cars and lawns piled high with fluffy, marshmallowy snow. The magic of a New York Christmas was long past, and I was left with a wet wind so cold it burned my cheeks and a half-inch of black slush that seeped through my boots and numbed my toes.

I had been in town to see a friend's show in Chelsea. The work was fairly good—she made modern versions of French history paintings. Hers depicted contemporary events already made iconic by ubiquitous news coverage. Rachel can really paint, and she had slaved over every canvas. But they lacked the power and immediacy of the thousands of amateur snapshots traveling the world through social media. Her giant canvases featured protesters confronting cops in riot gear. The layers of thick paint and minute detail made them look stiff compared to the shaky, grainy images captured by real street warriors. Rachel hadn't been near the protests, and it showed. She poured her sweat and tears into her work, but she didn't bleed for it.

Of course, I told her this and she freaked out. She asked for my opinion and I was honest. I don't know why everyone has to be so fucking sensitive. When people give me criticism, I listen and get better. Everything I said to Rachel was true, and she knows it. She called me a bitch and accused me of being unsupportive. I left the gallery, depleted. I'd flown across the country for her mediocre show, and now we probably wouldn't even be friends anymore. Another relationship I managed to ruin. I suck at maintaining friendships, especially with women. Meeting people and charming them is easy, but sooner or later I blow things by saying the wrong thing, or disappearing for a month in a depressive funk. I felt cold and empty and sad as I wandered the streets, no real destination in mind. The sky was so dark and gray that it already felt like evening.

I stepped off the curb and gasped. My foot plunged into a pothole filled with freezing, oily water and god knows what filth. Every nerve in my skin sent out alarm signals. I needed to get inside, quickly. I walked across the street toward a row of galleries. I wasn't in the mood to look at more art, but at least there'd be heat and I could wait for my shoes to dry without risking frostbite.

Sophie Calle was the featured artist. I'd heard of *Take Care of Yourself* but never given it much thought. Sophie had named the work after the last line of a breakup email from a callous ex—a grown man who couldn't face her in person and take responsibility for his decision to end things. The exhibit included the actual email, a self-indulgent, sniveling mess. The anonymous cad wallowed in self-pity, blaming his anxiety and existential crisis for his decision to contact "the others," presumably a reference to other women. He even scolded Sophie—mid breakup email—for refusing to remain friends after the demise of their love affair. At the end of the wordy disaster, he signed off with a cold, dismissive *Take care of yourself.*

As Sophie explained in the project, "take care of herself" was exactly what she set out to do. She carved out space for herself to grieve and analyze the relationship. Sophie found more than a hundred women to analyze the Dear Jane letter, chosen for their particular expertise. There was a judge, a Talmudic scholar, an etiquette expert, a copy editor, a clown, even a (presumably female) parrot. The end result was a Greek chorus of feminine condemnation.

Sophie displayed the analysis along with photographs of the analyzers. As I moved along the wall, reading critique after critique of her ex's paean to masculine blame-shifting, the specific nature of their relationship melted away. The email became less about the cowardly worm who sent it and more about the societal structures that let a man feel he can dismiss a woman so effortlessly—without experiencing a single consequence, or even giving a thought to the harm he caused. With such a simple concept, Sophie had completely shifted the power balance. She'd transformed her pain into a weapon, and ultimately used it to put out a work that was greater than her own experience, that felt almost universal in its truth.

I was mesmerized. Suddenly, my whole portfolio felt like a joke. I talked a big game about challenging power structures, but what had I done, really? I'd made some slightly embarrassing paintings of fancy people that ultimately gave them a fun party anecdote, even bragging rights. I'd palled around with an art forger in a trite exploration of "authenticity." It all felt derivative. My work was titillating at best and didn't really say anything. I needed to dig deeper. How could I use art to *change* something? To actually transform power dynamics—both on and off the canvas?

CHAPTER

14

Present Day—Kate

I GOOGLED JASON MARTINEZ on the walk back to my car. The first thing that popped up was a bio from his actual gallery, Bauman & Firth. It was mostly fluff about his short career and a statement mourning his loss. I forwarded the article to Luke. *Guess who has a posthumous show at Berkland?* He didn't respond. Luke was probably ten steps ahead of me, and I had my own investigation to worry about.

Next, I pulled up Jason's Facebook page. For an art star, his social media presence was surprisingly bare. He hadn't posted anything in the months leading up to his death. I scrolled through several congratulatory wall messages from various friends and acquaintances. Finally, I found a post in Spanish from someone name Elena Martinez. She was older than Jason, but the family resemblance was unmistakable. I made a mental note to contact her when I had a spare minute. But there were several other things on the day's agenda that I needed to handle first.

I drove to the office, retrieved Margot's devices, and headed over to meet my favorite hacker. Narek Badjanian and I had first crossed paths when he was a scared seventeen-year-old charged with killing his parents. The kid was well known to Glendale police: his penchant for computer hacking had landed him in juvie the year before, to the horror of his wealthy family. Then one day, officers got a call about screams coming from the house. They arrived on scene to find Narek standing over his mother and father, holding a bloody knife.

It seemed like an open-and-shut case: a teenage weirdo snapped and murdered his controlling parents. But Narek's lawyer was convinced of his innocence and hired me to look into things. It was one of my first cases as a PI. I canvassed the neighborhood and turned up a shy kid down the street who'd been flying his drone outside the house and captured footage of two burglars running out the door. We turned the tape over to the district attorney, who dropped the charges and eventually found the killers.

Narek later sold his parents' mansion and rented a run-down studio apartment. Now he lives off the inheritance and pursues his legally questionable hobbies full-time. I took a liking to the awkward young man during my investigation. From time to time, I check on him and bring him fruit, so he doesn't get scurvy from his diet of pizza and ramen. On two or three occasions, I've also brought a piece of encrypted technology with me. Despite my insistence, Narek refused to charge me for technical help.

I parked on the street and took the stairs up to Narek's third-floor unit. As I moved my hand back to knock, the door swung open. He'd probably rigged the hallway with some kind of surveillance system.

"Hi, Kate," said Narek, with his usual shoddy eye contact.

"Hey, Narek. How's it going?"

"Fine." He stepped aside to let me enter. I tried not to gag on the foul air. There was a mound of laundry on the floor and an ancient chicken carcass on the kitchen counter. It had probably been sitting there for days.

"Narek, you gotta crack a window in here, buddy. It's a little ripe."

He blushed. "Sorry, I haven't gone outside today. I guess I got used to the smell." Narek walked swiftly across the cramped living room and opened a door to the small balcony.

I scanned his kitchen counter and saw the collection of produce I had dropped off two weeks ago. Most of it was uneaten and had started to shrivel. "DEFCON's coming up, isn't it?" I asked.

His face lit up. The annual hacking conference was like Christmas for him. "I have a booth this year. I'm still working on my presentation."

"Just don't tell your probation officer, okay? You know it could get you in trouble."

"I know," he said sheepishly. Narek had been caught hacking an electric hazard sign on the 210 freeway. It was his first adult offense, so the DA gave him community service. There was a "no hacking" requirement of his probation, which he completely ignored.

"Listen, I'm looking into someone's death, and I need to get into her phone and computer. You think you can help me?"

"Sure," said Narek.

"Her parents emailed me words and dates that meant something to her. I'll forward you the list. Maybe it'll help you crack the passwords. And Narek—why don't you let me pay you? I don't have a ton of cash, but your time is valuable, and you should really be charging for it."

He shook his head. "Just bring me a pizza when you pick them up."

"All right, I appreciate it. And let me know if you apply to terminate probation early. I'll write you a letter saying you're doing great."

"Thanks, Kate," he said. "I'll text you when it's ready."

I took a deep breath as I closed the door to the acrid apartment. Maybe someday he'd meet a nice girl-hacker and have an incentive to get his housekeeping act together.

It was late afternoon by the time I got back to my car. There was just enough time left in the day to badger Barton Grigsby, Margot's banker ex-lover. This morning I'd spoken to his secretary, who informed me that Grigsby doesn't talk about Miss Starling. Still, I wanted to try my luck in person. You can learn a lot even from the precise way someone tells you to get lost.

Bank of America's Los Angeles office is headquartered on Bunker Hill. Downtown's most iconic skyscrapers are on this stretch, along with two art museums and the Disney Concert Hall. The strip of office buildings and luxury apartments appears to be populated mostly by a small community of attractive yuppies with little dogs. Lines of food trucks hawking gourmet popsicles and grilled cheese with smoked Gouda keep the busy locals supplied with quick and tasty meals.

Bunker Hill is the only part of LA that looks like New York, so they're constantly closing off the street to film a car commercial or a movie scene. Sure enough, I had to park down the street so a silver-haired actor could drive an Infiniti past the Broad Museum. I was panting by the time I climbed the steep hill and arrived at Bank of America. I took a seat in the lobby and redialed the number to Grigsby's personal assistant. "Private Wealth Management, Barton Grigsby's office. How can I help you?"

"Hi there," I said, still breathing heavily. "This is Kate Myles. I'm calling for your boss about Margot Starling."

She exhaled sharply. "I told you, he's not going to discuss that matter."

I pretended not to hear her. "I was in the neighborhood and figured I'd swing by just in case he could spare a few minutes. Can you let him know I'm in the lobby?" She made a little clucking sound, and I cut her off before she could protest further. "Tell him I'll just wait here until he's done for the day. I'm in no rush."

There was an awkward pause. "Hold on," she said finally. Then she actually placed me on hold, judging by the soft jazzy music that started playing through the receiver. Minutes later, the elevator doors opened and a stocky man with an impressive power paunch bounded toward me. He looked decidedly unthrilled.

"Are you Kate Myles?" he demanded.

"Yes," I said. "You must be Mr. Grigsby." I extended my hand, and he stared at it like I was offering him a dog turd.

"Let's take a walk," said Grigsby. He sped toward the revolving doors, and I had to jog to keep up.

Grigsby led me out the door and through a crowded courtyard to the quieter street behind the building before turning around to face me. "My secretary already told you that I'm not going to discuss her, so I don't know why you're here. You don't seem to be getting the message." My back was toward the wall, and he was leaning in a little too close.

"I'm not sure if your secretary told you everything. I'm not with the police. I'm a private detective working for Margot's parents—"

"Save it. I don't give a fuck who you are," he barked. Grigsby was so close I could feel the heat of his body, and little droplets of spittle were landing on my face. "You came to my place of work? My *work*." He paused a moment. "I have nothing to say about her. She's cost me enough. If you set foot in this building again, I'll call security. And if you say anything to my coworkers about me and Margot, I'll sue you within an inch of your life. Are we clear?"

"Crystal," I said, taking a step back to regain my breathing space. "But I'm curious, Mr. Grigsby. What does a man do to a woman to make her carve his name on her stomach? I've gone through a divorce and plenty of breakups and never come close to that kind of passion."

Barton shot me a look of pure hatred. For a moment, I felt like he was going to hit me. I blinked as he raised his hand and pointed a fleshy index finger in my face. "Stay away from me," he hissed, before turning and walking away.

I wiped his saliva from my face and watched as he disappeared. There definitely was a story here.

CHAPTER

15

Five Years Ago—Margot

Barton is not the type of man I usually go for: a rich alpha male with a master-of-the-universe job at a bank. The kind of guy who spends his Sundays golfing, pays fifty dollars for a steak, and has no ambition to travel farther than his multimillion-dollar vacation home in Lake Arrowhead. On paper, we had nothing in common, but somehow there was a chemistry there. He had an energy to him, and a sense of humor. It was the humor mostly— we didn't have conversation, not really. But we had repartee.

The sex was fine—proficient if unimaginative. I still remember his eyes growing wide the first time I climbed on top. Poor Mrs. Grigsby . . . and yes, there's a Mrs. Grigsby. He didn't mention her, of course. I discovered the wife when I Googled him after our first time together. At that point I should have deleted his number, but I've always had a self-destructive streak.

From the beginning, I knew my affair with Barton would run its course. After a couple months, the banter got repetitive and he started calling less often. I wanted to commemorate things before they fell apart, so I set up a camera in my bedroom. It's something I do when I sense the end is near. Posed photographs irritate me, and I like to remember things as they were.

Our fling was starting to fizzle out when I had to leave the country for a show in Berlin. When I came back, I texted Barton, hoping to pick up where we left off. He didn't bother responding. I sent him another text and called a couple of times, in case my messages didn't go through. I even wrote him an email. Nothing.

Barton's silence plunged me into a deep depression. It always happens when I split up with someone—even if I wanted out of the relationship. Even if I'm the one who leaves. It's just my fucked-up brain chemistry. And frankly, breakups are sad. You care about someone on some level. You're intimate with them, and then they're gone from your life like nothing ever happened. The way Barton disappeared made it even worse. A big ugly scene at least shows that you meant something to a person. That you registered as more than a blip on their radar. But Barton just crumpled me up and tossed me aside like a used candy wrapper.

A few weeks later I saw him from a distance, laughing and lunching with some young thing in business attire. They were sitting a little too close, and he made a point of touching her arm partway through an anecdote. If I'm honest, I could have predicted this exact outcome. Barton Grigsby is the kind of man who takes what he wants with no concern for the consequences. He dumped me exactly the way I'd always known he would dump me. And I still jumped in with both feet. But at this point in my life, I'm tired of navel gazing and trying to figure things out. I just ride the waves, knowing that someday one will pull me under.

I hadn't thought about Barton in a long time. Then suddenly his employer was all over the news. The FBI was investigating them for money laundering. Apparently, they were the preferred bank of a major Mexican drug cartel. And Barton's friends just looked the other way. I remembered Barton's blame-deflecting description of his profession. "I just move money," he said. "Doctors treat the sick and don't ask about their personal life. I'm the same way. What you do with the cash I manage is your business." He didn't care who got hurt. The collateral consequences weren't his problem.

A few days later, the protests started. There was a big story about a "die in" staged outside the bank's annual shareholder meeting in New York. Eighty young idealists were arrested for nothing more than asserting their First Amendment rights. The arrests galvanized the LA activist scene. Soon, a half dozen protestors showed up outside the LA office and chained themselves to the door. That's when Barton Grigsby took action. According to the *L.A. Times*, it was Barton who called the police. He admitted it in the paper, calling them immature hooligans and preaching that actions have consequences. Six young people were now facing criminal charges—including felonies—because Barton hadn't felt like waiting for the protest to end.

He was right. Actions do have consequences.

That's when I got to work. My anger was electrifying. I stayed up for days working, obsessively perfecting every detail. Then I opened my computer and sent Barton a message: *I've got something to show you. I think you'll like it.*

He responded a few hours later, probably expecting another round of fun and meaningless sex with no strings attached. *I'm intrigued*, wrote Barton. *When/where?*

5:30, my place, I replied. I pictured him sitting at his desk, erect and smiling like a schoolboy with an ice cream cone.

I put the finishing touches on my piece before settling down to wait. And then, just like that, my energy was gone. I've come to expect the crash that follows all my big projects. It would have been nice to get through the Barton meeting first, but c'est la vie. I curled into a ball on the couch, half watching daytime TV. Feeling too miserable to bother with food or a shower.

When I heard a knock on the door, I activated my camera system—insurance in case Barton responded badly—and then opened the door to let him in. He stood there, grinning like an idiot, holding a bottle of Macallan 18. There was a flicker of disappointment in his eyes when he saw me. I didn't exactly look my best—I wore an oversized sweatshirt, pajama pants, and no makeup. My three-days-unwashed hair was knotted in a tangled bun on top of my head. He was probably expecting lingerie.

Barton forced himself to smile and leaned in for a kiss. I turned away, and his lips grazed my cheek. They felt wet and slightly cold, like old sweat. His touch was repugnant. I couldn't remember what had drawn me to him. Barton handed me the whiskey, not sure what else to do. "Thanks," I said in a monotone. I turned away from him, set the bottle on the table, and grabbed two glasses.

His eyes bounced back and forth from me to the piles of crap littering my floor. "You could've picked up," said Barton, more than a little annoyed. He was a man used to having his expectations met, and I hadn't delivered.

I shrugged. "Sorry." Barton flinched at the lack of expression in my voice. He was losing his patience and having a hard time concealing it.

"What's this about, Margot?" he asked. "You email me out of the blue that you have a surprise you think I'll like. Then I show up with my dick in my hand, and you're dressed like my grandmother and talking in monosyllables."

I poured us each a drink and downed mine in a single gulp. "I finished a painting recently that I think you'll find interesting. I'd like to offer you a chance to buy it before I put it on the market."

Barton laughed and set down his glass. "Margot, I already own one of your paintings. No offense, but I'm not in the market for another picture. I came here because I thought you wanted to fuck. If that's not the case, then I have things to do."

"Just have a look. It won't take long," I said, walking over to a paint-stained tarp covering my latest work, and wrenched the cloth away.

Barton slammed his glass down and jumped to his feet. "What the fuck?" he shouted. "Are you trying to humiliate me?"

The painting was an image of him I'd made from a video taken during one of our last nights together. He'd never known I was recording. It was a nice memory, actually. Barton had been teasing me about the satiny robes I like to wear. He'd asked me what was with the kimonos. I'd shrugged and told him they were pretty and I liked the feel of the fabric on my skin. A drunk Barton announced that he wanted to see for himself. He'd slipped a robe from my closet over his naked body and jokingly sashayed around the room. He held a beer in one hand, and his limp dick swung from side to side as he pranced around. I remember laughing so hard I snorted.

"What the fuck is this, Margot?" Barton repeated. "Is this a shakedown?" He snatched a knife off the table and lunged at me, grabbing my shoulders and pinning me against the wall. It should have been terrifying. But I was so tired and numb that it mostly registered as surprising.

Barton took a step back, shocked by the force of his own reaction. Then he turned toward the painting. As his eyes traveled across the image, taking it in, he became enraged anew. Barton plunged the knife into the picture. The blade ripped through the canvas with a tearing sound, like someone unzipping a snow parka.

"You should know," I told him, "that I set up a security camera for my own protection. There's no sound, but it's recording everything visually. Don't touch me again. Like you, I have no qualms about pressing charges."

Barton's jaw dropped, and he stared at me in disbelief. "Is that what this is about? The fucking protesters? What was I supposed to do? Let the assholes in the building and offer them some goddamn lemonade?"

"This is about an opportunity to purchase a painting. It's strictly business," I told him.

"This is blackmail, Margot. It's revenge porn."

"No, revenge porn involves photographs, and this is an oil painting." I'd done my research. "I suppose you could try to sue me or press charges. But you'd have to prove that this painting depicts something real. I'm not so sure you want to go there."

That's when he hit me. A hard smack across the face. The noise of it shocked me even more than the sting. I could feel my eyes start to water. "If you touch me one more time, I'll take the tape to the police, and then to Forbes," I warned him. "My career can survive a little sordid gossip. How about yours?"

Barton was quiet then. His face slowly changed from anger to fear to desperation. The reality of his situation was sinking in, and he finally understood that he wasn't in control. His fists clenched, and I could tell he wanted to hit me again. Instead, he punched the painting and the hole ripped further.

"Please continue if it makes you feel better," I said. "I can always paint another one. But I need an answer. My Hong Kong show is in a month, and Peter needs a list of which paintings I'm planning to exhibit."

Barton stared at me. "You want to put this in an art show?"

I nodded. "Unless you're interested in collecting it."

"Collecting it? Let's drop the pretense, Margot. How much do you want, and how do I know this won't happen again?"

I walked back over to the table, refilled our glasses, and handed Barton his drink. His hands were making me nervous, and I wanted to give him something to keep them occupied. "Three hundred thousand. The bill of sale will include a clause that I won't make another painting containing your likeness or display any photos of you."

"I want them destroyed," he demanded.

"No. I'm keeping them as an insurance policy in case you do something stupid. But the contract says I'll have to refund the money if I disseminate a photograph of you for anything other than legal defense."

Barton set his drink down on the window ledge and stared at the painting. I wondered if he was thinking about his career or his marriage. Neither would survive a public display of him doing the naked cha-cha in women's lingerie. Too bad. Finally, he took out his checkbook and ripped one out. "Let's get this over with."

"Oh, it's not for me." I suppressed a smile. "I don't need your money. And for the record, my rate is way higher than three hundred thousand. You're getting the friends and family discount."

Barton glared at me. "Fuck you, Margot, stop playing games. What do you want?"

"I'm offering to sell you this painting. Don't worry, I'll repair the rip."

He shook his head. "Repair the rip? I'm going to burn it."

I shrugged. "It'll be yours. You can do what you want with it." I was drawing this out, finally starting to enjoy myself. "Anyway, I don't need your money, but other people do. There's a GoFundMe set up for the protesters arrested outside your bank. It's for the thousands in bail and legal fees they've incurred since you decided to involve police in a peaceful protest. And it has to be in your name, so they can see that you're trying to make amends."

"*You crazy bitch.* Do you have any idea what that'll do to my career? You want me to fund the assholes who chained themselves to our doors? I'll look like I lost my mind."

"Or like you felt guilty, which you should. You can always tell people that your wife used your card to make the donation."

He flinched at the reference to his marriage.

That's right, Barton. Your actions affect more than just you.

"I'll do it anonymously," he countered.

"No," I said. "This is restitution. It's in your name or no deal." I walked over to my desk, grabbed a copy of the paperwork, and handed it to him. "Take the contract and look it over. I need an answer by tomorrow. Several of the protesters have court hearings coming up, and I have to get Peter snapshots for the Hong Kong show."

He stared at the papers silently, scanning his brain for a way out that didn't exist. He'd sign. We both knew it, and I was getting bored with this exercise.

"If you'll excuse me," I said, "I have an appointment in an hour, and I need to freshen up. You can see yourself out."

16

Present Day—Kate

GOT INTO HER *laptop, still working on the phone*, texted Narek.
I glanced at the clock on my dashboard. He'd probably
cracked the code hours ago but waited till dinner to summon me.
I picked up a large pepperoni and drove over to his rancid apartment. Hopefully the tomato sauce and hot grease would mask the
stench of old laundry.

Margot's laptop was open and sitting on the kitchen counter
next to the chicken carcass. I walked over to retrieve it, trying
not to touch a damp bath towel slumped across a vinyl barstool.
Narek bore the shy smile of someone anticipating rare praise for a
peculiar talent. "I changed the password on her computer and her
email account," he said. "They're both just *Kate* now."

"You're the best, Narek. If you crack the phone, I'll throw in
breadsticks next time."

Back in my house, I nuked a box of mac and cheese and sat
down to read Margot's emails. I moved backward from the day her
body was found. There were several frantic messages from Garlington, threatening to drop her if she didn't "get her ass" to the gallery.
Jean Starling had forwarded some clickbait about pygmy goats. It
was kind of poignant. Everybody's mom loves animal pictures.

Nothing from the week before Margot's death jumped out at me. But about a month earlier, Garlington had sent an email with the subject line *Venice Biennale*.

I never approved that project, he wrote. *Are any of my clients implicated?*

Margot had responded within minutes. *It's fine. This won't come back on you.*

Well, *that* was certainly interesting.

After half an hour of sifting through junk mail, I remembered Margot's X-Acto knife project. I grabbed her catalog off my night-stand and flipped through it until I found the artwork in question. Names covered her torso, some large, some small, and blood dripped down her body toward the floor. She had on burgundy panties and fishnets. It was impossible to distinguish blood from fabric. According to the catalog text, the cuts were shallow and only a few had left light scars. I wondered if that was meant to be symbolic.

Some of the names in the photograph were obscured by blood and shadow. Others were clear as day. But Margot had also made paintings from the picture and carefully written out each name with a tiny brush. The catalog didn't include the identities of her subjects, and I didn't feel like searching her mutilated flesh for that information. Luckily, some art blogger had already done that for me. I Googled the painting's title and sifted through articles until I found one listing her lovers in alphabetical order. There were forty names in all. A few people were listed by first initial and last name. There was a *D Chernov*, a *BK Smith*, and a *Z Farabee*. I wondered who they were and why they got special treatment. Maybe some people were too dangerous to fully expose.

Barton Grigsby had a prime spot by her navel, next to Garlington. I typed Grigsby's name into the search window of Margot's email account. Several messages popped up from about a year ago. *My wife just filed for divorce. You've officially ruined my life.* Margot had responded by forwarding him an invitation to her next show. I was starting to like her. She was twisted, but she had a sense of humor.

About six months before the divorce exchange, Barton had sent a flurry of hysterical emails: *I'm going to KILL YOU. I already paid you, you evil bitch. NOW MY WIFE KNOWS. I HOPE YOU FUCKING DIE.*

She'd replied with a one-liner: *Hi Barton, please refrain from threatening me or I'll contact the police about your prior acts of violence.*

What did Barton mean, *I already paid you?* Was she blackmailing him? Did she blackmail him about an affair and then make it public anyway? That would make anyone feel homicidal. And what did she mean by prior acts of violence?

If Margot was extorting Grigsby, she could have done the same thing to other men. I picked a name from the list at random: Michael White. No emails. Maybe he didn't have any money. I started reading through the names, trying to see if any rang a bell. Shawn Hinkle sounded familiar. I typed his name into Google. No wonder I recognized his name; he was a freaking congressman. According to Wikipedia, Hinkle represented California's twenty-second district. As a married rep from the conservative Central Valley, he really didn't need an affair attached to his name.

I searched Margot's emails for the name *Hinkle.* Nothing came up. Next, I tried *Shawn,* and found messages between Margot and someone whose account was just a string of random letters. *You fucking blocked your phone?* said the first email. *You're trying to destroy me. I did what you asked. If you don't stop, I will MAKE YOU STOP.*

Margot had replied with a terse message. *Hi Shawn, please refrain from threatening me or I will contact the authorities. Best of luck at CPAC.*

CHAPTER

17

"Sit," ORDERED JOHN. He pulled a wooden chair out from the kitchen table and clutched the back of it tightly, waiting for me to comply. I sat down obediently. John had dropped Amelia at my mother's house so we could hash things out. I'd begged him not to tell her why.

He threw several pictures on the table along with two empty pill bottles—both in my name—from different doctors. They were for the same prescription, clear proof I'd been taking a double dose. I picked one up and examined the label. It was two months old. He'd been waiting for the right moment to make his move. The pictures were close-ups of bottles. And snapshots of me, passed out on the floor.

"You've been keeping tabs on me?" I had sensed him growing distant. Still, this took me by surprise. For months, I had practically begged him for help, or even the slightest hint of emotional support. But instead he'd been collecting evidence.

"Look at yourself, Kate." He shoved one of the pictures at me. I was shocked by my own appearance. Colorless skin, stringy unwashed hair. How had I let myself go to this degree? "Of course

I've been keeping tabs. We have a daughter—a daughter you could have killed today."

I put my head in my hands, and hot tears dampened my palms. "I'm so sorry," I whispered. It was all I could manage. I'd fallen asleep driving Amelia to the dentist and hit a parked car. She was fine—she didn't even have whiplash. But that wasn't the point. The doctor had told me not to drive on painkillers, and I'd done it anyway. I'd remembered the appointment at the last minute and jumped in the car with Amelia. I'd never thought about the medication in my system until I woke up with my front bumper compressed against a neighbor's Subaru. I was worse than the asshole who hit me. I could have killed my own child. What kind of mother does something that?

"Sorry isn't good enough," snapped John. "You're an unfit mother, and I want a divorce."

I looked up from my hands and met his eyes. He was not going to waver. Today I had done something monstrous. But I knew he'd made up his mind about leaving the moment he snapped a picture instead of helping me off the floor. It was futile, but I had to try anyway, for Amelia's sake. "John, let's talk about this."

He shook his head. "No, I'm done. I've been patient for months. All you do is lie around, and you're out of it half the time. Today was the last straw."

"I'll do whatever you want," I pleaded. "I'll quit cold turkey. We were fine before I got hurt."

My argument sounded hollow, and John smiled cruelly. We'd been far from fine before my injury. I'd been walking on eggshells for years. He'd been swallowing his contempt for just as long. I'd never been able to measure up to his lawyer friends' snobby wives. John resented being trapped in a marriage to a sloppy, spacey woman he looked down on. And I was tired of being judged inadequate because I didn't have a white-collar job and my bed-making didn't involve hospital corners. If it hadn't been for Amelia, I would have left years ago. We'd never have gotten married in the first place. But neither of us had ever given voice to the constant low-grade tension that hung around our household like a nagging electrical hum.

"Give me a break, Kate," said John. "We were going through the motions and now you're not even doing that. You're a junkie and a danger to Amelia. I want a divorce, and I don't want you around her."

My stomach seized up. He'd been planning his escape and collecting evidence for a custody fight. "No," I said. "You want to leave, then go. But you're not taking my daughter."

John stood over me with his arms crossed. His stance was slightly wider than normal, the position he took when cross-examining a defendant. I'd seen him do it when we worked a case together a lifetime ago. He'd told me he liked to create a power dynamic with his body language. That was exactly what he was doing. He'd spent months building a case against me, and I'd just delivered the closing argument with my reckless stupidity.

"John," I pleaded. "I messed up. Terribly. I know that. And I know you don't love me—that's been pretty obvious for a long time. But you know I love Amelia. I'm a good mother. You've seen me. Before the accident, I spent hours every night putting her to bed. I read to her. I took her to the beach and the park. You know I've done everything to give her a good childhood." I could see that my pitch was falling on deaf ears. John held the cards. If he brought the pictures and empty pill bottles before a judge, I could lose Amelia altogether.

"You used to be a fine mother," he conceded. "Now you neglect her and get in the car with her while you're high."

"That will *never* happen again." I got up, walked around the table, and reached for him. John flinched as my hand made contact with his arm. He looked like I'd touched him with a hot iron. The intensity of his physical reaction was a shock, and I let go.

"There's no point talking about this anymore," he said. There was a terrifying flatness to his voice. "Here's what's going to happen. You're going to agree to a divorce. And you're going to sign a custody agreement giving you two weekends a month with Amelia."

I grabbed him by the arms again. "No, you can't do this. I'll fight you in court."

"And," he said, raising his voice but keeping the same icy detachment, "if you take me to court, I will show the judge everything I've collected. I'll bring the empty bottles and pictures of the car you just wrecked. And you'll be lucky to get supervised visitation."

"John—" I started, but he cut me off.

"And then I'll take everything I have to your boss, and you'll lose your job."

I couldn't believe he would stoop low enough to threaten my work. I was out on temporary disability but still held out hope that I'd be fit enough to return someday. Not that I gave a damn about my job when he was threatening to take Amelia. If John thought his threat would deter me, then he had never really known me at all. "You're a bastard," I said. "Do the last five years really mean nothing?"

John got up and walked toward the door. "You've left me no choice. I'll have my lawyer draw up the paperwork."

"How long have you been planning this??" I stammered. "No—it doesn't matter. You can leave; I won't try to stop you. I'll give you everything. You can have my half of the condo and our bank account. Take both cars. It doesn't matter. Just don't take Amelia—she's all I have."

"Well, you should have thought about that before you got high and drove into a parked car," he snapped. He grabbed his keys off the counter and walked toward the door.

I ran after him, grabbed him by the shoulders. "Please, just talk to me. We can work this out." He shoved me off him and walked out of the apartment, leaving me crumpled and sobbing by the door.

18

Present Day—Kate

MARGOT'S EMAIL HISTORY was a curiosity cabinet of wounded male egos. I found five blackmail victims, and her phone would probably reveal even more. Each of these men had a motive to kill her. But as any cop will tell you, a victim's current beau is most often the culprit.

After hours of sleuthing, I hadn't found a single message from Margot's DJ paramour. It was time to talk to Blaze. According to his Twitter account, Blaze was scheduled to perform tonight at a downtown club. I texted Luke about the event, hoping he would join me. Luke had access to police reports and possible 911 recordings that weren't available to me. By now he would have reviewed whatever evidence the LAPD had collected against Blaze. If I saw Luke around Blaze, his face and line of questioning would tell me a lot about whether a domestic violence murder was a lead worth pursuing.

Blaze would be busy with his performance but would probably take a break between sets. We might be able to catch him off guard if he went out for a smoke or something. We wouldn't have time for a real interview, but I wanted to get a feel for the guy and see how he reacted to hearing Margot's name. That microsecond before self-control sets in can tell you everything you need to know.

I threw on a pair of black jeans and my leather jacket and headed out the door. Traffic wasn't bad, but downtown parking is the world's biggest rip-off. I handed a wad of bills to the attendant and started the quarter-mile trek to the club. It wasn't hard to find. A line of cold-looking young people stretched down the block. The music was so loud I could feel the beat in my thyroid.

This would probably be a good time to mention that I hate clubs. I hated them when I was twenty-one, and they haven't grown on me in the ensuing fifteen years. I don't like getting hit on by gross, drunk strangers. I don't like painful ringing ears. I don't like overpriced watery drinks. I don't like sticky, pee-stained bathroom floors. If I'm really bad, I expect to end up in a club after I die, because that's my personal version of hell.

The line took forty minutes to get through. All the while, a miniskirt-clad woman in front of me bobbed up and down, doing the universal *I have to pee* dance. Her boyfriend ignored her and chatted up a bruiser who I'm pretty sure I once arrested.

Someone tapped me on the shoulder. I spun around and saw a grinning redhead in a Lakers jersey. He smelled like beer and cheap cologne. "Hey, doll, where's your man at?"

"I don't have one, and I'm not looking for one," I said.

"Why not?" asked Don Juan. So much for taking a hint.

"Because my fondest wish is to be left alone so I can die alone."

The stranger put up both palms and took a step back in exaggerated defensiveness. "Wow, whatever, bitch. I was just making conversation."

"Okay, good chat."

"Fuck you," he hissed. "You're old and ugly anyway."

"Cheers to that." I turned around and pretended not to listen while the redhead talked smack about me. The line was moving at a snail's pace. I tried to telepathically persuade the bouncer to hurry things along, but he herded young-and-lovelys to the front while the rest of us waited. Eventually, my ordeal was over. I paid a ridiculous cover, the bouncer stamped my hand, and I walked down a flight of stairs to the subterranean purgatory.

The ceiling was claustrophobically low, and the music was deafening. I wandered over to the bar and ordered a gin and tonic that was basically just tonic with a dehydrated lime wedge floating on top like a dead insect. I looked at the stage and recognized Blaze from my internet stalking. He was a handsome metrosexual type. A little wimpy looking for my taste, but I could see the appeal. I wanted to watch him do his thing to get a feel for his personality. Afterward, I'd try to find the back entrance and wait for him to come out.

I looked around and spotted a familiar face in the back corner. Luke was chatting up a pretty, doe-eyed brunette. I kept my distance, not wanting to mess up his game.

Suddenly, I felt someone grab my arm. I spun around and saw the grinning redhead. He'd picked up two asshole friends and a beer. The combination had emboldened him.

"Hey, look, it's the asexual," he announced. "Wanna dance?"

"No," I said, shaking myself free.

"Come on." He grabbed my arm again. I pulled away from his sticky fingers with more force this time and accidentally splashed a bit of my drink on his jersey.

He looked down at his wet chest and then chucked his glass of beer on me. My training and my reflexes kicked in. I punched him in the windpipe, and as he doubled over, I kicked him in the groin. He dropped to the floor and several people around us took a step back.

One of the asshole friends started coming toward me, and I unzipped my jacket to show them my holster strap. "Try it," I said. They backed away obediently. The bigger of the two called me a crazy bitch before squatting down to tend to his boy.

I looked up and saw the three-hundred-pound bouncer jogging over to us. "Time to go," he ordered, grabbing my arm.

"Are you kidding me?" I protested. "He attacked me."

"Now," barked the bouncer, shoving me toward the exit. I caught Luke's eye as he headed in our direction. He put an arm around the bouncer and whispered something in his ear. The bouncer shrugged and walked away.

"Are you okay?" asked Luke.

I nodded. "Just sticky."

"Come on," he said, putting one arm behind my back and gesturing toward the door with the other.

"It's fine," I told him. "I'm gonna go outside and wait for Blaze to come out. You should stay and talk to that girl."

Luke rolled his eyes. "Don't be an ass, Myles. We need to move. I don't know if your friends are packing."

He had a point there. We walked outside, and I looked down at my wet jacket, assessing the damage.

"There's an alley behind this place where the talent enters and leaves from," said Luke. "Let's go wait for Blaze."

"You've been here before?"

He shrugged. "I worked downtown years back. I probably came here twice a week when a fight got out of hand."

We walked along the side of the building to a garbage-strewn alley that smelled of piss. An emaciated young woman with pig-tails and meth sores was talking to a man in a parka. He reached into his coat pocket and pulled out something wrapped in plastic. Luke flashed his badge, and they ran off.

I leaned against the brick wall, trying to get comfortable. My back hurt, and we could be here for a while.

"You kicked that guy's ass," said Luke. "What was that about?"

"We had a miscommunication."

He laughed. "About what?"

"Whether I should commune with a fine specimen like himself."

"Glad you set him straight."

Luke leaned next to me against the wall. He was close enough that I could sense the warmth of his skin. He smelled incredible.

"You smell like beer," said Luke.

"It covers up the other perfumes in this alley," I told him.

My mind flashed back to the night of the gallery opening, and I felt a fresh wave of humiliation. "By the way," I said, "thanks for driving me home the other night. I clearly had one too many, and I'm sorry if I said anything stupid."

Luke looked amused. "You mean like when you told me I was the hottest piece of ass you know?"

I gasped. "Oh my god, I said that?"

He laughed. "No, Myles, I was kidding. Though you did mention something about cloning me."

My cheeks burned.

"No worries. I had a nice time."

I glanced at him. He was hard to read. "Who was that girl in the club?"

Luke shrugged. "I have no idea. I was just passing the time. I hate this place."

"Tell me about it," I said. A gust of wind blew past me, and I shivered inside my damp jacket.

"You cold?" asked Luke.

I shook my head. "I'm good." I wished he'd put his arm around me. He didn't.

We lapsed into silence. The music was still so loud that I could feel it as much as hear it. A drunk wandered over to the brick wall across from us and fiddled with his belt. Luke held up his badge again, and he moved out of view.

Somehow Luke had drifted a little closer, and his arm was touching the sleeve of my jacket. I imagined what it would feel like if he leaned in. *Stop it*, I ordered myself. *You have a professional relationship, and being single and horny is not an excuse to let go of your faculties.* It had been more than two years since I'd had sex. Probably a decade since anyone shoved me against a wall in a fit of passion. I tried to think of something to say. Naturally, I came up with the perfect topic to break the spell.

"Luke, how did you end up in fraud?"

He flinched and looked away. *Brilliant, Kate, brilliant.*

"We don't have to talk about it," I backtracked. "It's none of my business, but you're obviously still obsessed with solving murders, so I was curious."

"It's fine," he said. "About a year ago, I was working late, catching up on reports. A couple officers—Bennett included—came back to the station after taking a few of the cadets on a ride-along."

The cadets are local teens that cops mentor as part of a community outreach effort. The thought of Bennett taking a minor under his wing raised major alarm bells. "They shouldn't let Bennett near the cadets," I said. "That's a lawsuit waiting to happen."

Luke smiled darkly. "Yeah, no shit. And he's not the only one. Anyway, one of the officers, Bill Jackson, brought out a couple of six-packs and invited me to join them for a drink on the roof. I declined, but I pulled him aside and asked what he was doing after hours with kids and booze. Jackson assured me the beers weren't for the cadets, so I let it go. But I had a bad feeling. One of the girls was really pretty, and he has a reputation for being a sleaze."

"I think I see where this is going," I said.

"I'm sure you do. At any rate, I left pretty soon after that. One of the girls later claimed Jackson got her drunk and had sex with her in a squad car. She was sixteen."

I winced. "That's gross, but it still doesn't explain why you're the one in fraud."

"Jackson gave my name to Internal Affairs. He claimed I could confirm that the cadets went straight home after the ride-along. But when IA called me, I told them the truth—I'm not gonna cover up that shit. Turns out Jackson's uncle is a captain in Robbery-Homicide. Jackson was briefly investigated and then returned to duty. I was written up for not reporting the drinking."

"No one else got in trouble?"

"Nope. Bennett backed Jackson, and the girl withdrew her claim. I don't know if they intimidated her or if there was some kind of payout. But Jackson was returned to duty, since it was my word against his. Bennett got rewarded with a transfer to RHD, and I got sent to fraud."

"That's outrageous," I said.

He sighed. "It is what it is." We lapsed into silence. I scanned my brain for a more cheerful topic of conversation but came up empty.

"Okay, my turn to ask a question," said Luke after a few minutes. I flinched, but turnabout's fair play. "Back at the gallery, why did John ask if you were on something?"

I tried to keep a neutral expression, but my heart pounded against my rib cage. "Because he's an asshole and he wanted to hurt me."

"That's what I thought at first," said Luke, "but after your second margarita, you mentioned that he has custody of your daughter. I don't see you letting that happen without a reason."

I turned away so he couldn't see my face. "Yeah, not exactly the normal custody split."

"Then there's something to it?" he pressed.

So much for a second chance with Luke. I couldn't blame him for prying. We were working together—sort of. He should know what he was dealing with.

I stared down the alley, trying to find something to focus on. A jar of peanut butter was spinning around in circles. If not for the tail poking out, you'd think it had a mind of its own. I sucked in a deep breath of air and let it out slowly.

"After I got T-boned by the guy evading arrest, I had six herniated disks and a cracked vertebra. I was in pain all the time. Sitting, standing, laying down—it didn't matter. My doctor prescribed something to help, and I got hooked. Between my fucked-up back and my fucked-up marriage, I needed to feel better, and the pills did the trick." I paused, waiting for Luke to say something, but he stayed quiet. "At any rate, I got off the pills after the surgery, and I haven't had an issue in a long time. There's nothing you need to worry about." My voice sounded strange, like it belonged to someone else.

"So that's why John left?" asked Luke.

"No, he left because we're incompatible and he was already sleeping with his twenty-six-year-old associate. Mind you, I didn't know that until she posted about their one-year anniversary five months after our divorce. But you live and you learn."

"And the pills—is that why John has custody?" he asked.

I focused on the spinning jar, keeping my eyes away from Luke. "To make a long story short," I said. I thought about telling him the rest of it. How I'd fallen asleep behind the wheel and endangered my daughter. How I'd signed away my custody rights out of fear that a judge would only allow me supervised visits. But I couldn't bring myself to say it. Not to him. Luke had seen me at my best—as a great detective with a stellar solve rate. As someone with a career on the rise, someone who had their shit together. It was impossible to reconcile that image of me with the unwashed addict who'd driven her child into a parked car. I was no longer the person Luke used to know, but working with him brought me a little closer to who I used to be. I didn't want to completely shatter that connection to my past. Besides, he wasn't entitled to every detail of my sordid history.

"Is the custody situation permanent? If you haven't had an issue in a while, can you challenge it?"

I glanced over at him. He was looking at me like a concerned friend. It wasn't the way I'd hoped he'd look at me, but I didn't detect any judgment or pity.

"I'm planning to challenge it, but I need to wait till I can prove I'm in control."

The jar had switched directions and was now rolling back toward the dumpster. I could feel Luke's eyes on me. My mind turned to a show about astral projection I'd watched once when I couldn't sleep. I imagined leaving my body and flying out of here and away from this conversation. Luke opened his mouth to speak, but before he could say anything, the music stopped. I jumped at the opportunity to change the subject. "They must be taking a break. Judging from Instagram, Blaze is a smoker. Hopefully he'll come out for a puff."

Luke nodded.

The back door to the club swung open, and Blaze emerged. "Hey, can we talk to you?" I asked.

He reached into his pocket, pulled out a cigarette, and lit it. "What do you want?" he said with mild annoyance. I studied his face. Up close, he looked like a baby. He must be at least ten years younger than Margot.

Luke held up his badge. "We want to ask you a few questions about Margot Starling."

Blaze grimaced at the sound of her name. "Fine, but I don't have much to say."

"Were you romantically involved with her?" I asked.

"Yeah, we broke up maybe a month before she died."

"Why'd you split up?" pressed Luke.

"I told her I loved her. She didn't feel the same. End of story. I didn't kill her, if that's what you're after."

Blaze looked like he was in a considerable amount of pain. My instincts told me he was telling the truth, although I've been wrong before. "Did you keep talking to her after she left you?" I asked.

"Yeah, we hooked up once or twice," he said. "I was hoping she'd change her mind about things, but she didn't."

"When was the last time you spoke?"

"Um, maybe a week before she died. Margot asked me to come over. Some cops had just been there. She was really freaked out and wanted me to spend the night."

Luke and I exchanged glances. "Did she describe the cops?"

"Um, she said there was a white guy and an Asian guy."

"Did she tell you anything else?" I asked. "Did she say why the police were at her place?"

He stubbed his cigarette out on the wall behind him and tossed it on the ground. "Something about old business. She just seemed shaken and wanted someone there with her. She asked me to stay the next night too, but I told her I was busy. I think about that every day."

Blaze pulled out his phone and checked the time. "I gotta go. It's only supposed to be a five-minute break." He knocked on the heavy metal door, and someone let him back inside. Luke and I exchanged glances. I knew we were thinking the same thing.

19

Present Day—Kate

WHEN I WOKE up the next morning, my ears were still ringing from Blaze's set. I forced myself to put Luke and my evening of revelations out of my mind. No more wasting time fantasizing about something that was never going to happen. Last night had been a badly needed reality check, and it was time to get my head back in the game.

I rolled out of bed and made coffee. The machine was covered in faded Disney stickers, courtesy of Amelia. I like them because they remind me of her. Sometimes I leave a little bit of her mess around so I can pretend she's just in the next room.

After pouring myself a cup, I sat down to make my daily to-do list. I needed to ask Garlington about the Venice Biennale, interview Jason Martinez's mother, and talk to Margot's neighbors. Unfortunately, my various stops were all over the county. Depending on traffic, I could be in for six hours of driving. My back would be on fire by the end of the day, and I'd promised Amelia an evening of bowling. I preemptively popped two Tylenol.

Garlington was my first stop of the day. Kelsey's sister was sitting at the front desk, wearing some kind of weird architectural shirt that tied in a bow. She turned crimson when I walked

through the door. Kelsey had probably shared some choice anec-
dotes about John's frumpy, hysterical ex with a pill problem. This
was bound to be awkward, but maybe I could use that to my
advantage. I gave her my best attempt at a warm smile. "Hi, Anya!
It was nice meeting you the other day. How are you?"

"Fine," she said, struggling to maintain eye contact. "How are
you?"

Good, forced politeness instead of the cold shoulder. "I'm
doing great," I said. "Thanks for asking." I looked around and
didn't see any customers. "It's kinda slow in here today, huh?"

"Yeah, afternoons are usually busier." She was nervously playing with her hair now, which made a strange contrast with her
sophisticated outfit.

"Great, then you'll have a few minutes to catch up." I didn't
pose it as a question, and I didn't wait for an answer. "Hey, I need
to ask you a few questions about one of your artists. Did you know
Margot Starling?"

Anya flinched, which I took as a yes.

"Did you ever meet her in person?"

"Yeah, a few times," she said. "I was going to pick her up for
the opening when I found her . . . like that."

My eyes widened. The coroner's report hadn't said who discovered the body. "You found her hanging in her bedroom?"

Anya nodded. "It was horrible. She was purple—her head was
swollen, and her eyes were kind of bugging out. The whole apartment smelled like rotten meat. It's the most awful thing I've ever
seen." Her voice was animated, and there was just the tiniest spark
of excitement in her eyes.

"I can imagine," I said. This girl had a flare for the dramatic.
She probably turned her macabre discovery into a favorite party
anecdote. *The time I walked in on a decomposing art star.* "Why
were you picking up Margot? Is that something you normally do
before an opening? Like a door-to-door service for artists?"

Anya shook her head. "She didn't show up at the opening,
so Peter gave me his key and told me to go get her." This detail

caught my attention. Garlington had told me their affair ended years ago. He shouldn't have still had a key to her digs.

"Was the door open when you got there?" I asked. "Was it damaged, like someone had forced their way in?"

She shook her head. "No, it was normal. I had to use the key." So Margot was killed by someone with a key or someone she'd let in.

"What did her apartment look like?" I asked. "Did you see any signs of a struggle?"

Anya shrugged. "I wouldn't know what I was looking for. The place was messy, if that's what you mean."

"Like normal messy, or something more?"

"Very messy. She'd just thrown her clothes on the floor like she didn't care. And there were tubes of paint on the ground. I stepped on one. It actually ruined my favorite pair of shoes." Clearly the biggest tragedy of her evening.

"Was anything damaged?" I asked.

Anya nodded again. "There was broken glass by the front door. I had to walk through it. And one of her paintings was slashed through, like with a knife."

I'd heard of Margot cutting herself but never mutilating her own work. On the other hand, if the killer had used a knife on a picture, why not on the artist?

Anya was looking past me, scanning the gallery for someone to save her. I needed to cut to the chase before she blew me off. "There's something else I wanted to ask you about," I said. "Tell me about the Venice Biennale."

"Um, it's an art show in Venice that's held every two years. Each country nominates an artist to represent them. It's a huge honor, a career high for any artist."

"And Margot was supposed to rep the U.S.?"

"Yes," she said. "We were all really excited about it."

I heard footsteps behind me and swung around to see Peter Garlington's unsmiling face. "Mr. Garlington! Anya and I were just chatting about the Venice Biennale. Incidentally, we just learned that we're related by marriage. What a small world!" I'd probably hear about this later from John, but he could shove it.

"Okay," said Garlington, shooting an icy glare in Anya's direction. She turned crimson once more but stayed silent. I got the sense she was terrified of her boss. He was probably a real peach when no witnesses were around.

"At any rate," I continued, "Anya was telling me that it's been a slow morning and you might have a few minutes to chat?"

"Um, that's not exactly what I said," she protested.

Garlington rubbed his temples, like my mere presence was giving him a headache. "What do you want to know?"

"Let's talk about Margot's project for the Biennale and why you were concerned about its effect on your clients."

He shot Anya a death glare before ushering me into his office and closing the door. "I don't know what my idiot assistant told you."

"Not much. Although I've been sifting through Margot's emails, which were very informative. Can you tell me about the blackmail?"

Garlington flinched. He was probably scanning his brain, trying to remember what he'd been careless enough to put in writing. "Technically, she wasn't blackmailing anyone," he said finally. "And to be clear, I didn't know about Margot's little hobby until after the fact. I got an angry call from a former client, which is how I learned about her hit list."

"What's his name?" I asked.

Garlington let out a single chuckle. "I'm not going to tell you that."

"Then tell me why it wasn't technically blackmail. She was sleeping with men and asking for money to keep it under wraps."

He shook his head. "Not exactly. She was sleeping with men in positions of power, taking embarrassing pictures, and then making paintings from the photographs. Margot never asked for money, but she offered them first dibs on purchasing the art."

"I don't understand," I said. "I've seen her auction prices. She obviously didn't need the money."

"The proceeds didn't go to her. She made them donate to some cause preselected for maximum impact. She called it restitution."

"What do you mean by maximum impact?"

"Maximum embarrassment. We're talking Republican politicians donating to Planned Parenthood. A lawyer for the archdiocese giving to a fund for children abused by priests. That kind of thing."

"And they agreed to this?"

"Yes," he said. "The first couple had to donate in their own name. When she hit on more pushback, she let them make the donations in her name."

"Why would they agree to do this?"

"They thought it was their only way out. Margot signed a contract assuring them that she wouldn't make another painting in their likeness or disseminate the photographs she'd taken of them—unless it was for her own legal defense."

"But then she did her little X-Acto project, and they got exposed anyway," I pointed out.

"Yes, that was a nightmare. People who'd paid hundreds of thousands to keep her quiet were publicly humiliated. And of course they couldn't deny it, because Margot kept receipts."

"So where does the Biennale come in?" I asked.

"The contracts prevented Margot from disseminating photographs of the men or making additional paintings of them. But it said nothing about sharing photographs of preexisting paintings. Margot had thought through every detail and built in a loophole."

"What was she planning to do exactly?" I asked.

"When Margot was selected for the Venice Biennale, the timing worked out perfectly. The statute of limitations on extortion had run. She was going to show blown-up photographs of the paintings next to copies of the contracts and records of her lovers' embarrassing donations."

"So she was preparing to humiliate a bunch of jilted VIPs for the third time. First the blackmail, then the painting with their names on her torso, then the Biennale."

Garlington nodded. "Pretty much. And there was nothing they could do about it besides complain to me. I begged her to come up with a different project, but Margot was stubborn as a mule. She always did what she wanted."

"Did anyone besides you know about the project?"

"An art blogger got hold of the broad outline of her plan—not the names or the details but the general idea. I suspect Margot leaked it herself to get people talking. After that, a number of her subjects started calling me, desperate to shut it down."

"Can you tell me who called you?" I pressed.

Garlington looked annoyed. "I already gave you Grigsby's name, which was more than I should have. Go back to her *Homage to Tracy Emin* piece. Most of the people involved are included there."

"Why was she out to destroy these people?" I asked. "Was it some kind of personal vendetta?"

Garlington hesitated and ran a hand through his thick white hair. "Yes and no. At some point, Margot had a friend who was raped in jail. He'd been in for just a few days for some minor offense—probably drugs. Afterwards, she became a bit radicalized about certain issues. Prisoner rights were front and center, but other civil rights too. She wanted her work to matter. But it wasn't all about her ideals," he continued. "Margot understood the market. When she first started, it was all about shock art, pushing boundaries. Everything had to be violent, obscene, confessional. Margot was good at that. But there was a shift in tastes, and people became more interested in art about social justice and less focused on sex and violence."

"Was that shift around the time she started this project?"

"Yes," said Garlington.

"So you think it was just business for her?"

He considered this. "I wouldn't say that. Margot was a brilliant woman, but she got bored easily. She needed to constantly reinvent herself and watch the world's reaction. At the same time, she genuinely cared about what she viewed as injustice. She was an icy bitch, but she felt things deeply."

"Not that any of that would matter to the men she was black-mailing," I pointed out.

"No," agreed Garlington. "Like I told you before, if you're making a list of her enemies, it'll be a long one."

I had a feeling he was right about that. And I'd barely scratched the surface.

20

Present Day—Kate

Jason's mother had responded right away to my Facebook message. After a brief back-and-forth, she'd agreed to meet me at a coffee shop near her house in Long Beach. Unfortunately, that was about an hour and a half from the gallery without traffic. It was gonna be a long day.

As I drove, my thoughts turned to Margot. I'd pictured a sensitive arrested adolescent who lucked her way into a glamorous life. But in her own crazy way, Margot was in control. Take Blaze—I'd thought he was using her, but it was the other way around. And then there was her blackmail project. What she did to her exes was fucked-up, but there was something delicious about her talent for revenge-as-self-promotion. Even Garlington couldn't rein her in. I tried to imagine going through life like Margot—planning my ascent, taking what I wanted, never apologizing. She was only a few years older than me, but our lives couldn't have been further apart.

I arrived at the coffee shop early and selected a table in the corner. The scent of freshly roasted beans triggered my late-morning caffeine headache. I ordered a large Americano and settled down to wait. Before long, a petite woman with salt-and-pepper hair walked in. I instantly recognized her from her son's social media accounts, but she looked about twenty years older than the person I'd been expecting.

I rose to my feet to greet her. "Mrs. Martinez?" I asked, catching her eye.

"Please, call me Elena," she said, taking my outstretched hand. I could see the family resemblance. She had the same beautiful dark eyes as her son, but the skin around them was crisscrossed with fine lines and the hollows underneath were as dark as a bruise. She probably hadn't slept through the night since Jason died.

"I'm Kate. Can I get you a coffee?"

Elena shook her head. "Now you said this was about my son?" There was an eagerness in her voice, and I felt a pang of guilt. I should have been more specific in my message.

"Yes, I have some questions about Jason. First of all, I'm so sorry for your loss."

"Thank you." Her tone said to get to the point.

"I'm working for the family of another artist—Margot Starling."

Elena nodded. "She and Jason were at UCLA together."

I'd been wondering if Margot and Jason had known each other. They were both successful, LA-based painters in the same age bracket. The art world seemed pretty claustrophobic. Those two were bound to run into each other at the occasional cocktail party. But the fact that they were actually classmates in a tiny MFA program felt like more than a coincidence. And their mutual connection to a C-list dealer in Venice was definitely suspicious. "Were they friends?" I asked.

Elena flushed and looked uncomfortable. I had a feeling she didn't want to speak ill of the dead. "No. Jason didn't like her. He said she could be nasty, but he respected her work."

I felt slightly disappointed. Maybe it was a coincidence that they'd both ended up in the same gallery. "I contacted you because I've been hired to look into Margot's death," I told her. "In the process, I came across a gallery called Berkland that started selling Margot's paintings after she died. A lot of people think they're forgeries. Now Berkland is selling paintings he claims were made by your son. Did you know anything about this?"

Elena frowned, and I could tell this was news to her. "Jason sold a few pieces through Berkland when he was struggling after art school," she told me. "But he hasn't shown there in years. Bauman & Firth represented him."

I didn't know what to make of Berkland's past connection to Jason. On one hand, a prior affiliation could explain how the gallerist ended up with Jason's paintings. On the other hand, he hadn't exactly acted innocent when I confronted him. And it was weird that he never mentioned Jason's history with the gallery.

"Berkland claims your son gave several paintings to a friend, who's now selling them through his gallery. He told the exact same story when he was selling what we think were Margot Starling knock-offs. Did Jason have anyone special he might have given paintings to?"

She thought for a moment. "Possibly his boyfriend, Mike Moreland. But Mike would have gone through Bauman & Firth."

If so, the boyfriend should have gone to the fancier gallery, which charged higher prices. But if there was something shady about the sale, unloading them through Berkland made sense. "Tell me about Mike," I said. "What was their relationship like?"

Elena's face lit up. "Mike is wonderful. He was so good to Jason. I'd hoped they'd get married someday. He still calls to check on me sometimes." Her eyes started to shine.

"I'm so sorry," I said, placing one hand over Elena's. She nodded and dabbed at her eyes with a napkin. My heart went out to her. To see her son find love and achieve his dreams—everything a person wants for their child—and then for him to die a sudden violent death . . . "How long were they together?"

"A couple years. Jason moved in with Mike a few months before he died. The boys would bring me with them to buy things for the house. They'd ask my opinion on furniture, but I don't think they really needed my help. It was just an excuse to take me on an outing."

"Did Mike go to UCLA with Jason and Margot?" I asked.

She shook her head. "Mike's not an artist, he's a lawyer."

"I'd love to talk to him. Do you think he'd be willing to speak to me?"

Elena shrugged. "I can ask him." She pulled her phone out of a small backpack and read me his phone number from her list of contacts. I scribbled it down on a napkin.

"Mrs. Martinez, would you be willing to go to the Berkland gallery and let me know if you think your son made those paintings?"

"Of course," she said. "If someone is taking advantage of Jason, I want to know. I can give you my opinion—he grew up following me around, sketching and painting as I worked. But I'm no expert."

"Well, you're his mother. Your opinion matters."

"I'll go. I'll go right away," she promised. "And thank you for letting me know about this." Elena shook my hand and headed for the door.

After she left, I picked up my phone to call Jason's boyfriend. He picked up with a brisk "Moreland here."

"Hi, Mr. Moreland," I said. "I'm a private detective looking into the death of an artist named Margot Starling. I was wondering if I could ask you a few questions about Jason Martinez?" The line clicked off. I called back twice in case the disconnect was accidental, but it went straight to voice mail. Dodging my calls could be a sign that he was hiding something. Or that he didn't want to talk about his grief with a pushy stranger.

After draining a second cup of coffee, I hit the road. My phone chimed, alerting me to a new voice mail. I hit the speaker button and was treated to a minute and a half of John yelling at me for "harassing" Kelsey's sister. This had nothing to do with him, and I didn't need his permission to do my job. Hopefully he wouldn't try to punish me for the intrusion into his life. I was well aware of how passive-aggressive John could be.

I pulled into a pay lot down the block from Margot's place and walked over. I'd noticed the building before. It was a funky, art deco skyscraper with the kind of historical detail that people pay through the nose for. I crossed the street and entered the impressive marble lobby. The wrought iron elevator looked original to the building, so it had to be at least ninety years old. I stepped inside and held my breath as it groaned to life and slowly carried me to the ninth floor.

From a brief conversation with the building manager, I'd learned that Margot had been leasing her condo. After the police released the scene, her landlord had had it power washed and put it back on the market. I wondered if he had told the new tenant about the woman found hanging in the bedroom. Maybe I would do the honors.

I knocked on Margot's door, but no one was home. Next, I tried the unit on either side. No answer. It was fairly early, so they could still be at work. I pounded harder in case the inhabitants were elderly or hard of hearing. A door across the way swung open. I turned around and saw a young woman peek into the hallway. She was wearing a chocolate-milk-stained T-shirt and bouncing a toddler on her hip. In the background, a little girl sat openmouthed in front of the TV. "Well, you're not the delivery guy," the woman said.

"Sorry to disappoint." I stepped toward her before she could close the door and handed her my card. "I'm a private investigator working for Margot Starling's parents." She glanced reflexively at Margot's old unit. "Can I ask you a few questions?"

She nodded. "Sure, at least until the pizza gets here. Then I have to feed my kids."

"I get it. I have a seven-year-old," I told her, feeling a stab of jealousy. My little girl should be home watching movies on the couch. At least she was coming over tonight. "Did you know your former neighbor?"

"I wouldn't say I *knew* her. We spoke a couple times." From her tone, it was clear things hadn't been friendly.

"What about?" I asked.

She shrugged. "Nothing worth mentioning. Nods in the hallway, that kind of thing. We weren't buddies or anything. She was a shitty neighbor, always blasting music late at night. We thought about calling the police a couple times."

My ears perked up. "Did you call them?"

"No," she said. "My husband wanted to, but I thought it would make things more tense."

"Did the police ever come?" I asked.

She nodded. "About a week before they found her, two cops came to her door."

"Do you happen to remember what they looked like?" I still knew a lot of people on the force. If she remembered something distinguishing, it might give me another officer to bug for information besides poor Luke.

"Yeah," she said. "There was an Asian guy and a white guy with tattoos."

The mention of tattoos brought Bennett to mind. But I could be letting my dislike of him cloud my judgment. "What happened after the cops showed up?"

"They went inside her apartment." She smiled sheepishly. "My husband and I stuck our heads into the hallway to eavesdrop. We were sick of Margot's bullshit and felt a bit of schadenfreude at the thought of her getting in trouble."

"What did they say?" I asked.

She shrugged. "As usual, Margot had music on in the background, so I couldn't make out most of it. But the conversation sounded heated. At one point I heard a slap. We thought maybe she was resisting arrest or something."

"You're sure it was a slap?" I asked. The coroner investigator must have misunderstood. She'd written that the police came *after* a slap. But the neighbor seemed to think they were already there.

"It sounded like a slap, but I can't say for sure. It could have been a clap for emphasis, or a high five or something." She adjusted the kid on her hip.

"You said you couldn't hear most of the conversation, but did any words jump out at you?"

She cocked her head, trying to remember. "One of the cops said, 'It's not going to happen,' or something like that. It sounded like a warning."

"Do you think you'd recognize the officers if you saw them again?" I asked.

"Oh, I did see one of them again. The one with the ink came back the day they found her body. I told someone about it at the time. I think she was a crime tech or something."

It took me a second to process what I was hearing. *Oh my god, it was Bennett.* This explained why he hid the coroner investigator's report from Luke. "You're sure it was the same guy?" I pressed.

"Pretty sure, but not positive. Maybe seventy percent."

I opened my mouth to inquire further, but the elevator chimed, and a pimply teenager in a delivery uniform stepped out holding a pizza box.

"Sorry, I gotta feed my kid," she said.

"Can I call you later to finish this conversation?" I asked.

She scribbled her number on a piece of paper and handed it to me. "Sure, but I've told you all I know."

I felt shell-shocked as I walked down the hallway. When I took on this case, I'd expected to confirm that the LAPD got it right. Now I couldn't shake the feeling that the cops were somehow involved. It would explain the rush job on the investigation and Bennett's shifty behavior. I needed to talk to the coroner investigator. And to tread very, very lightly.

CHAPTER

21

Six Years Ago—Zack

"THIS IS BULLSHIT," I told my sergeant. "If she already admitted it, why can't I just go pick her up?"

He frowned at me in that hangdog way of his. The loose skin on his brow furrowed like it does on those bloodhounds we send out to sniff for corpses. "The DA says it's not enough," he told me. "You need more than a confession to charge someone. Otherwise we'd be locking up every hobo who thinks he shot Reagan."

Jesus, even his analogies were decades out of date. "I don't get it," I said. "Some artist weasels her way into a tour of Men's Central Jail, admits she snuck in a camera to film the inmates, and then makes *paintings* of them. Why isn't this open-and-shut?"

He sighed and rubbed his temples, a sign that it was time for me to stop talking. I was scheduled to take the sergeant's exam in a month. With a stellar arrest rate, I was a shoo-in for the promotion. That is, if I could keep my attitude in check. "It's cool, Sarge, I'll go. You just want me to show up at the gallery, look at the paintings, and try to talk to her?"

"Yes. And take pictures of the art for evidence. Diaz said the painting they reproduced in *LA Weekly* looks like that attempted homicide you brought in last month."

"Why aren't the sheriffs investigating this?" I asked. "If this is their fuck-up, why does LAPD have to clean it up?"

He took off his glasses and cleaned them on the front of his shirt: another sign I was fraying his nerves. "Internal Affairs over there asked us to look into it as a favor. This has the potential to be a publicity case, and they want to show they're impartial by inviting in an outside agency."

Now things were making sense. It's illegal to film inside a jail. If some brand-new deputy got distracted by a hot artist and let her into custody with a camera, the shit was gonna hit the fan. "I got it, Sarge, but tell me this: wouldn't this whole headache go away if it turns out she made the whole thing up as a publicity stunt?"

"Sure, if that's the truth," he snapped. He was done talking about it, and that was fine by me. I had nothing better to do tonight anyway. I'd stop by the gallery toward the end of the opening reception. Hopefully she'd be nice and boozy by then and start confessing.

I thought about my brother, Chris, recently hired by the sheriff's department. They start their new recruits in the jails before putting them on the street. It makes sense, to be honest. You learn how to manage the animals while they're disarmed and confined. By the time the deputies are assigned to patrol, they're not as jumpy and trigger-happy as some of our rookies. That's the idea, anyway.

A nasty thought popped into my head. Chris was one of the grunts they'd probably assigned to do jail tours. And he was always shy around pretty girls. I could see him half-assing a search: skipping the pat-down and never finding the camera stashed in her bra or snatch or wherever.

It was the kind of thing that could happen to anyone, and the kind of scandal that could end a career before it even started. Maybe even land you on the DA's list of problem officers. I doubted this bitch ever thought about the lives she was messing with. Probably some spoiled liberal who thought every cop was a racist murderer.

Once inside my car, I pulled up a picture of the artist online and texted it to Chris. *Does she look familiar?* I asked.

A little, he wrote back. *Why?*

Fuck. *Is it possible that you gave her a jail tour?* I stared at my phone, impatient for a response.

Maybe? he wrote. *Definitely looks familiar but I can't place her. She's pretty.*

It didn't necessarily mean anything. He could have seen her picture in the paper. And sometimes beautiful people just look familiar. It's almost like you wish you'd seen them before.

Why? texted Chris.

Don't worry about it, I wrote. No reason to upset him prematurely.

I parked in front of the gallery. It was huge, like a strip mall painted white. The rent must cost a fortune. I walked up to the door and held it for an ancient couple. The old man was stooped over and walked with a cane. His wife clutched his arm tightly. Loose yellow skin coated her hands, like a turkey before you skin it. All that money can't buy you time, gramps.

The crowd was starting to thin. I grabbed a glass of wine and scanned the room for the artist. She was easy to spot. Long, fit body, sleek dark hair, a red dress that fit like a glove. I could see how she might con some poor kid working security. Once she was alone, I'd make my approach. I had worn my court suit to blend in. She'd think I was just another rich mope ready to drop a pile of cash if she smiled enough.

I walked around and looked at the paintings, waiting for her to finish her conversation. They were really good; they could almost be photographs. But it was depressing seeing giant picture after giant picture of men in jail cells. I couldn't believe anyone would actually buy one of these and put it in their living room. The setting was clearly Men's Central. One work was even titled *The Gay Men's Wing*. The sheriffs separate them out for their own protection, and they have their own accommodations. She'd captured it all right.

Next, she'd done the child molester wing. Those guys have to be kept apart too, since they'd be the first ones to get shivved in gen pop. True to form, it was men of all ages and backgrounds. One guy, who'd probably been a teacher or doctor before getting busted, was reading the *Wall Street Journal*. Another just lay on his bunk and stared into space.

I found the painting my sergeant had mentioned, and it was one hundred percent the guy I'd arrested. Will Francis had gotten mad at his girlfriend for texting another guy. She refused to let him see her phone, so he decided to teach her a lesson with a seven-inch butcher knife. She should be dead; with her injuries, it would have been a blessing. But she wasn't.

That was Francis all right. Down to his widow's peak and the red lips tattooed on his neck. It was the injury on his hand that convinced me the portrait was copied from a photograph. Will's knife had slipped while he was going to town on his old lady, and he'd cut himself with the blade. In the painting, he clutched the bars defiantly. You could see a deep red gash on the fleshy part of his palm. On his left cheek, he had three scratches, where the vic had clawed him in self-defense. No way this woman could have remembered those details so perfectly after seeing the asshole for just a millisecond.

I looked down at the title: *Feeding the Animals*. The artist probably meant it ironically. She had no idea. I felt a wave of repulsion and spun around to catch a glimpse of her. She was grabbing a glass of wine from the drink table. Our eyes met, and she smiled and walked over.

"Hi, I'm Margot," she said.

She was even hotter up close. Green eyes, red lips. I smiled back and shook her hand. "I'm Zack. Did you make these?"

She nodded.

"I was wondering if the rumors were true." I tried to sound casual and flirty. It wasn't hard, since she was so attractive.

"What rumors?" she asked, sidling up to me.

"Now you're being coy."

She laughed, and her face lit up like a Christmas tree. "No, I'm serious. I've been the subject of a lot of rumors over the years."

"That you snuck in a camera. They look so real—I can't imagine how else you could've made these without a camera."

She grinned mysteriously. "I did tour the jail," she admitted. "I had been studying the work of German artist Käthe Kollwitz. You know her?"

Obviously not. "Sure," I said.

"She made this incredible serious of etchings of prisoners in the nineteenth century, and it inspired me to set up a jail tour to see if things have changed."

"Have they?" I asked.

"No, it was appalling. People were just living on top of one another, and the smell was beyond belief."

"How'd you set up the tour?" I asked. "You just called up and said, 'I want to see inmates'?"

She smiled. "No, I have a friend who's an ACLU lawyer. They were already going, and she asked me if I wanted to join the tour."

"What was it like?" I asked.

"Truly horrible. They had this sweet young kid giving the tour, a tall beanpole of a thing with a mop of frizzy hair."

Fuck, that sounded like Chris. "He was one of the guards?"

"Yes. This kid looked like he could barely grow facial hair, and he was caging human beings for a living."

"So the kid took you on your tour. But how did you get the pictures? They're so detailed. You must have brought a camera." I was playing dumb, like I didn't already know that cameras were banned. "Did you just snap pictures with your phone or something?"

"I'll tell you a little secret," she said. "Well, I told *LA Weekly* already, so it's not really a secret. You're not supposed to, but I did have a camera."

I smiled and pretended to be impressed. "Wow, did you hide it or something?"

"A girl can't give away all her secrets," she said.

I forced myself to laugh. "Now you're definitely being coy. Come on, you can tell me. My lips are sealed."

"Fine, if you promise to keep it to yourself." She'd probably been "confiding" her crime to people all night. *The arrogance of this woman.* "I had a button disguised as a camera. You can buy them on the internet."

"Tell me," I said. "Did you make any paintings of that young deputy you were talking about?"

"No," she said, to my great relief. "I thought about it. He really was poignant, but it didn't go with the theme."

This was a problem. If we booked her for a felony, we'd have to follow up with a warrant for the pictures. If Chris had been her tour guide, he'd be exposed. Not only that, I would get in trouble for hiding the conflict of interest from my boss. Bye-bye, promotion. There was no way I could report this. But I needed her to stop blabbing about it.

"Tell me about this picture," I said, pointing to Will Francis.

"When we walked by, he kept looking at me," she said. "He had this quiet dignity to him. And he kept saying things like 'Welcome to the zoo.' He was basically accusing us of gawking at him like he was an exhibit at SeaWorld. And he was right, in a way. I felt really terrible about it."

"You wanted to free him?" I asked. I was having a hard time keeping the contempt out of my voice, and Margot looked taken aback by my change in tone.

"Yes, of course," she said.

"What if I told you that guy stabbed his girlfriend forty-five times and she's disfigured for life. The nerve damage is so bad, she can't even smile any more. Does that change your perspective?"

The artist looked shocked. "I'd say that regardless of what a person's done, I don't believe in caging another human being. Now, who are you? You obviously didn't come here to support my work."

"Detective Zack Farabee, LAPD," I said. "Did you know that filming in the jails is a serious crime?"

"I knew it was against the rules," she said.

"It's not just against the rules. It's a felony that carries up to three years in prison." I doubted a judge would give her more than a slap on the wrist, but she didn't need to know that. I was making a point. She looked genuinely afraid. Good. She was messing with people's lives as a publicity stunt. She deserved to be a little fearful.

"Of course, you love prisoners so much, it should be a breeze. A beautiful girl like you, you'll have no problems making friends inside."

The bitch was finally speechless. She just stared at me with those big green eyes. I liked seeing her squirm. "And guess what else?" I said. "You're not the only one with a secret recorder." I pulled my phone out of my pocket and hit play, treating her to the first few seconds of our encounter. Her eyes grew wide with panic. "I have you on tape talking about how you committed a felony, and I can personally identify your friend in this picture, since I arrested him."

She took a step back from me and was now inches away from bumping into the painting. I held up my phone and prepared to hit record. Putting a little fear of God into her might be fun, but I didn't really care about Margot. What I really needed was for this case to go away. If it was Chris who fucked up, I wasn't about to let some liberal hack ruin his career, pontificating about shit she didn't know a thing about.

"Now let's try this again," I said. "Maybe you just have a really good memory. Maybe your interview in the *LA Weekly* was just a publicity stunt." I showed her the screen of my phone and hit record. "Miss Starling, as a fan, I have to ask, did you really sneak a camera into the jails?"

There was an awkward pause, and I wondered whether I'd made myself clear. She faked a laugh. "Of course not," she said. "The truth is, I have a photographic memory. It's served me well as an artist. I see something—I just remember it in great detail, so I can replicate it later in my studio. That's what I did here. But I'm flattered that anyone would think otherwise."

I hit stop and put my phone away. She sounded natural enough. With that recording, no DA would ever bring charges and Chris was safe. Then a thought occurred to me. A woman like this wouldn't give me the time of day in any other setting. But now I held all the cards. And after all, I was doing her a favor. Shouldn't I get something in return?

"Now I have both versions, and what happens next is up to you," I told her. "Maybe we can work something out. Maybe you do something for me, and that first recording goes away." My heart was pounding. I'd tried this kind of thing in alleys with whores, but not a famous artist in Beverly Hills. On the other hand, a criminal is a criminal.

She was silent as my meaning sank in. I knew she wanted it. This bitch had been flirting with me from the moment we locked eyes. Fine, she might not have chosen to go home with me if I hadn't forced her hand. But she enjoyed coming over here and doing her little presentation.

When she finally met my gaze, her expression was totally blank. "I was going to take an Uber home, but why don't you give me a ride?"

"I think I can do that." I couldn't believe my good fortune. I'd just made the case go away and was about to nail the hottest piece of ass I'd landed in years.

22

Present Day—Kate

SURE ENOUGH, JOHN punished me for visiting Anya by planning a last-minute sleepover on my Friday. I was about to fetch
Amelia from school when I received a text informing me that
she'd be staying over at her friend Michelle's. There was nothing I
could do. If I canceled, I'd disappoint my daughter and look like
a flake to her friend's parents.

I thought about calling her to say good-night but decided
against it. I'm not sure if that's something most mothers would do
when their kid sleeps over at a friend's house. I was probably overthinking it. But these days, I'm constantly trying to make a good
impression with the other parents. I know John bad-mouths me to
some of them, and I can't control that. But I try to act as average
and nondescript as I can, so I don't become known as the unstable
druggie mom who lost custody.

Normally I wouldn't care what random people think of me,
but I worry about how my reputation affects Amelia. Parents gossip; children overhear things. When I was in elementary school,
everyone knew Eileen Warfield's mother had slept with Rachel
Schmidt's father, and the bullying was merciless. I hate how my

divorce affects Amelia, and I try to at least keep the fallout away from her school life.

I had planned to make a real dinner tonight: shepherd's pie, which Amelia loves, and broccoli, which she tolerates. But the idea of cooking for one made me feel even lonelier. Instead, I spent Friday night eating frozen beef stroganoff and drinking wine in front of the TV.

Before the accident, I never drank alone. Then I quit the pills and developed chronic insomnia. Every night for months, I lay awake in pain, wondering whether it would hurt less if I changed positions or mentally rehashing the myriad ways I had managed to screw up my life. A glass of wine or two was often the only way I could fall asleep. It didn't seem like a big deal at first. After growing up with a cop for a dad—a happy, more-or-less functional alcoholic with a posse of drinking buddies—daily alcohol felt normal to me. Plus, I was used to drinking at cop hangouts, where the only teetotalers refrain for religious reasons or because they truly can't control themselves. After a while the glass of wine went from a comfort to a habit to a crutch. I never touch the stuff in front of Amelia, and I don't usually let it interfere with my work. But if I'm honest with myself, it's probably past time to cool it.

Saturday and Sunday were still reserved for my daughter, but my plan of showing her a good time was not meant to be. Amelia caught a nasty stomach bug from her friend. She seemed fine on the drive home, if a little pale. But as I pulled onto my street, she leaned forward and heaved liquid pancake all over the upholstery. I texted John to let him know she was under the weather. He tried to get me to bring her back to his house, which was not going to happen. I had precious little time with her, and she could convalesce just as well at my place.

The rest of the weekend was a fog of thermometers, chicken soup, and cartoons. When Sunday night rolled around, I felt incredibly sad. Normally, I let Amelia stay up late to squeeze in a few more precious hours with her. I figure it won't kill her if she's a little sleepy at school every other Monday. But she'd been sick all weekend and needed to rest. I tucked her in after dinner and read her a chapter of *The Secret Garden*. When she finally passed out, I closed the book and watched her sleep. If only I could read to her every night like a normal mother. I wondered what kind of relationship we'd have when she grew up. She'd think of me as an immature weekend parent who fed her too much candy and let her stay up past her bedtime. Maybe it was time to call a lawyer. At this point, no reasonable judge would view me as a safety risk.

I stayed by her side until my back ached from sitting on the rigid, child-sized bed. Then I wandered over to my room. It was still relatively early, so I decided to try Mike Moreland again. He didn't pick up. I left a message telling him that Jason's mom had given me his number. Elena had made it sound like they were close. Hopefully, hearing her name would reassure him.

After hanging up, I flipped through crap TV for an hour and then went to my room to toss and turn and try to sleep.

On Mondays, I normally take Amelia directly to school. But she'd forgotten her backpack at her dad's house. We got up at the crack of dawn to get her there before John had to leave for work. As soon as he opened the door, he started interrogating me about what I'd fed her and how much TV I'd let her watch. I wish he wouldn't use that tone in front of the kid. He can be as condescending as he wants when we're alone, but around Amelia, it reinforces his narrative that Daddy knows best and Mommy is an incompetent ass. I told him I was late for a nonexistent meeting, kissed my daughter, and walked away.

Once in the car, I cursed and slapped the wheel. I hardly see the kid. When she finally comes over, she's sick as a dog and I get put through the third degree about what type of bread I use for her sandwiches. John had been freaking out lately, saying Amelia was getting plump. Like it matters at age seven. Kelsey had even enrolled my uncoordinated little girl in ballet class "for the exercise." The two of them are going to give Amelia an eating dis-order before she hits puberty.

I forced myself to mentally change channels and focus on the case. Elena Martinez had texted me, telling me she went to see Berkland and "gave him a piece of her mind." I'd forwarded the message to Luke. His silence confirmed that I was onto something. I decided to swing by the gallery and see if Elena had spooked Berkland enough to hide the inventory. If the paintings were gone, I'd know they were forgeries.

Before setting out, I tried Mike Moreland again. He didn't pick up, so I left another message. "Hi, Mike, it's Kate Myles. I'd really like to talk to you. Please call me when you get a chance." I'd now been phone-stalking him for days. If he didn't get back to me by tomorrow, I'd track down an address and show up at his door.

I stopped at a drive-through coffee place and took the 405 down to Venice. It was a beautiful day with a delicious ocean breeze. The gallery wasn't open yet, so I decided to kill time at the beach. The parking lot was almost empty. It was too early for tourists, and the locals hardly come here anymore.

I pulled into a spot and hit the alarm button on my key chain. The beachside homeless encampment had doubled since the last time I was out here. The *L.A. Times* had been covering the war between homeowners and activists, which hit a fever pitch as property crimes reached a multiyear high. I walked past the rib-bon of garbage and makeshift tents and stepped out onto the sand. It felt cool under my feet, not yet baked by the LA sun. I walked down to the water's edge. In the distance, a young mother was lowering her baby's toes into the freezing Pacific, laughing as he recoiled from the shock. I smiled, remembering when Amelia first discovered the ocean. The gulls screamed overhead, and I sipped my coffee, letting my mind go blank.

After twenty minutes, I turned around and walked back to the car. I drove to the gallery and found a parking spot across the street. The lights were off, and it looked like the place was still closed. I tried the door handle just to be sure. It didn't budge. There was a glare of reflected light on the window, and I pressed my face against it to see inside. The wall of so-called Martinez paintings was intact. As I scanned the room, my eyes hit on the empty front desk. A few days ago, the table had sported a MacBook Pro, now nowhere in sight. Other than the missing computer, everything looked the same.

I turned around to leave and saw a scowling man heading in my direction. "Kate Myles?" he barked.

"That's me," I said. "Who are you?"

"Gus Vargas, FBI." He was right out of central casting, with a dark, freshly pressed suit and close-cropped hair. Vargas had an athletic build and a no-nonsense face. The only thing out of sorts about him was his left eyebrow, bifurcated by a two-inch-long scar.

"What's this about?" I asked.

"Let's take a walk," said Vargas. It sounded like an order.

Something felt off. I didn't understand how this guy recognized me or why the FBI was interested in a low-rent private eye. "Can I see some ID?" I asked. He scowled at me, as if my request was out of line. "I don't know you, and I'm not going to follow you anywhere until you show me an ID."

Vargas looked annoyed, but he pulled out his badge. It appeared to be the real thing, and I had my gun if I was wrong. "How did you know who I was?" I asked.

He swiveled his head to either side, scanning for anyone watching us. "I don't want to do this in front of the gallery. There's a dog park a block west of here. We can talk there."

I hesitated but decided to follow him. My curiosity was piqued, and I could turn around if things started to feel hinky.

We walked in silence. Vargas didn't bother making small talk, and I followed his lead. The park was surrounded by a chain-link fence and bordered by a fairly busy street. On the other side of the field, a young woman was playing catch with an expensive-looking poodle hybrid. She was out of earshot but would be able to see if things took a bad turn.

"What's this about?" I asked. "And how did you know who I was?"

"I need to know what you said to Aksel Berkland," he demanded.

The question caught me off guard. I'd only had one conversation with the gallerist and had no idea how Vargas would even know about that. "Berkland? I met him once."

His eyes narrowed. "I've spent the last six months working up a case, and suddenly I'm told that a prime figure in my investigation disappeared after talking to a PI named Kate Myles. Why do you think that is?"

I couldn't tell what he was insinuating, but I didn't like his tone. "Told by whom? And what kind of investigation?" I asked. "Is it related to the forgeries?"

"I can't tell you that," he snapped. I took that as a yes. "What did you say to Berkland?"

I crossed my arms over my chest. "Who gave you my name, and how did you recognize me just now?"

He let out an exasperated sigh. "Luke Delgado from the LAPD said you talked to Berkland. I ran your DMV and recognized you from your picture. Now, you said you only met Berkland once. What was the meeting about?"

Luke was the last name I expected to hear. "How do you know Detective Delgado?"

"I'm not here to play twenty questions," Vargas snapped.

"That's fine. I'm happy to end this conversation right now." Luke should have given me a heads-up before siccing this macho asshole on me. I was happy to share information, but I didn't appreciate the surprise interrogation.

"I've worked with Detective Delgado in the past," said Vargas cryptically. "My sources told me you talked to Berkland this week and sent Jason Martinez's mother to harass him. Berkland was seen leaving the building Friday evening, and the gallery has been shuttered ever since. I have reason to believe his life is in danger, and I need you to stop playing tit for tat and answer my questions."

I had a sinking feeling at this. Clearly, there was more going on here than just art forgery. And I needed to know what I was dealing with. "Why do you think Berkland's in danger?" I asked. "Did someone find out about the fake paintings?"

Agent Vargas rolled his eyes toward the sky like he couldn't believe my arrogance. Fine, I was being difficult, but he just dropped a bombshell on me, and he wasn't exactly brightening my day.

"Obviously, I can't tell you that."

I wasn't going to get anything else out of this guy, and pressing him further would just waste both of our time. "I'm investigating the death of the artist Margot Starling. Berkland sold several pieces that he claimed were painted by her. He said he was selling them on behalf of her friend, who wanted to stay anonymous. I went to the gallery to talk to him, and he started pitching me the Martinez paintings. He told me an identical story about the anonymous owner, so I gave him my card and asked if it was the same person who supplied the Starlings. Then he threw me out. That's pretty much it."

"Did you accuse him of selling forgeries?"

"Well, I kind of implied it. He was, wasn't he?"

Vargas glared at me. You can't blame a girl for trying.

"How did Berkland react?" he asked.

I thought back to our encounter, remembering Berkland's tight jaw and clenched fists. "He got extremely defensive and claimed to be busy. But the gallery was empty."

"Did he say anything about going somewhere?"

It was a dumb question. We'd met once; obviously Berkland wasn't going to share his itinerary with me. On the other hand, maybe Vargas thought I was leaving something out and wanted to catch me in a lie. "Why would he tell me that? He doesn't know me, and I just confronted him about his shady sales tactics."

"What did you say to Elena Martinez?" asked Vargas. I described my conversation with Jason's mother while he nodded along, looking increasingly displeased. "And then you sent her to the gallery?"

"I just asked her to take a look at the paintings and tell me if she thought they were real. I never told her to confront Berkland. But she texted me that she gave him a piece of her mind. That's all I know." I took out my phone and showed him the text.

"I'm going to need to borrow your phone," said Vargas.

I laughed. "That's not happening. You can see the text message."

"I'd like to take a look at other relevant contacts you've had."

"Not gonna happen," I said. He had no legal basis for taking my phone, and I didn't appreciate being bullied. Besides, I didn't want him to see my calls to Mike Moreland. If Vargas got to him first, he'd instruct Moreland not to talk to me. I took a quick screenshot of my text from Elena. "What's your number? I'll send it to you."

His eyes narrowed. Vargas seemed like a man who was used to getting his way and didn't take well to pushback. He reluctantly gave up the digits, and I forwarded the screenshot. "Now that I have your number, I'll call you if I learn anything else, but I could be a lot more helpful if I knew what this was about."

"I don't want you digging around; I just want you to answer my questions. And I need you to stay away from the gallery. You have no idea what you're dealing with."

"What *am* I dealing with?"

He glared at me.

"Kidding," I said. "I know, you can't tell me. Is there anything else you want to ask me, or can I go?"

"Who else have you spoken to about Berkland?" asked Vargas.

"Renate Rossi," I said.

Vargas flinched at the sound of her name, which made my think I should follow up with Renate sooner rather than later.

"Anything else?" I asked. "I'd like to get on with my day."

He shook his head. "Not for now, but I'll be in touch. We should walk back separately. I don't want anyone to see us talking—for your sake as much as mine." I opened my mouth to speak, but Vargas cut me off. "I mean it, Kate. You're playing with fire, and you need to back off before someone gets hurt." He motioned for me to go first. I walked quickly, unnerved at the thought of him trailing behind.

I got in my car and drove around, taking random turns in case anyone—FBI or otherwise—was following. Once I was sure no one was behind me, I pulled into a strip mall parking lot and called Luke. He picked up right away. I wondered if Agent Charming had already briefed him on our chat.

"Who is Gus Vargas, and what did you tell him about me?" I demanded.

Luke sighed. "He's someone I work with. I really can't go into it."

"Luke, it's not fair to play the principled secrecy card after siccing an FBI agent on me. You could have at least given me a heads-up. I'm happy to share anything I find, but I don't like being surprised by a fed who orders me around and tries to take my phone. What the hell?"

"He took your phone?"

"No, I didn't let him. I'm not an idiot. But he made ominous statements about danger and how I didn't know what I was getting myself into. I couldn't tell if he was warning me or just shoving his weight around."

"Probably a little of both." Luke's tone was flat. He was being careful not to give anything away. That alone told me something serious was at stake.

"What's going on? Why does he think Berkland's in danger?" There was an awkward silence. "Is Vargas involved in the forgery investigation?"

"Myles, stop," said Luke. "You know I can't discuss it."

"Fine, then just tell me what you told Vargas about me." I was really getting frustrated now, and a little worried. "I have a federal agent who's all but accusing me of obstructing justice, and I need to know why. I don't want to get myself in trouble here."

He let out a long, slow exhale. "I can't go into it without revealing case information."

This was too much. I got why Luke was playing his investigative cards close to the vest, but now he was interfering with my case and my livelihood. "You can't go into what you told the FBI about *me*? You could have just called me yourself. I would have told you everything I know." I paused to give him a chance to apologize, or at least say something. He stayed silent. "Fine, Luke. I was hoping we could help each other unofficially, but that's clearly not going to work if you're gonna flag me to the feds and then give me the silent treatment. Have a good one."

I hung up. There was no point in continuing the conversation. He wasn't going to tell me anything, and I might end up sniping at him and regretting it. What really stung was that Luke hadn't approached me himself. The surprise FBI visit felt tactical, like he and Vargas had wanted to get answers before I had a chance to think through my responses. Luke was handling me like a civilian informant.

My mind flashed on our conversation at the club and all of my awkward revelations. When I first approached Luke, he was guarded but seemed to trust me. Maybe now he was having second thoughts. I should never have contacted him in the first place. And after involving him, it was clearly a mistake to open up. I'd talked to him like a friend, but truthfully he wasn't even a colleague anymore. I'd put Luke in an awkward position and added another layer of complexity to my case. And now things would be weird between us personally. Just one more thing I'd managed to screw up.

I wondered how Luke knew Vargas. The LAPD didn't do a lot of work with the feds, so it seemed like a weird connection. I Googled Luke's name along with *Gus Vargas, FBI*. An article came up about a casino sting from last year. I skimmed the piece until I hit on *Gus Vargas, FBI, and Luke Delgado, LAPD—part of the Southern California Money Laundering Task Force*. Was that what this was about? If Berkland was laundering money, maybe Margot had figured it out and tried to blackmail him. But that didn't explain how she'd gotten mixed up with him in the first place.

And if Margot had been working with Berkland, wouldn't that suggest that the paintings were real?

At any rate, I had a strange feeling that Mike Moreland could fill in some of the blanks. I decided to swing by his law firm and try to catch him before lunch.

CHAPTER

23

Present Day—Kate

UNSURPRISINGLY, THE RECEPTIONIST at Moreland's firm gave me the brush-off. According to her, he was working from home, but she'd tell him I stopped by. I wondered if Moreland was really out of the office or if that was just what he'd instructed her to say. There was a Starbucks directly across from the building with a view of the entrance. I decided to hunker down for a few hours and try to catch him on a coffee run. It would also give me a chance to type up my case notes.

I pulled up Moreland's picture on the firm website. He was a handsome Black man in his early forties with a confident smile. I remembered his face from a picture I'd seen of Jason online, laughing with friends at an art opening. They must have made an attractive couple.

About an hour later, I spotted Moreland coming out of the front door. I threw my laptop in my tote bag, abandoned my coffee, and raced across the street. A middle-aged woman in a silver Prius slammed on the brakes to keep from hitting me. I raised my palm in a half apology and jogged over to the sidewalk. My target was heading toward the crosswalk.

"Mr. Moreland!" I called. He spun around and met my eye. Moreland's expression caught me off guard. I'd expected him to look startled or annoyed, but what I saw was closer to fear. Maybe he did have something to hide. I stuck out my hand and smiled, trying my best to temper his anxiety. "Kate Myles," I said. "I left you a couple messages." He turned away and started walking quickly across the street. I followed alongside. "Elena Martinez suggested I contact you."

"I don't know why she would do that," he snapped. "I don't want to talk to you, and I'd appreciate it if you left me alone."

"Did you sell any of Jason's paintings through Aksel Berkland?" I asked.

He turned around and glared at me. "Look, I asked you nicely, please go away. I don't know you. My partner died; I don't feel like reminiscing about it with a strange woman who keeps leaving me intrusive messages." He changed direction and headed back toward his law firm. I trotted after him, but Moreland whispered something to the security guard at the door, who put a hand out to stop me.

"Ma'am, this is private property."

"This is an office building," I protested. "There are dozens of businesses in here."

"Just leave, all right?" he said. "I don't want any trouble."

Pushing my way in wouldn't have helped. I shook my head and headed over to the bar at the Biltmore Hotel. It had been a long, unproductive day, and I needed to think and regroup. I like hotel bars for the people watching and the privacy. It's always a strange mix of random outsiders, temporarily emboldened by the anonymity afforded by travel. I like to disappear in the background and watch the short-term groupings: sports talk between lonely businessmen, emotional confessions to strangers, preludes to one-night stands. But best of all, I like the downtown hotel bars because there's a markup on drinks, so I know I won't run into any cops.

I ordered myself a sapphire gin and tonic and let my thoughts turn to Mike Moreland. If I took his words at face value, the brush-off made total sense. He was grieving and didn't feel like spilling his guts to a pushy stranger. But I had a feeling there was more going on. There had been a hint of panic in his eyes when I mentioned Berkland. Moreover, he hadn't denied knowing Berkland, and his tone had all but confirmed their acquaintance.

I still couldn't picture the two of them in league together. Moreland was a partner at a major law firm and probably made a fortune. He didn't need the cash, and he had a stellar career to protect. On the other hand, most attorneys hate their jobs, and the prospect of a one-time payout to help him reach early retirement might have compromised his judgment.

If Moreland was really selling fakes through Berkland, he might have first tried his luck at Bauman & Firth, Jason's real gallery. I pulled up their website to check the hours and was pleased to see they were open late for a curator's talk about some artist I'd never heard of. Judging by the pictures online, his paintings were little more than splashes of color on dark backgrounds. I couldn't imagine there'd be too much to say about the canvases, but I guess I'm a bit of a philistine.

I paid the check and walked over to the gallery, which was just a few blocks away. Like Garlington, Bauman & Firth took up almost a whole city block. The main building was a two-story, nineteenth-century structure with wide windows and a giant arched entryway, but the gallery consisted of a huge quadrangle surrounding an open-air courtyard. They weren't just hawking fancy art; there was a design store with colorful knickknacks, a posh café, and even a wine bar.

The central courtyard was taken up by a giant art installation. Some wannabe genius had assembled a dozen tents against a brick wall. The tents were big, clean, and expensive looking. They would probably have been very popular with the unhoused Angelenos a few blocks over on Skid Row. Behind the tents, the artist had hung a neon sign reading *Everything will be all right.*

Several lithe hipsters wandered around, admiring the installation. I wondered how many actual homeless people they'd walked past on their way to the artificial camp.

I went inside the main gallery and tried to find someone who looked like an employee. The gallery was beautiful, with a high glass ceiling and tons of natural light. The floor looked as if they'd poured concrete around the ruins of an old mosaic. I wondered what this place had been before they bought it—maybe a high-end department store, or a public bath from a different era.

A gazelle-like woman in a wrap dress was setting up cups by the refreshment table. "Excuse me, do you work here?" I asked. She nodded. I introduced myself and mentioned that I'd learned about the gallery's relationship with Jason from his mother. She introduced herself as Reece Bernstein and escorted me up the stairs to an office where we could speak privately.

Reece ushered me into the small, windowless room and motioned for me to sit down on a tiny metal chair that looked like kid furniture. "You know, I knew Jason personally," she said. "I'm friends with his boyfriend, Mike."

I tried to hide my excitement. "I didn't know that. Did Mike ask you to sell any art on his behalf after Jason died?"

She shook her head. "Mike adored Jason, and he doesn't need the money. He has several of Jason's paintings, but I'd be shocked if he was willing to part with them."

I explained the situation with Berkland, and she nodded grimly. "Yes, we heard that he's been doing that. I have serious doubts about the authenticity of the pieces, but there's not much we can do. We had an exclusive agreement with Jason while he was alive, but that doesn't cover resale."

"Why do you think they're fake?" I asked.

She looked at me like I was an idiot. "Because if they were real, no one in their right mind would take a seventy percent cut on the sale price when they could just come to us."

"Any idea who might be behind the pictures?" I asked.

"None," said Reece, "but if you find out, we'd love to know."

"Understood," I told her.

"Do you mind if we continue this conversation another time?" asked Reece. "We're having an event pretty soon, and I'd like to go freshen up."

"No problem," I said. "But can I ask you a small favor?"

Her eyes narrowed, but she smiled politely. "What can I do for you?"

"Can you tell Mike I stopped by?"

She looked puzzled but nodded in agreement. "Sure, that's no problem." Maybe one more nudge from someone he knew would get Mike to talk to me. It was a long shot, but I hadn't exactly made a lot of progress.

I thanked Reece for her time and saw myself out of the small office. The second floor of the gallery consisted of a narrow hallway that wrapped around the four sides of the building like an indoor balcony. The wall facing the middle of the structure was only a few feet high, just enough to keep customers from losing their balance and falling onto the concrete and tile below.

As I headed for the stairs, I spotted Jason's signature gold leaf on the wall on the other side of the gallery. A tall, blond man was standing in front of the canvas, leaning in to admire it. I made my way along the narrow hallway toward the picture. It would be interesting to see a real Martinez in person. I wondered if I'd be able tell the difference. Probably not.

The blond man caught my eye and smiled as I approached. Up close, he was amazingly handsome. His face was slightly weathered, with little lines crossing his forehead and extending down from his eyes. He wore a baggy flannel shirt over paint-stained jeans. It was an odd uniform for someone well north of thirty, but it felt authentic and not like an affectation.

"Hi," I heard myself saying. I tend to get tongue-tied around very handsome men, and the gin and tonic wasn't helping.

"Hi," he replied with a warm smile.

I reminded myself that I was here to do a job, not to fraternize with hot bohemians. "Do you work here?" I asked.

He shook his head. "I just came for the talk."

"Did you know the artist?" I asked, nodding toward the painting.

"No, I'm just killing time," he said with a smile.

There was an awkward silence. For half a second, I thought about taking a page from Margot's book and trying to pick him up. He was prettier than me, but a little confidence can go a long way. And why not? I was single and had nothing to lose. Then reality set in. I tried to imagine sitting next to him through a lecture about abstract art and making halfway intelligent conversation about color and composition. I could sooner picture myself flying a plane or baking a soufflé.

"Well, enjoy your night," I said, turning to the stairs. I felt my cheeks turn pink as I made my way down. Once I reached the bottom, I glanced back up at the artsy guy. He was still looking at me. I smiled awkwardly and headed toward the door.

Walking back to my car, I felt somewhat deflated. Maybe I should have stuck around and tried to broaden my horizons. At the very least, it might have been nice to snack on canapés instead of a frozen dinner. But it was getting dark, so I focused my attention on the stretch ahead of me. Navigating downtown LA at night can be dicey. Blocks go from tony to sketchy and crowded to empty without much rhyme or reason. I kept my phone in my pocket, out of sight, and my bag clutched against my body.

When I finally got back to my car, I took out my phone to see if I'd missed any calls. To my surprise, there was a message from Moreland.

CHAPTER

24

Three Years Ago—Mike

*F*IVE MINUTES AWAY, I texted Jason. This would be my first time
visiting his place, and I was a little nervous. I'd never been
with an artist before, and my practical side had a million questions.
Like, what does an artist do, and can he even support himself? I
was worried that I'd get there and find he lived in a mouse-ridden
hovel with bars on the windows.

It's not that I'm a snob or anything, but I don't want things to be
awkward. I make good money as a lawyer. It's a trade-off. The work
is boring and the hours are terrible, but you're basically guaranteed
a comfortable life. I didn't have much growing up, and I'm not the
type to romanticize following your passion at all costs. All of my boyfriends since law school have been white-collar professionals, and for
the most part, they made the same calculation as me. Relationships
have a certain ease when both people are on the same wavelength.
And on a more selfish note, I've worked hard for what I have, and I'm
not interested in attaching myself to someone I have to support.

But then I met Jason, and we connected on a totally different
level.

On Fridays, after work, I walk over to The Last Bookstore
before heading home or going out with friends. I'm a bibliophile,

and this place is nerd paradise. It's housed in a huge old loft in the heart of downtown, with giant columns and carved wooden ceilings. The walls are painted dark blue and adorned with a life-size sculpture of a mammoth head. Upstairs, things get even more magical. A chunk of space is leased to small artist studios, and the rest is devoted to genre books. There's even an antique vault filled with true crime volumes.

I don't go there to pick up men. In fact, I usually turn off that part of my brain and revert back to a fifteen-year-old geek looking for a new graphic novel or fantasy read. But this time I spotted Jason and could barely tear my eyes off him. He was sitting on the floor cross-legged and leaning against a book-shelf in the sci-fi section. His nose was bent over a novel, and he looked totally absorbed. I used to scrunch myself into that same position when I was younger, before I became conscious of image and dignity and all that stuff. There was something attractive about the way he'd tuned out the outside world and lost himself in his read.

He must have sensed my eyes on him, because he looked up and shot me a warm, dazzling smile before returning to his novel. Sensing an invitation, I drifted over to the wall of books where he was sitting. I pretended to browse the volumes as I slowly made my way closer to him, hoping he'd speak to me.

"Am I in your way?" he asked, standing up.

"No, you're fine," I said. When he was on his feet, I saw that his body was beautiful as his face, thin and long-torsoed, with strong arms and shoulders. I looked down at the book in his hand. "Ursula Le Guin. I've heard she's great." Le Guin had been on my list of must-read authors for a while, but I'd never gotten around to it.

I wasn't prepared for his level of enthusiasm. His face lit up, and he looked upward like he was searching the heavens. "She's fantastic. A visionary." He slid the book he was reading back on the shelf, grabbed one next to it, and handed it to me.

"*The Left Hand of Darkness*," I read aloud.

"I know the title's cheesy, but it's brilliant. She used sci-fi to explore gender fluidity back in the sixties. Can you imagine? She was like a half century ahead of her time."

"That's awesome," I said.

"You should get it. I promise you won't be disappointed."

I'm usually pretty reserved when I meet strangers, but his warmth was infectious. "I'll tell you what," I said. "I'll get the book if you let me buy you a drink."

Jason grinned. "Here's a counteroffer. You get the book and pick one out for me, and we go Dutch on drinks."

"Deal," I said, feeling energized by this charming stranger.

Choosing a book for him was harder than I expected. He'd read everything. I tried to impress him with my knowledge of more intellectual sci-fi. He responded to every selection with that same enthusiasm before laughing and telling me he owned it and I'd better pick another. Eventually, I gave up and tried to think outside the genre. I led him into the crime vault and handed him a copy of Truman Capote's *In Cold Blood*. I gave him my best short summary, describing the beautiful writing and psychological insight.

Books in hand, we made our way downstairs and paid for our new reads. Then Jason suggested a cocktail bar nearby. On the way, we talked about books. I was blown away by his passion and insight. "You sound like you teach this stuff," I told him. "Are you a professor or something?"

Jason laughed. "Just an avid reader. I'm an artist, actually."

It was the first red flag I'd gotten. But frankly, I wasn't surprised. He didn't exactly talk like an accountant. Over drinks, I made him show me pictures of his paintings, which were gorgeous. He proudly told me about his gallery and suggested I stop by sometime.

We stayed for hours, almost until closing. At the end, when I reached for the bill, Jason snatched it up before I had the chance. "I've had the best time," he said. "You made my night, so let me treat you." Maybe he was actually supporting himself with this art thing.

I invited Jason back to my place on Bunker Hill. We made out in the elevator like teenagers. In my apartment, I quickly learned that our chemistry extended well beyond conversation.

He left the next morning, and we agreed to see each other soon. For the rest of the day, I couldn't get him out of my head. I even went to his gallery, which was crazy, since it was all the way in Venice and I had a million things to do. I went in feeling like a bit of a stalker. It was small and somewhat dingy. Only a couple of Jason's paintings hung on the wall. They were more stunning in person, but the prices seemed low. If he sold one in a month, that would net him fifteen hundred dollars and the gallery would probably take half of that. It didn't make sense. Maybe he had a side hustle to make ends meet.

Jason came over twice that week, and we had a fantastic time. When I pointed out that I hadn't seen his place, he invited me for dinner the following Saturday and offered to cook. All week long, I was distracted by thoughts of him. My productivity took a nose dive, and I ended up staying late at the office to make up for the daydreaming.

When Saturday finally came, I selected a bottle of white and walked over to his place. Standing outside his building, I was pleasantly surprised. It was in a nice part of downtown and even had a doorman. I slid the wine bottle under my arm and texted Jason that I was in the lobby. He sent me back a smiley face and his apartment number.

I rode the elevator, feeling giddy with anticipation. Jason must have heard me coming, because he opened the door before I even knocked. The whole place smelled of garlic and melted butter, and there was a relaxing bossa nova CD playing in the background. Jason handed me a cocktail and told me to make myself at home while he put the finishing touches on dinner.

I walked around the loft, trying to see what it could tell me about Jason. It was a great apartment, with high ceilings, lots of light, and a killer view. His gallery would have to sell a half dozen paintings a month for him to afford this. He must have family money. I walked around the space, admiring the art and his floor-to-ceiling bookshelves, filled with everything from Tolstoy to Toni Morrison.

Cocktail in hand, I wandered over to Jason's giant windows and watched the sun set over Los Angeles. I needed to chill. I'd just met this incredibly smart, sensual, gorgeous man who was in the process of cooking me Chilean sea bass. His finances were none of my business. Why question a good thing if it feels right?

"Dinner," called Jason. He shot me another of his beautiful smiles. This had promise, and I wasn't going to mess it up by overthinking things.

25

Present Day—Kate

MIKE SOUNDED PETRIFIED when I called him back. He finally agreed to meet me the following day on condition that I "stop harassing Elena and everyone else" in his life. I suggested a coffee shop near his firm, but he proposed that we meet at the Santa Monica Pier, of all places. The guy had either seen too many old-time detective movies or he had a serious hankering for funnel cake.

The pier was crawling with tourists by the time I pulled up. Mike probably wanted a public place, but this seemed a bit much. But we could ride the Ferris wheel if it got him to talk.

I spotted him by a souvenir stand. In a Dodgers cap, sunglasses, and sweatshirt, he looked like a different person from the fancy-suit-clad lawyer I'd seen the day before.

"Mike?" I asked. He nodded and offered me a cold, jittery hand to shake. His fear was palpable, and I needed to do something to calm his nerves. "Let's take a walk on the beach," I suggested. "It's still public but a little less stressful."

"Yeah, okay," he said.

We left the pier and walked down to the powdery white sand. Mike was looking over his shoulder the whole time. "Are you okay?" I asked.

"Not really, no," he said.

"Is this good?" I asked. "I can see that you're scared. I want to make sure you're comfortable."

"Yeah, it's fine. Let's just keep moving."

We started walking along the water. Mike was silent. "I'm sorry about your partner," I told him.

"Thank you," he said. "Listen, Elena—Jason's mom—she doesn't know anything. I'll talk to you if you promise you'll leave her alone. She told me you sent her to see Berkland. I don't think you understand how dangerous that was."

"She doesn't know anything about what?" I asked.

He sighed. "Any of it. Jason shielded her from the mess he got himself into. She still thinks he fell off a freaking cliff."

I felt queasy. The story of Jason's death had seemed a little fishy, but I wasn't expecting this.

"If you promise to leave her out of it, I'll tell you everything."

"Fine," I said. He obviously had a story to share, and this was the only way I was going to hear it. "Now let's back up. What did Jason get himself into?"

Mike let out a long, slow exhale. "We were together for three years, but I had no idea what was going on till the end. A lot of the time, I just kick myself and wonder why I didn't figure it out sooner. I'm a tax lawyer, for heaven's sake. If I didn't have my head buried in the sand, maybe I could have saved him."

"Slow down, Mike. I'm not sure what you're talking about. Was Jason in trouble?"

He stopped walking and faced the ocean. A tear rolled down his cheek, and he wiped it away.

"Can you start at the beginning?" I asked.

He nodded. "I can do that." Mike inhaled slowly, filling his lungs with the salty air. "If you Google Jason, you'll see that he was a really successful artist. But that's pretty recent. Jason struggled for years. He was so talented, and his work was beautiful. But no one was buying oil paintings of fruit vendors and old Hispanic women on porch stoops. For years after he graduated, he was working minimum-wage jobs and spending all his money on art supplies. Which are ridiculously expensive, by the way."

"Yeah," I said. "I imagine the gold leaf wasn't cheap."

Mike smiled bitterly. "Jason was spending hundreds every month on that stuff and making the minimum payment on his art school loans. It wasn't even enough to cover the principal, so his debt just ballooned. He was about to give up and get a so-called real job when he met Aksel Berkland."

A young couple was walking along the beach from the opposite direction. Mike stopped talking as they neared us, eyeing them suspiciously until they passed. The poor guy was barely holding it together. I thought about telling him that I was carrying, but that would probably just freak him out more. "What happened when he met Berkland?" I prodded.

"Jason thought it was his big chance. Aksel was going to give him a solo show. But in exchange, Jason had to forge other people's work."

I nodded. So Berkland was dealing forgeries after all. "How did they meet?"

"Aksel was trawling for talent at a local art fair when he spotted Jason. He was looking for a starving artist with great technical skills who'd do anything for a break. Jason fit the bill. Aksel told him he owned a gallery and invited him out for drinks. He got him sloshed and dangled the prospect of a solo show. Jason had been struggling for years, and he jumped at the chance."

"Who was he forging?" I asked. "Did the name Margot Starling ever come up?"

Mike shook his head. "Dead artists from the late twentieth century. Berkland was too smart to go for real heavy hitters. That would have brought too much scrutiny. He stuck with artists whose work was valued in the high-five- or low-six-figure range. Enough to make money, but there wasn't much risk that something would get resold at Sotheby's and examined by experts."

"Didn't the buyers ask for provenance?" I asked.

"Berkland created a paper trail for every piece. Fake bills of sale, gallery stamps, that kind of thing. Enough to pass muster with shady middlemen who weren't interested in asking questions. It was a pretty simple operation for a while. But at some point, Berkland got greedy and teamed up with some really dangerous people. Then the art became secondary, and it was all about moving money."

"You mean money laundering?" I asked.

Mike nodded. "I was the one who finally put it together. They had the perfect patsy in Jason." He laughed grimly. "Clearly they didn't expect him to fall for a tax lawyer."

"How did you find out?"

He sighed. "If I'm honest, I always knew something was off. Jason was showing his work in this shithole gallery and selling maybe one painting a month. But he lived in a great apartment and always had spending money. Sometimes I'd go over there and see him working on a painting that was totally different from his style. The truth is, I didn't ask because I didn't want to know."

"Who was Berkland moving money for, exactly?" I asked.

Mike stopped walking and looked at the ocean. "The Russian mob," he said, biting his lip. "The fucking Russian mob."

"You're sure?" I asked.

He nodded. "When he eventually told me about the forgery, I started digging around. I wanted to see exactly what he'd gotten himself into. I managed to get my hands on some transfer documents. Don't ask me how. I couldn't believe what I was looking at. Over and over again, it was a painting consigned by shell company A and sold to shell company B. Then, sometimes, the same work was resold for more money to a third shell company. The whole thing reeked."

"How do you know it was the Russian mob?" I pressed.

"Like I said, I did a little digging. All these shell companies are incorporated in Nevada, which is basically money laundering mecca, and they all list California-based directors with Russian last names. Then I started looking up those names, and all kinds of crazy stuff popped up—we're talking mug shots and racketeering indictments."

"But why art?" I asked. "There has to be an easier way to hide money. Why go through the trouble of forging a painting?"

"It's actually the perfect vehicle for fraud," explained Mike. "They're taking advantage of a gap in the law. The Bank Secrecy Act doesn't apply to art."

I worked murders when I was on the force, not financial crimes. And you really don't need to know much about banking regulations to catch cheating spouses. Mike must have sensed my confusion. "If you go to a jeweler or a casino and spend more than ten thousand dollars," he explained, "the business has to report it to the government. There's a significant paper trail. None of that exists for fine art. You can waltz in and drop a million in cash on a piece of canvas, and the government never has to know.

"On top of that, prices fluctuate wildly in the art world. If you sell me fifty gold bars for the price of one gold bar, that's going to get flagged. But people inflate the price of mediocre paintings every day. So, say you want to pay your hit man. Or a corrupt local politician. He can sell you a lousy painting—or a fake painting. You pay way more than the painting's worth, and everyone's happy. You've just washed your money, and no one's the wiser."

"Why even bother forging paintings at that point?" I asked. "Why not just create a bill of sale?"

Mike shrugged. "Plausible deniability in case there's ever a government investigation? Anyway, at first, everyone was satisfied with this arrangement," he continued. "But then one of the mobsters stumbled on an article about recent auction sales, and they started getting greedy."

"What do you mean?" I asked.

"Why stop at transferring money back and forth? They had a world-class painter at their disposal and a shady gallerist who knew how to create a fake provenance. They started upping their game—making Jason forge higher-caliber artists and then reselling them for more at a local auction house."

"Was this Hughes?"

He nodded.

"What about the shell companies?" I asked. "Wouldn't that make the auction house suspicious?"

"Not at all. I've handled dozens of art sales for clients with tax problems, and they usually request anonymity. You don't want to publicize that you're selling mom's lithographs to pay child support. It's embarrassing. Anonymous deals are standard. Besides, Hughes has a reputation for being lax on due diligence."

"It's like the art market was designed with laundering in mind," I observed.

Mike shrugged again. "Ever wonder why a painting of a square sells for three hundred million to an anonymous buyer? Maybe it's a rich guy with boring taste. But a lot of the time, something else is going on behind the curtain."

"So you told me Jason started forging pictures when he was young and broke. But when he died, he was a star. How did that happen?"

"Jason was brilliant, and no one appreciated him," said Mike. "I wanted to do something to change that. One of the top sellers at Bauman & Firth is a client—Reece. Apparently you met her yesterday. So I organized a dinner party and invited her. I covered the walls with Jason's art, and of course, she was blown away. She put things in motion, and they agreed to sign him."

"Did he quit forging at that point?" I asked.

Mike turned away and wiped his eyes. He was swaying a bit and didn't look totally well. "Do you want to sit down?" I asked.

He waved me off. "It's fine." Mike was quiet for a minute as he regained his composure. "Anyway, Jason broke down one night. Bauman & Firth has galleries all over the world. The output expectations were enormous. I knew he was behind schedule, and I nagged him about it. Then suddenly, he started sobbing and told me about the forgery. He was behind on his own work because he was still making these shitty knock-offs for Berkland."

"What did you say when he told you?"

"I told him to quit. I even threatened to leave him. This was my client, after all. I'd put myself out there for him, and a forgery scandal could blow up both our careers. He begged me not to go, and he promised to stop. I made him call Berkland in front of me and quit on the spot."

"How did Berkland take it?"

"Not well. God, if I'd known back then that he was dealing with mobsters—Berkland made it clear that his partners wouldn't let Jason quit. Jason just hung up on him. I thought it was over, but that's when the threats started."

"What kind of threats?"

"People following us home. Someone broke into our apartment and poured blood all over several finished canvases, which probably cost Jason a hundred thousand dollars. That's when I started looking into the shell companies."

"And you realized who Berkland's partners were."

"Exactly. We were trapped. I met with Berkland on Jason's behalf. Jason was hysterical, and I was afraid of what he'd say if he went alone. I didn't tell him we were together, I just said I was Jason's lawyer. But Berkland isn't stupid. You look up Jason online, and there's a dozen pictures of me with my arm around him at parties. We negotiated that Jason would keep forging for six more months. It gave Berkland half a year to find a replacement. Then Jason would have his freedom back."

"When was the six months up?" I asked.

He turned and looked me in the eye. "Two weeks before he died."

Mike reached into his pocket and pulled out a flash drive. "Here," he said. "There's an Excel chart I put together of the art sales, shell companies, and phantom directors. A lot of it is publicly available information if you know where to look. You can't tell anyone where you got it or I'm a dead man."

I took the flash drive and slipped it into my pocket. "What do you think happened to Jason?" I asked.

"I *know* what happened. They killed him. Jason had tendonitis in his knee. He would tolerate flat, wimpy hikes for my benefit, but he always complained about it. There's no way in hell he fell off a mountain."

"Jesus," I said. Agent Vargas was right; I had no idea what I was dealing with. "So, you think Berkland killed Jason. But I spoke to someone in law enforcement who thinks *Berkland's* life is in danger."

Mike shook his head. "Berkland is just a two-bit con man who knows his way around paperwork. His partners killed Jason, and when Berkland ceases to be useful, they'll kill him too. These aren't the kind of people who like to leave witnesses. Hell, maybe they already killed him, and I'm probably next on their list."

I couldn't believe what I was hearing. No wonder Mike had looked like a deer in headlights when I first mentioned Berkland's name. "What are you doing to keep safe?" I asked. "I used to be a cop, and I still have a few connections. Maybe I can help you."

He shook his head. "You know what these people do to snitches?"

I did know. There was nothing I could say.

"Don't worry about it. I'm keeping my distance, and I've been working remotely for months. It was pure chance that you caught me yesterday—I had to go to the office for a client meeting."

"Well, I'm certainly glad I did."

"Anyway, I need to go, and I've told you everything," he said.

"Can I call you if I have follow-up questions?" I asked.

"You won't be able to reach me, but I might check in again if I think it's safe. Take care, Kate." And with that, he jogged off across the sand. I watched him chuck his cell phone in a trash can by the road and disappear out of sight.

26

Present Day—Kate

Panic set in as I walked back along the beach. On top of bankers, cops, and blue-chip art dealers, I now had the Russian mob to contend with. Fan-fucking-tastic. What was next, NASA? The Illuminati?

When I finally got back to the parking lot, my car was a sauna. I turned the AC on full blast, but the air felt like a hand dryer in a public bathroom. It dawned on me that I was supposed to be somewhere. I looked down at my to-do list and read *Interview Stephanie Sung, coroner investigator*. The appointment was in twenty minutes. Mike's story had been so captivating that I'd lost track of time. I texted Stephanie that I was running late and flew down the I-10.

I'd worked with Stephanie—like Dr. Greco—once or twice on murder cases. The coroner investigators are an interesting bunch. They tend to have a fascination with crime but little interest in law enforcement's machismo culture. Their job is to show up at a murder scene, document things for a cause-of-death determination, and remove the body. A typical day might involve examining a bullet-riddled corpse, extracting a five-hundred-pound body from a bathtub, and cataloging bone fragments found in an abandoned suitcase. It takes an unusual person with a penchant for the dark side to do this work. Not surprisingly, I tend to like them.

I pulled into the guest parking lot at the coroner's and texted Stephanie. She met me at the breezeway and took me through a back door to her subterranean office. The windowless room was the size of a large storage closet, and she shared it with another investigator named Katrina Phelps. I'd seen Katrina's name on paperwork but had never worked with her.

Stephanie's work space was decorated with different pictures of skulls and skeletons. She even had a life-size diagram of a flayed body tacked to the strip of wall between her computer and the doorway.

"Don't you ever get tired of looking at bones?" I asked.

"No," she said, grinning. "We need to be really familiar with the skeleton. Just last week I had a case in Lancaster where a rancher's dog came home with someone's femur. You get a lot of dead cows out there, so we have to be good at telling human bone from animal."

"Lovely." It actually sounded kind of Zen: being out in the desert, working with your hands to methodically reconstruct a body. If my PI business didn't pick up, maybe I'd put in an application.

"You said this was about a case," said Stephanie. "Do you have the case number?"

I read it to her off my notepad. "The victim's name is Margot Starling."

She nodded. "The artist. I remember her." I waited while she pulled up her report and skimmed it.

"Did you talk to the handling detective—Ron Bennett?"

Stephanie looked over her shoulder to make sure no one was in earshot. "Kind of an arrogant prick," she whispered.

I laughed. "Yeah, that's him. Did anything about his behavior at the scene seem strange to you?"

She rested her chin in her hand and scrunched her brows in thought. "Well, actually, yes. When I got there, I talked to Starling's neighbor—I think she lived across the way."

"Pretty woman in her thirties with two small kids?" I asked.

Stephanie nodded. "Sounds like her. She told me the police had been there the week before and she heard a slap. Anyway, I told Bennett what the neighbor said, and he basically blew me off. He looked at me like I was telling him about my last manicure."

Of course he didn't want to hear about it. He was the cop from the prior week. "Did she say if the slap happened before or after the police arrived?" I pressed.

"Um, she was holding a crying baby, and she wasn't that clear. I think she said the police came and she heard a slap. I just assumed it must have happened earlier. I meant to go back and clarify, but she left the apartment soon after, and I thought I'd leave it to the cops to iron out."

"Did you see if Bennett interviewed the neighbors?" I asked. Normally a homicide detective would have questioned Stephanie thoroughly and then immediately talked to the woman across the way. Of course, Bennett had his reasons for taking a different approach.

"I wasn't there the whole time, but I don't think so," she said. "It was weird. At one point, a guy with a mustache peered over the crime scene tape and watched us before walking off. I think he was another neighbor. I told Bennett about that too. He thanked me, but I didn't see him follow up."

Bennett should have immediately knocked on Mustachio's door, while the witness was home. If he had an innocent reason for being at Margot's apartment the prior week, he'd have had nothing to fear from talking to the neighbors. Something was wrong. "What about the rest of his investigation?" I asked. "Did anything seem off?"

Stephanie shrugged. "He kept saying things like 'This looks like a suicide.' I mean, in his defense, it did look like a suicide. But he said it like it was a foregone conclusion and we should just wrap things up and move on."

I shook my head in disgust. Bennett had half-assed the whole investigation when the coroner's team was practically begging him to dig deeper. At first, I'd thought he was just being lazy, but it was really starting to seem like he had something to hide.

Stephanie started to speak again but stopped midsentence. A tall, athletic blond woman walked in and sat down at the computer across from us. Stephanie flashed me a warning look that told me our conversation was over.

"Hi, Katrina," said Stephanie. "I thought your shift started at three?"

"No," said Katrina. "It's two today." Her voice was cold and unfriendly. I wondered what her deal was. Was she just a snitch who followed procedure, or did she have a connection to the case? I glanced over at Stephanie's Día de los Muertos–themed clock on the wall. It was two fifteen. Katrina could have been listening to our whole conversation.

"Well, it was great seeing you, Kate," said Stephanie. "Let's do lunch soon and catch up."

I stood up and shook her outstretched hand. "Sounds like a plan."

As I walked back to my car, I mentally ran through the conversation. Stephanie had confirmed what I already suspected: Bennett had a connection to Starling. I wasn't convinced he had killed her, but he might know who did.

I've heard of cops making extra cash by providing security for rich people. A buddy of mine at Anaheim PD makes a fortune on his off days searching Disneyland for perverts and ejecting them before they hurt any kids. Maybe one of Margot's blackmail victims had hired Bennett to scare her into dropping the Biennale project. Then, when it didn't work, Mr. Victim had her killed.

My phone chimed, and I looked down at the screen. It was a new text from Stephanie. *Sorry, Katrina flirts with him a lot. I think there's something going on.* Well, that cat was out of the bag. If Katrina had overheard anything, I could expect a nasty call from Bennett at the very least. I had an uneasy feeling. I'd been hoping to discreetly poke around and try to uncover Bennett's reason for being in Margot's apartment a week before she died. But if he found out I was snooping, he'd do everything possible to stop me. Bennett could get wildly defensive if you made a lighthearted joke at his expense. I couldn't imagine how he'd react to being investigated.

I thought about Luke and felt a stab of guilt. If Bennett was involved in all this, Luke needed to know. I should probably tell him about Jason's involvement in the forgery too. But Luke would just turn around and call Agent Vargas, and I had enough on my plate without the FBI breathing down my neck. Besides, I'd promised to keep Mike's name off the record. I could give Luke the flash drive after downloading its contents. Mike had requested anonymity, but he never told me not to share his trove of information.

Back at my house, I copied the flash drive onto my computer and started reading through files. There were detailed spreadsheets and charts showing who owned what shell companies. Mike must have spent hundreds of hours putting this together. He'd organized the information around specific art sales. Whenever he thought a work was fake, which was most of the time, he'd put the artist's name in quotes. As time went on, sales involved increasingly important artists and larger amounts of money.

Just like Mike had said, every transaction was done through shell companies. One "Twombly" was sold by Dickson Import LTD. The director of the company was listed as Cy Petrov. Dickson appeared to be owned by another company called Kingfisher, which was registered on the island of Niue. At this point, Mike had hit a brick wall. Instead of listing an owner for Kingfisher, he'd typed in three question marks.

The third entity, called Rainmaker LLP, purchased the "Twombly." The company was registered in Nevada, and strangely, Cy Petrov was also the director. Rainmaker appeared to be a front for a Wyoming-based shell called Beluga, with a director named Anatoly Lebedev. At this point, the trail went cold.

I Googled *Cy Petrov* and found nothing explicit about a mob connection. He had a four-year-old conviction for identity theft, and his mug shot quickly came up on the Long Beach Police Department website. Cy had mean eyes, small features, and a round face. He'd probably been handsome at twenty, but by his thirties he looked unhealthy and worn out. A few other old arrests popped up. Meth, unsurprisingly. There was also an assault with a deadly weapon charge that had been pled down to a misdemeanor. Typical tweaker stuff. Cy made a good patsy. He probably needed drug money and was happy to sign his name on some forms for a small but steady paycheck.

Anatoly Lebedev was a completely different story. As soon as I typed his name into the internet, I hit on a federal racketeering indictment, charging him and fifteen others with crimes ranging from fraud to murder. An article in the *L.A. Times* mentioned that the case was dismissed after three witnesses disappeared.

One of the other names on the indictment sounded familiar— Dmitry Chernov. I Googled him and found several articles about his work as a high-profile developer in Los Angeles. An anonymous blog post explored his possible Russian mob connections.

Where have I heard that name before? I turned back to the list of Margot's X-Acto knife lovers and scanned the page until my eyes hit on *D Chernov.* That could be Dmitry. I doubted that Margot would have been reckless enough to blackmail this guy. But she had a masochistic streak and suffered from bouts of depression. Maybe she'd committed a different kind of suicide by trying to shake down a mobster.

I turned to the other names from the project and cross-checked them against Mike's data. Nothing. Then a thought hit me: Margot had listed several people by their first initial. If I was right about Chernov, these were her most dangerous conquests. I still hadn't identified BK Smith or Z Farabee. I tried Googling each person with a series of buzzwords: *CEO Smith, Farabee executive.* Nothing useful came up. That last name was kind of unusual, and there aren't a lot of first names that start with Z. My cousin Ellie married a guy named Zeke, so I tried that first—nothing. Next, I tried Zane, then Zach, Zachary, and when I tried Zack, I got a hit. The LAPD website popped up with a year-old press release about personnel changes, including Captain Zack Farabee's transfer to the Robbery-Homicide Division.

27

Present Day—Kate

Aften my morning coffee, I placed three calls to the Berkland gallery. Each time, the line went to voice mail. If I were
still a police officer, I'd do a door knock at Berkland's residence
and then, if that didn't work, get a warrant. That was no longer an
option, but I could at least drive by and see if he was home. And
breathing, for that matter.

I ran a LexisNexis search on Aksel Berkland. The internet
data retrieval service is expensive, but it lets you look for addresses
associated with people and has paid dividends in several cases. I
found an address for Berkland in Venice Beach and an apartment
associated with Cy Petrov in Koreatown, complete with a roommate, some guy named Soren Allinder. I wondered if the roommate had any idea Cy was a low-level mobster.

According to a real estate website, Berkland bought his
home five months ago, paying a healthy seven figures for the
1,300-square-foot bungalow. The house had sold two years earlier for substantially less money and was probably a flip. In the
crazy LA housing market, speculators often buy neglected prop-
erties, slap on a coat of white paint, and up the price by half a
million.

I called the Berkland gallery a fourth time. Still no answer. I decided to go see for myself if he'd really closed up shop and then swing by his house and check whether anyone was home.

Traffic was light, and I got to Venice in no time. I drove slowly, scanning the street for Agent Vargas's car. Maybe he was taking a day off from surveillance or had delegated the task to some underling. I slowed my car to a crawl and peered in the gallery window. All the lights were out. I called one more time and could see the phone on the desk light up. No one came to answer it.

I plugged Berkland's address into my GPS and headed over to the house, just five minutes from the gallery.

Ruth Avenue was a quiet street of manicured lawns and a mix of ranch and Spanish-style houses. The neighborhood looked middle class until you remembered that the beach was a short drive away. With my windows rolled up, I could still hear a buzz from the nearby freeway. The residents probably pretended it was ocean waves.

I drove slowly around the block. Berkland's house was painted stark white and surrounded by a brand-new teakwood fence. The front yard was xeriscaped in a nod to LA's desert climate. The ground was covered in gravel and polka-dotted with small succulents. An enormous, beautiful agave grew by the front door.

There were no vehicles in the driveway, but there was a one-car garage. I got out of my car, walked up to the front door, and knocked. No answer. As I walked back toward the street, I noticed the garage door was only partially closed, suspended about half a foot above the ground. Berkland didn't seem like the kind of guy to absent-mindedly leave his garage open. His front yard was perfectly maintained, and he'd been immaculately dressed when I met him. I thought about the missing laptop back in his gallery. Maybe he'd fled in a hurry and hadn't taken the time to close the door properly.

I glanced behind me to see if anyone was watching, then walked quickly up the driveway. It would only take a second to peek under the garage door and see if the car was gone.

I got on my knees and peered underneath the garage door. As I expected, it was empty, save for some boxes and a few paintings leaning against the wall. Luke should get a warrant for this place. There was no telling what he might find. I turned to head down the driveway.

At the back of the house, I could see a large wooden deck with a barbecue. It would be nice to live in a place like this. I imagined drinking a margarita in a lawn chair, enjoying the ocean breeze while Amelia worked on her coloring books. If she got bored, we'd just zip down to the beach.

I stopped: one of the French doors leading onto the balcony was open, just an inch. I walked onto the deck and knocked on the partly open door. "Mr. Berkland?" I called. No answer. I peered through the glass into a spotless kitchen. Everything was white and blond wood. Any evidence that someone regularly cooked or ate in there had been hidden from view. Then I saw a wallet and a set of keys lying in the middle of the floor, as if knocked off the counter. All my cop instincts went on high alert. If Berkland had been planning to fly the coop, he wouldn't have left his keys and wallet behind.

I pushed open the door and took a step into the kitchen. "Mr. Berkland?" I called.

Other than the few items on the floor, there was no sign of a struggle. I quickly moved from room to room, calling Berkland's name and feeling like an idiot. No one was here, and the place looked immaculate. I should have left immediately. But I'd never have another chance to look around Berkland's private digs. I thought about Mike and what had happened to Jason—I needed to find some answers.

I scanned the living room. The walls were adorned with colorful modern paintings. One of them looked distinctly like Margot's style, and another bore Jason's signature gold leaf. I snapped a picture of each. There were other canvases with signatures by artists even I recognized: Keith Haring, Basquiat, Dali. They were probably all fakes. When you have a pet forger and a house to decorate, why not go nuts?

Berkland had transformed the second bedroom into an office, also immaculate. It was almost too orderly, like someone had snooped around and cleaned up to cover their tracks. One of the file cabinet drawers was open, and I could see it was empty. There was a desktop computer, which looked brand-new. But the laptop I'd seen at the gallery was the machine Berkland kept with him and would be what held anything incriminating. I nudged open a desk drawer, using a tissue from my pocket—nothing. There was a paper shredder by the desk, but even that had been emptied.

The main bedroom looked a bit more lived-in. The queen bed was freshly made, but there were books on the nightstand. A navy sweater was draped across an overstuffed white armchair. I glanced inside the large closet. As I stepped inside, I heard the distinctive sound of a gun being racked. "Hands up," said a voice behind me.

28

Present Day—Kate

I SPUN AROUND AND met the eyes of a baby-faced police officer.
"Put your hands up!" he barked.

I did what I was told. "I'm a private detective," I said, trying
to keep my voice as calm as possible. "My name is Kate Myles. I'm
licensed; you can look me up. And I should probably tell you, I
have a concealed carry permit and I'm armed."

His eyes widened a bit at this last piece of information. Fuck,
this rookie was going to freak out and shoot me. "Step out of the
closet and put your hands against the wall!" he ordered.

I moved slowly and deliberately, trying not to make any sudden movements he could misinterpret. My face turned beet red
as he patted me down. He removed my gun, wrenched my hands
behind my back, and cuffed me with too much force. I winced
as my wrist twisted at an unnatural angle. It took every ounce of
willpower I had not to cry out. He ordered me to lean over the
bed. For half a second, I wondered if he was going to get frisky.

The kid pulled out his radio, and I heard him ask about my
name. "Kate Myles?" said the dispatcher. "I think she used to be a
cop." I felt my face grow hot.

"She says she's a PI now," added the rookie.

"That's right, I think I heard that." The dispatcher's voice sounded amused and vaguely familiar. We'd probably worked together at one point. I was going to be the day's gossip for sure.

The officer pulled me up by the cuffs, painfully wrenching the ligaments in my shoulder. "Can you be a little more careful?" I asked. "I had spinal surgery, and my back's in bad shape."

"Just move," he ordered.

He took me out through the front door and sat me on the curb. A blond woman across the street was watching us through her living room window. The bored housewife probably had nothing better to do than stare out the glass and call the police. Two years ago, I'd have commended her for being a responsible citizen.

"Why were you in there?" asked the rookie.

I looked down at the ground and tried to think of what to say. I could tell him I knew Berkland, which was sort of true, and that I'd been checking on him because the door was open. But this was LAPD, where I used to work. It was bad enough that my arrest was about to be the day's hot gossip. I wasn't going to talk myself out of this, and I didn't want to blurt out something that could be used against me. But I didn't want to get cited for a felony.

"I'm a private detective, former LAPD," I told him. "I had no intention of taking anything. I don't have anything else to say without a lawyer." This was clearly just a trespass. My pockets were empty, and I wasn't carrying a purse or bag that I could slip something into.

"Okay, I have to take you in," he told me.

"Why? I have no record, and a 602 is supposed to be a routine cite out," I said, mentioning the penal code section for trespass.

The rookie's eyes narrowed. "You were rummaging around in someone's house and carrying a loaded gun."

Oh my god, the gun. If he charged me with burglary and added a gun allegation, I'd be facing years in prison. My bail would be impossible. I was fucked.

The drive to the Pacific Community Station felt like an eternity. I stared out the window and willed myself not to cry. I'd never survive in prison. It's better to go to jail as a pedophile than an ex-cop. I'd arrested countless people over the years. One was bound to recognize me and shiv me in a dark corner. Even if I survived, I wouldn't see Amelia for years. John would probably tell her I was dead.

We pulled into the station, and the rookie led me inside. A couple of cops silently watched me. One, who looked vaguely familiar, was pointing in my direction and talking animatedly.

A female officer, whose name tag read *Sanora*, came over to search me. She patted me down, running the back of her gloved hand along every crevice of my body. I gritted my teeth as her knuckles grazed my crotch. I'd never felt this humiliated.

When she was done, Sanora informed me that my bail was set at $50,000. That meant the rookie had gone with burglary but hadn't known to add the gun allegation. I was screwed, but at least I could afford to get out of custody.

I called the bondsmen, who said they were backed up, so it would take a few hours to get me processed.

Sanora walked me over to the small jail in the back of the station. "I have a bondsman coming," I told her.

"Uh-huh," she said. "If he's not here by the end of my shift, you're getting transferred to Lynwood." My heart sank. I'd been a cop for a decade and made hundreds of arrests. There was no telling what might happen if someone recognized me in gen pop.

The small station jail consisted of a handful of cells on either side of a narrow hallway. Every unit was full. Sanora brought me over to a cell in the far corner that held the only other female inmate, an elderly woman who looked like she was homeless. Her smell was wretched. She'd probably soiled herself. "What's she in for?" I asked, nodding toward the old lady.

Sanora shrugged. "She stole a chicken from Ralph's."

The cells were designed for one person, and the old woman had already claimed the only seating, a narrow metal bench. I sank to the floor, leaning my back against the stained cinder block wall. Across the way, a scruffy blond guy had pressed himself against the bars of his cell. His erect penis was out, and he was stroking it so hard, you could hear the skin slap as his fist met his groin.

"Chester, that's another 314 charge," said Sanora, rolling her eyes. "You're not helping yourself." Her tone was almost bored. As a female working in custody, she'd probably seen her share of exposed genitalia.

Sanora locked me in and walked away. I moved my eyes away from the weenie wagger's little display, and my gaze landed on the elderly woman. She caught me looking at her and started cursing. I stared at the floor, trying to avoid a confrontation.

After a while my companion forgot about me, and her ramblings turned inward. She griped about devils and demons and occasionally addressed someone named Lucia, who she seemed to think was in the cell with us. This woman shouldn't be here, I thought. She was hungry and out of her mind. They should have let her walk off with the chicken or taken her to a hospital. I hoped she was sane enough to plead guilty and take the probation. If the public defender declared a doubt about her competence, she'd spend the next two months getting forcibly medicated until she was capable of standing trial.

After almost three hours in purgatory, the bail agent showed up. Relief flowed through me as Sanora liberated me from my cell. I took a momentary glance back at the old woman. "What's her bail set at?" I asked Sanora.

She glared at me. "That's none of your business."

"Maybe I can pay it," I said.

She looked at me like I was insane but checked the woman's citation. They hadn't bothered to charge her with the chicken theft. She was in for trespassing, and bail was set at $1,000. "I'll pay it," I told her.

"You know she's never coming to court?" said Sanora. "You're flushing your money down the toilet."

"I know."

I forked over ten percent of my own bail and paid another grand for my cellmate. Thanks to my pension, I had a rainy-day fund, a chunk of which was now going up in smoke. It hurt, but at least I was getting out. To my great relief, the custody clerk gave me my wallet and phone back. Rookie mistake. My phone had pictures of Berkland's house. He should have booked it and gotten a search warrant for the contents. They'd kept my gun, but that was to be expected while the case was pending.

After my release, I walked several blocks away from the jail before calling a rideshare. I had a feeling the driver wouldn't be keen on fetching me from the police station—or maybe I just didn't want to be thought of as someone just released from jail. Which I was. A young woman in a gray Prius picked me up. Once I was in her back seat, I fought hard to hold back tears. I'm not one for making scenes in front of strangers, but I was near my limit.

My car was still parked at Berkland's. I stared out the window until we pulled onto Ruth Avenue, feeling nauseous as his house came into view. Hopefully the nosy neighbor wouldn't recognize me and call the police again. I couldn't take any more mortification.

Keeping my head down, I got into my car and drove out of the neighborhood. Once I'd driven a few blocks, I pulled over and let myself break down. I was screwed. *How could I have been so stupid?* Best-case scenario, I'd get felony probation and they'd take my PI license. But with the gun, that hardly seemed likely. I was probably heading to prison.

Looking down at my phone, I saw that I had two missed calls from Bennett and three from Luke. Apparently word travels fast. My phone started ringing, and Luke's name flashed on the screen. I pressed the decline button. I couldn't talk to him now.

At home, I took a long hot shower, scrubbing hard to remove whatever germs and filth I'd come in contact with at the jail. After boiling my skin to a lobster red, I wrapped myself in my robe, sat down at the kitchen table, and reached for an open wine bottle. I took a healthy swig, and a ribbon of Cabernet dribbled down my chin. I was past caring.

After another sip, I forced myself to think. I needed a lawyer, and I wouldn't qualify for a public defender. The county reserves

PDs for the truly indigent. If you have a bank account, you can spend it on an attorney. If you're broke but you have a house, you can take out a second mortgage. It always seemed messed up to me. You want someone to plead guilty because they did it, not because the alternative is financial ruin.

I called my friend Angela Washington, who had represented Narek. Angela was a prosecutor in the DA's elite Major Crimes unit until a few years back. She'd had the audacity to report to HR that her boss was getting handsy, but instead of firing him, the office transferred her to an unglamorous position filing misdemeanors in El Monte. She quit and opened her own shop. From what I could tell, she was making a killing.

Angela listened as I explained, interrupting now and then to ask questions. She agreed to let me work off her fee by doing investigations on other cases. She made it sound like a fair trade, but I knew it was a gift.

I hung up the phone and saw that I had five missed calls and a voice mail from Bennett. I also had four text messages from Luke, the last of which said, *I'm coming over. Be there in ten.*

Great. I was sitting here with wet hair in a bathrobe. It was bad enough that Luke would now know me as a felon. I didn't need him to see me looking like a complete degenerate. I threw on a pair of jeans and a wrinkled T-shirt to make myself marginally more presentable. Then I heard a knock.

I opened the door and was shocked to see Bennett, not Luke, glaring at me. "What the hell are you doing here?" I asked.

"You're asking around about me now?" he shouted. "Have you fucking lost your mind?" He pointed an index finger at my chest, and I leaned back to keep him from touching me. Bennett stepped forward, and his foot landed on the wood of my floor.

"Back off," I said. "Get out of my house."

"I'll leave when I'm ready," sneered Bennett. "What are you gonna do, call the police?" He shot me a knowing look. I guess news of my stunt had already reached him. "Or have you wasted enough police time today?"

"Why were you at Margot Starling's apartment a week before she died?" I shot back. I might as well try to get something out of him.

Bennett's eyes narrowed. "Get this through your head. You're not a cop anymore, you're nobody, just a common criminal."

"You didn't answer my question. Why were you at Margot's apartment? Did Captain Farabee send you? Let me guess, he didn't like being blackmailed."

The look in Bennett's eyes told me I was dead right. He lunged forward, grabbed me by the throat, and shoved me against the door. Pain radiated up my neck into the base of my skull. "You have no idea what you're messing with. You think you're going to get probation? One call from the right people and you'll be doing real time."

It's hard to think when someone's holding you by the throat. Your first instinct is to grab their hands and pry them away. But it's hard to get a good grip, and chances are you'll just end up clawing yourself. Instead, I grabbed his left wrist with one hand, yanking down as hard as I could. As Bennett's face lowered, I jabbed him in the nose with the base of my left hand.

Bennett let go and staggered backward. He pressed a finger to his nose and, when he saw that it was bleeding, reached over and slapped me hard enough that my head wrenched to the side. I swung my face around and locked eyes with him. "Is this the playbook you used on Margot?" I asked. "Dr. Greco found hemorrhages in her eyes. Did you strangle her?" His face was pure rage, and I wondered if he was desperate enough to kill me. I wished I still had my gun.

"You're just a crazy bitch, making up stories to feel important. I should arrest you right now for assaulting an officer."

"Yeah?" I put my hands on my hips and willed myself to look unafraid. "Have fun explaining what you're doing at my house after I ignored your calls all afternoon. Now get the fuck off my property."

Bennett gave a nasty little laugh and stepped toward the stairs leading down to the pavement. I had a fleeting impulse to push him and watch his head crack open on the concrete like an egg. He turned back one final time and grinned at me. "You know, felons lose their PI license. You might want to dust off your dishwashing skills."

He sauntered down the steps like he had all the time in the world. As he reached the bottom, I saw Luke getting out of his car. Luke and Bennett stared at each other, and Bennett let out a chuckle. "Figures," he said, loud enough for me to hear. "I always knew you two were screwing."

Luke glared at Bennett and silently watched him get into his car and drive away. Once Bennett was halfway down the street, Luke climbed the stairs, two at a time. "We need to talk," he said.

I sighed and motioned for him to come inside. My neck was killing me. With my three fused cervical vertebrae, hopefully Bennett hadn't jolted something out of place. I didn't feel nerve pain in my arms, but that might come later.

"What was Bennett doing here?" asked Luke as I closed the door behind him. He frowned and gently took my chin between his thumb and forefinger. "Did he *hit* you?"

"Take a seat," I said, ignoring his question. "You want a drink?"

Luke shook his head. "No. And I don't think you should have one either."

"Well, you don't get a vote," I snapped. "In the last five hours, I've been arrested, slapped, threatened, and strangled. So, if you don't mind, I'm going to finish my Cabernet." I sat down and held up my glass to him in an imaginary toast.

"Strangled?" said Luke. "Who strangled you?"

"Who do you think? Apparently, I've been sticking my nose where it doesn't belong."

Luke shook his head in astonishment. "Bastard. I'm going to report this."

"No, you're not," I said. "You already torpedoed your career once by reporting another officer; you're not doing it again on my account." He flinched, and I realized that my comment had thrown him. "Luke, I'm sorry if that was insensitive, but I don't think I can take it if you turn against me right now."

He nodded quietly. "What were you doing at Berkland's house?"

I laughed. "I'm charged with res burg, and you're LAPD. I'm not gonna go there."

"You think I'd testify against you?" There was a look of genuine hurt on his face.

I sighed and put my head in my hands. Pain radiated up the back of my skull. Tomorrow would be even worse. "No," I said finally. "I don't think you'd testify against me. Listen, I think someone else might have broken in. Berkland's back door was open and he was gone, but his wallet and a set of keys were still in the house. Vargas said he might be in danger, so I looked around."

"Is that why you went in?" he asked, shaking his head. "This is my fault. I should never have gotten you involved."

"Stop it," I said. "I'm an adult, and I'm responsible for my own bad decisions." I broke Luke's gaze, and there was an awkward silence. My eyes landed on Mike's flash drive. I reached over to the far side of the table and pulled it out of my computer. The files were already copied onto my laptop. "Take this, and don't ask me where I got it," I said, handing Luke the little plastic fob. Our hands touched as he grabbed the drive. His skin felt nice.

"This isn't from Berkland's house, is it?" he asked.

"No, I didn't take anything from the house. That's the last thing I'm going to say about it."

Luke nodded. "Okay." He walked over to my kitchen, poured two glasses of water, and set one in front of me. My mouth felt parched, and I realized I hadn't had anything to drink besides wine in hours.

"What do you know about Captain Zack Farabee?" I asked.

"Farabee?" Luke cocked his head in surprise. "He's running RHD. What about him?"

"What do you know about his connection to Bennett?"

"Farabee supervised Bennett when he was a sergeant and Bennett was still on patrol. They got along really well. Farabee is the one who pulled him into RHD. He has a reputation for"—Luke paused, trying to find the right words—"doing what's necessary."

"What do you mean?" I asked.

He shot me a knowing look. "You know what I mean. Holding the line, protecting the troops. He does what needs to be done. You know, what I'm apparently not so good at doing. Now I need to know why you're asking about an RHD captain after his detective showed up at your doorstep."

I sighed and downed the rest of my water. "How much time do you have?"

"All night."

That's a tempting prospect, I almost said, but I restrained myself. I told Luke about Margot's blackmail project and the upcoming Venice Biennale. I told him about the money laundering, leaving out my conversation with Mike Moreland. He'd have to figure that out on his own. Hopefully, Mike would be out of harm's way by then.

I opened Margot's catalog and pointed out where *Z Farabee* was carved into her flesh, right below her left breast. "As soon as I mentioned Farabee, Bennett freaked out," I said. "I think she had something on him."

Luke stared at me in wide-eyed amazement. "You think Bennett killed her, don't you?"

I shrugged. "I honestly don't know. She had a lot of enemies. But I wouldn't put it past him, would you?"

He paused and thought for a moment. "No," he said finally. "Bennett's broken the law before to help a cop. I can see him going to extremes to protect the captain who made his career. Plus he always had a bit of a violent streak."

"And we already know he threatened Margot," I added. "The neighbor told me a tattooed white cop showed up a week before her death, and she heard a slap."

"What?" said Luke.

Apparently I'd forgotten to mention that tasty morsel. "It explains why he never bothered to interview the neighbors and why he never sent you the coroner investigator's report."

"Maybe he did kill her," said Luke. "It's certainly convenient that he was put on the case. And it provides cover if his fingerprints turn up at the scene."

"So what do we do now? We need more evidence on Margot's link to Farabee. Right now, it's all speculation."

"*We* aren't going to do anything," said Luke. "You're going to focus on not ruining your life over what you did today."

"First of all, I don't report to you," I reminded him. "And I'm going to keep working this case, since I just depleted my bank account to make bail and I need to pay my mortgage."

He shook his head in frustration. "Just focus on your case and put Bennett on pause. As you already pointed out, we have no idea what he's capable of."

I sipped my water and looked down at the table. Luke had a point. Bennett was out of control, which made him dangerous. But I couldn't shake the feeling that whatever secret he was hiding lay at the heart of this case. I needed to keep pressing. I'd just have to be smart about it.

CHAPTER

29

Seven Months Ago—Blaze

WHEN A GIRL breaks your heart, she waits eight to fourteen days before reaching out. It's mathematically calculated to enhance your torment. Think about it: after a week or so of licking your wounds, you start noticing girls again—maybe even join a dating app. You're still sad, but you can see the light at the end of the tunnel.

Then she drops a line and reels you back in. Maybe she asks you to come by and get your stuff. Maybe she calls to see how you're doing. Or worse, she wants to sit down over coffee for the sake of "closure." Then, after tearing off the scab, she disappears, leaving you alone to lick your wounds.

Margot was right on time. Exactly eight days after she dumped me, I got this crazy text saying she didn't want to be alone. I was supposed to drop everything and rush over like a lapdog. My show had just ended, and I was talking to this cute bass player with purple hair. We'd been having eye sex all night, and I was minutes away from an invitation to her place. Then Margot reached out across space and time to grab me by the balls.

Our relationship had been doomed from the start. Margot was a thirty-five-year-old artist with a master's degree who'd traveled the world. She spoke fluent German and followed world politics. I was a twenty-six-year-old college dropout who'd found moderate success slinging records. She was the most fascinating woman I'd ever been with. I was—as Margot put it—a palate cleanser.

On the drive over, I practiced my speech. I was going to let her have it. She was treating me like her errand boy. She couldn't just crook her finger and expect me to come running.

By the time I got to her door, I was filled with righteous indignation. I should have told her to shove it and nailed that bass player. What was I even doing here?

But my anger evaporated when I saw her. She was holding an ice pack to her cheek, and she'd clearly been crying. "What happened?" I asked, stepping inside.

Margot brushed past me, closed the door, and threw the dead bolt. "Please stay with me tonight," she said. "I'm scared." Her voice was quiet and had none of its usual confidence.

"Of course," I stammered, "but you have to tell me what happened."

She poured glasses of whiskey for both of us, and we sat down at the table. Margot took a long gulp and winced. "I forgot I bit myself," she said. "The liquor's not helping."

"What happened, Margot?" I repeated.

"The police were here," she said in that same low monotone. I waited for the rest of the story, but it didn't come. When Margot's up, she'll talk your ear off. When she's low, you have to pick through her monosyllables and half sentences for information.

"Did they hit you or something?"

She nodded and took another sip.

"Why were the police here?" I prodded, taking her hand in mine. She didn't stop me.

"An officer did something to me a long time ago," said Margot. "And I wanted to bring it to light."

"What did he do to you?" I asked.

She shook her head. "I don't want to talk about it. But it happened. I don't think I ever got over how angry it made me. And it wasn't okay."

"What did he do exactly?" I repeated, although I had a sick feeling I already knew.

"It doesn't matter right now," she said. "But pretty soon the world is going to know about it. So he sent a couple of his minions to shut me up."

"Cops? And they hit you?"

She nodded again. "They told me if I so much as breathed the name of their friend, they'd come back and do their own X-Acto knife project on my face. They said they could kill me and make it look like an accident. No one would ever know."

"You have to call—"

"Who?" she interrupted. "The police? They *are* the police. They said no one would believe me, and they're right. But people will believe me about their friend. I kept receipts." Margot pressed her index finger into her lower cheek and frowned. "I think my tooth is loose. That bastard really got me."

I winced. "There has to be someone we can report this to."

Margot shook her head. "I'll get my revenge. When the time comes, I'll talk to the press. I made a point of memorizing his tattoos. The one who hit me had a cartoon tiger on his forearm and the word *corazòn* with the accent slanted the wrong way."

Her level-headedness was chilling. Margot had really thought this out. As freaked out as she was, she wasn't crying. She was sitting there calmly plotting retribution.

"I'm tired," she said. "I want to go to bed. Would you stay with me and just hold me? I don't want to be by myself."

30

Present Day—Kate

O N THE NIGHT after my arrest, I lay awake, imagining shivs, baloney sandwiches, and the fecal smell of state prison. I thought about Amelia. John would never take her to see me in a place like that, and frankly, I couldn't blame him. Maybe he'd let me call once a week to hear her voice.

After a while, the light trickled in through my blinds. I buried my head under a pillow and stayed in that position until hunger drew me out. When I sat up, my neck screamed at the sudden motion. The muscles were so stiff that I could barely turn my head. Still, I was grateful it wasn't worse after my encounter with Bennett. I'd be fine in a day or two. Physically, at least.

Most of the day was a haze of wine, ice cream, and trash TV. In the late afternoon, my phone rang, and I let it go to voice mail. It was Milt Starling calling for an update, which I desperately owed him. I started to call him back but hung up, realizing I didn't have the bandwidth to carry on an adult conversation. By then I was a bottle in, and he might even detect a slur in my voice. Milt called back a few minutes later, and I stared at my phone, watching it ring. *In a meeting*, I texted him. *I'll call you tomorrow.*

I exited the text screen and looked at the background picture of my daughter. She was wearing the purple Rollerblades I'd found at a flea market, practicing her moves on the flat stretch of sidewalk that runs along Manhattan Beach.

What am I doing? I'd just gotten arrested, and now I was ignoring a client so he didn't find out that I was drunk in the middle of the day. I needed to get my shit together—fast—if I was going to salvage what was left of my career and be a decent parent.

I picked up the bottle of Cabernet and poured the remnants into the sink. I forced myself to start cleaning the house. Two hours later, I'd created some order in the chaos. That night I cooked a healthy-ish dinner for once—steamed vegetables with melted cheese on top. When I was done, I walked into Amelia's room and lay down on her bed. It might be a long time before I saw her again, and I wanted to feel her presence. Sleep wasn't going to happen—I was too anxious for that. So I tried to push thoughts of shackles and orange jail uniforms to the back of my mind, focusing on memories of good times with my daughter. I'd have to deal with the darker stuff soon enough.

On the morning of my arraignment, I straightened my hair and wriggled into my court suit. It was a little tighter in the hips than I remembered. Angela wanted to pick me up so she could lecture me on the drive about courtroom behavior. I tried to explain that I've testified dozens of times, but she wouldn't hear it. "It's different when your ass is on the line," she told me.

She pulled up in a cream-colored Audi. Private practice had been good to her. "You look nice," said Angela. "You wouldn't believe what most of my clients wear to court."

"Thank you for doing this," I said. "I'd be taking out a second mortgage if it wasn't for you."

She waved it off. "Consider it payback for turning up that witness on the Esposito case. You saved him from doing twenty-five to life for a crime he didn't commit."

Angela told me about her conversation with the filing DA on my case. When they last spoke, he'd been struggling with the idea of a misdemeanor because of my gun, but he promised to run it by the head deputy in charge of the branch court. Angela told me not to get my hopes up. If I got lucky, they'd let me plead to a felony and "earn" a misdo after a year of good behavior. It wouldn't be enough to save my license, but it would keep me out of state prison.

We pulled up to the west side courthouse. Angela parked at the far end of the lot, away from the other vehicles. "You know how many people are here for a DUI?" she said. "I'll defend them, but I'm not getting near their cars."

I'd been too nauseous to eat breakfast, and I was starting to feel light-headed. I followed Angela into the courthouse and through the metal detector. My belt set off the alarm, and I stood still with my arms extended as the sheriff ran a wand over my body. Last time I'd gone to court, I still had my badge and skipped the security routine. And now here I was as a criminal. I felt numb.

Angela had gone ahead of me and was looking for my name on the flat-screen TV that paired defendants with assigned courtrooms. She looked back at me and grinned. "You're in Department 72. That's a misdemeanor court." Angela paused to let the full meaning sink in. "The judge is a nice old lady who used to be a public defender. Kate, you're not out of the woods yet, but this is exactly what we were hoping for!"

I followed her into the crowded elevator, which smelled like marijuana and sweat. The guy behind me was pressed against my leg a little too closely. I resisted the urge to forcibly reposition him. Angela had said I had to be on my best behavior.

Department 72 was packed. Dozens of defense attorneys swarmed around an overwhelmed misdemeanor DA. The young man, who'd probably been on the job for about a month, was working hard to scribble down offers and respond to the judge's questions while an ancient public defender in New Balance sneakers shout-whispered in his ear. I studied the line of attorneys waiting for their turn to yell at the DA. One of them looked vaguely familiar, but I couldn't place him. We made eye contact, but he quickly looked away.

Angela left me seated on a bench in the back row while she checked in with the court clerk. A few minutes later, she returned with a copy of the complaint and the police report. "Come outside with me. Let's talk in the hall," she said, placing a hand on my shoulder.

I followed her down the corridor until we were out of anyone's earshot. "It's your lucky day, Kate. They charged you with trespass. Honestly, I can't believe your luck, but whatever they offer, I'm going to need you to take it today before they come to their senses."

I felt relief wash over me. I could stay out of jail and keep my license. John wouldn't even find out about the incident to use it against me.

"I'm not going to waste time talking to the baby DA," Angela continued. "I'm going to see if the head deputy will give me five minutes and try to get you a diversion."

Diversions are frequently given out on low-level misdemeanors. It means that if you stay crime-free for a year and do some community service, they dismiss your case and you keep your clean record.

Angela squeezed my hand and disappeared down the hall. I sat on one of the benches outside the courtroom and looked around. A barefoot baby was crawling on the floor while his mom ate a bag of Doritos. Across from me, a young woman sporting a black eye was draped all over a bald guy in a wifebeater. He had the domestic violence look. It sticks to some guys like a bad smell.

The ancient public defender in the sneakers emerged from the courtroom and flagged down a Spanish interpreter. I watched them explain to a fiftyish woman that her son would likely get six months in jail for his eighth driving-on-a-suspended-license case. Of course, Men's Central was so crowded, the sheriff would probably release him after a night or two. The mother started to cry. Poor guy probably couldn't afford to pay a speeding ticket.

When he hadn't come up with the money, his license had gotten suspended. By now, the fines and fees had skyrocketed. The state would never get him to stop driving, so they arrested him once a year. He immediately got back in the car because he had to drive to work. In ten years, his mom would be back here supporting him on his fifteenth suspended-license case.

After what felt like forever, I heard the rapid-fire clack of Angela's stilettos. Our eyes met as she hurried down the hall and gave me a thumbs-up. "I got him to agree to a diversion," she said. "You have to do a hundred hours of community service, stay away from Berkland's house, and not possess any weapons. Do that for eight months and he'll dismiss the case. I asked for six, he wanted a year, but I whittled it down."

Relief flowed over me. I tried to speak but felt a lump in my throat. The weapons condition was not ideal, but I knew better than to push my luck.

"I need you to take this today," continued Angela. "Before he changes his mind. Until you agree to the diversion, they can revisit the felony."

I nodded. "Of course. But why are they doing this?"

"They got a call from an LAPD detective. The owner of that house is a suspect in an FBI case, and apparently he's vanished. They doubt he'll ever turn up, and if he does, he'll probably take the Fifth. Without him, they can't prove you didn't have permission to be inside."

Luke.

"Kate, I need to be straight with you. The DA thinks he can't prove his case. If you want to fight the charge, chances are we'll set it for trial, they'll fail to produce the homeowner, and you'll get a dismissal. But there's a small chance that they'll solve their witness issue and up it to res burg with a gun allegation. Then you'll be in a world of trouble. We can fight this, but no way is it worth the risk."

"I'll take the diversion," I reassured her. "It's better than I deserve, and I can't risk getting locked up." She nodded approvingly.

I followed her into the courtroom. Angela pranced up to the baby DA and showed him the offer his boss had handwritten on the face of her complaint. The young man nodded, relieved that there was one less battle for him to fight this morning. He announced to the clerk that we had worked out a disposition and were ready to call the case.

My elation was tempered when I heard the judge call my name. As I stepped forward, I caught the eye of the defense attorney who had seemed so familiar. He was staring at me with his mouth hanging open. Who was this guy?

The judge asked me a series of questions that I barely heard. I responded yes to each of them. They set a proof of completion date for the community service three months from now, and the clerk handed me some paperwork. I was free to go.

Angela hugged me when we got back to the hallway. I thanked her profusely and promised to work for free on her next major case.

On the drive back, she told me about a death penalty trial she was gearing up for. Her client was a famous serial killer who enjoyed stabbing young women in their apartments. "Between you, me, and the wall," she said, "he did it because he's evil. And they're going to convict him, because he's guilty. And then they'll vote to execute him, because he's the devil. I can't even get his family to testify for him."

I started to ask how she could defend someone like that. Then I remembered that she'd just saved my skin and thought better of it.

"Someone's gotta do it," she said, reading my mind. "And no state should convict someone who hasn't had the advantage of a rigorous defense."

I felt my phone vibrate. As I pulled it out of my pocket, the screen flashed with two missed calls from John. That lawyer I'd recognized in the courtroom probably knew him. Maybe he was an ex-DA from John's prosecutor days.

As I stared at my screen, a text came through. *Kate, you got ARRESTED??????? Pick up your phone.*

My cell started ringing again. I moved to decline the call but accidentally answered instead. I winced and put the phone up to my ear. I'd rather do this in private, but Angela was divorced. She knew the drill.

"John, I can't talk right now," I told him.

He ignored my comment and lit into me. "Don McCready just saw you entering a plea at the Airport Courthouse. What did you do? Do you have any idea how humiliating that is?"

As usual, all about him. "Sorry to put a damper on your morning."

"What did you do, Kate?" he repeated. "I have a right to know."

I sighed. "Actually, you don't have a right to know anything about my personal life. You forfeited that a long time ago." Out of the corner of my eye, I saw Angela nodding approvingly.

"As the father of your child, I need to know if you're losing it. I need to know if my daughter is going to be in a safe environment. If you're not going to give me a straight answer, maybe we should talk to a judge about it."

"Nice try," I said. "It was a diversion on a trespass for something work related. No court takes away kids for that. But if you want to share it with the judge, go ahead. I think it's well past time we revisit our custody agreement."

I hung up and looked over at Angela. "Sorry. Apparently John's buddy saw me in court."

"Don't apologize," she said. "It sounded like you showed remarkable restraint."

I laughed.

"And if you ever need it," continued Angela, "my former officemate does family law now. She's a pit bull in the courtroom."

CHAPTER

31

Present Day—Kate

I HUGGED ANGELA GOOD-BYE and climbed the stairs to my house. My emotional reserves were sapped, and I could feel a headache coming on. All I wanted to do was turn off my phone, heat up a frozen pizza, and eat it in bed with the lights off.

There was a rustling noise as I opened the door. I looked down and saw that I was standing on a thick manila envelope. It lacked a return address, but someone had typed up a label with my name on it. I picked up the envelope, tore open the sealed edge, and pulled out a series of black-and-white photographs. To my shock, I was in every image.

The pictures looked like they'd been taken with an expensive wide-angle lens. Whoever did this was experienced and well resourced. There was a picture of me talking to Agent Vargas outside the Berkland Gallery. Then me again walking on the beach with Mike Moreland. Were they following Mike, or had I led them to him? I felt sick. A third picture showed me getting arrested. Maybe the photographer called the cops, not the neighbor lady I'd thought was responsible. It was a smart move. He'd stopped me from snooping and destroyed my credibility in one blow. The last picture showed Bennett yelling at me outside my house, mouth curled into a snarl and finger pointed at my face.

Who could have taken these pictures? Bennett obviously hadn't photographed himself. And even if he had a shady partner with a camera, he wouldn't hand over photographic evidence of Bennett's attempt to intimidate me. Vargas wasn't a likely suspect either; FBI agents don't slip pictures under your door. That left whoever Berkland was in bed with.

Mike Moreland's words echoed in my ears: *Jason didn't like to hike, and he didn't fall off a mountain.* My legs felt weak, and I slid down the wall onto the floor. I flipped through the pictures again and again, hands trembling. Macho cops trying to keep me in line were one thing, but this was something else entirely. The worst part was that I had so little information about Berkland's associates. How do you assess a risk that you barely understand?

It might be time to bow out of this case. Things were spiraling out of control. I'd just gotten arrested for acting like a fool trying to find out what happened to Margot. And I had a daughter to worry about. If these goons decided to stick a bullet in my brain and throw me in a cement mixer, she'd grow up without me. She'd come of age knowing nothing about her mother besides the grim picture John painted for her.

But business was slow, and I'd just forked over a chunk of my savings to a bail bondsman. My mortgage was due every month, and I needed money if I was going to hire a lawyer to challenge my custody arrangement. And these assholes had gotten me arrested, taken my gun, and murdered one, maybe two brilliant artists at the peak of their careers. I couldn't let them get away with it. And they could kill again. Mike seemed to think they were just getting started.

My phone rang, and Milt's name flashed across the screen. It had been days since we'd spoken, and I desperately owed him an update. I was worried he'd be annoyed, but he sounded as patient and midwestern-nice as ever. As I started to fill him in, it dawned on me that my place could be bugged. Whoever delivered those

pictures obviously knew where I lived and probably had no com-
punction about breaking in. "Hey, can I call you back in ten minutes?" I tried to sound casual, but my heart was racing.

"No problem," he said.

I ran down the stairs to the sidewalk. Was I losing it? If I
voiced my thoughts out loud, I'd sound like a crazy person. But
the FBI had just warned me to steer clear of a Russian mob investigation, and someone had been following me for days taking glam-
our shots. I was pretty sure that one of Berkland's associates had
witnessed my arrest. So they knew I had an arraignment coming
up and could easily have looked up the date, giving them a perfect
opportunity to sneak into my place while I was in court. Maybe I
was being paranoid, but I had already put Mike Moreland at risk
by being sloppy. If they were targeting me, they could easily target
my client.

Every few seconds, I looked over my shoulder to see if I was
being followed. When I reached the end of my block, I turned
onto a quiet side street where I could talk without much traffic
noise. I sat on a retaining wall and called Milt. He listened as I
explained that Margot had probably blackmailed a police supervi-
sor and two cops had threatened her a week before she died.

"Is it the officer assigned to her case?" asked Milt. "Bennett?"

I winced. "Yes. Not the one she was blackmailing, but the one
who came to her apartment." I implored him to keep things quiet
for now, promising that we'd figure out what to do when the time
came. I didn't tell him about Mike or the Russian mob. It was too
dangerous to even mention at this point.

After ten minutes of persuading, Milt agreed not to contact
LAPD. I hung up and felt a wave of dread wash over me. Like it
or not, I'd just committed to finishing the investigation. If I quit
now, Milt might start talking about how a PI blamed the police
for killing his daughter. Or worse, he might believe me and start
talking to the press in the hope of ginning up renewed interest in
the case. Either way, I'd sound like a lunatic and lose whatever was
left of my business and reputation.

I walked back to the house, staring into the windows of every parked car for some brooding gangster with a wide-lens camera. One more week of this case and I'd be ripping off my clothes and howling at the moon.

As I turned onto my block, I thought about Mike Moreland. I had to warn him about the pictures. He was already taking safety precautions, but he didn't know a stealth photographer was snapping candids of him. I called Mike's number, and it went straight to voice mail. "Hi there, it's Kate Myles. Call me when you get a chance." He might not be checking those messages. After all, I'd watched him toss a cell phone into a trash can.

I pulled up his law firm website and called the number listed for him. No answer, just a recording telling me he was working remotely but checking messages. I left another voice mail, asking him to call me.

Once I was back at my place, I grabbed a spoon and a carton of coffee ice cream and binged until brain freeze kicked in. My phone chimed with a message from Luke: *Trespass?*

I wanted to call and thank him but realized I couldn't trust myself to sound dignified. I'd probably start blubbering away like a buffoon. *Thank you*, I texted.

Luke wrote back a minute later. *No idea what you're talking about, but glad things worked out.* He'd never confess to interfering in the case. This was the most I'd ever get out of him.

Once my spoon scraped cardboard, I returned the dregs of the ice cream to the freezer. I sat down at my kitchen table and put my head in my hands. The room felt smaller than usual, as if the wood-paneled walls were closing in on me. I needed to get out of here.

After John left, I'd spent the better part of a year trying to regain control over my life. Getting arrested and finding those pictures brought back dark emotions that I'd fought hard to put behind me. It was a feeling of impotence, like spinning your wheels when you're stuck in the mud. The more you try, the more trapped you get. I needed to pick myself up before I sank further.

Being productive would take my mind of my problems, help me lose the sensation of waiting around for something bad to happen.

My thoughts turned back to the case. I needed to figure out if the mob angle had anything to do with Margot's death. Cy Petrov was definitely involved in the forgery scheme—his name cropped up all over Berkland's art sales paperwork. But I didn't know how deep.

I typed Cy's address into Google Maps. The building was a sterile, yellow-brick rectangle pockmarked with air-conditioning units. I pulled up the floor plan from a rental agency website. The layout looked cramped but functional, hardly the luxurious den of a criminal mastermind. Especially if Cy was sharing it with a roommate.

I'd drive over and check it out—maybe I'd see him coming or going. And surveillance required minimal brain activity. Before driving over, I wanted to find a picture of the roommate as well so I'd know if I came across him. I Googled his name, Soren Allinder, and my jaw almost touched the floor. The first hit was an artist's webpage. The opening screen showed a picture of the smiling painter and a blurb about his work. He was good-looking in a dissipated kind of way.

I scrolled down and saw dozens of beautiful paintings of women. A lithe brunette sat naked in front of the mirror, brushing her long strands. A dark-skinned Black woman reclined on a sofa. A curly blond perched invitingly on a bed. There was nothing unusual about these works. They were lovely and poetic— the kind of thing you'd hang on your wall if people hung nudes anymore.

The Russian mob needed a world-class forger, and the straw director of their shell companies was bunked up with a talented artist. It couldn't be a coincidence. *Soren had to be Jason's replacement.*

By now, whoever was keeping tabs on me could probably identify my car. I decided to get a rental for a few days in the hopes of staying anonymous. I fished through my closet until I found a pair of binoculars and an old wig, curly and dark and relatively un-fake looking. I picked up some sunglasses off my desk and threw them in a tote bag. Not much of a disguise, but it was better than nothing.

After assembling my surveillance kit, I took a rideshare to the nearest rental agency and selected a gray Volkswagen Jetta. The windows were already tinted. Some burglary crew who'd rented the car before me had probably darkened them, and the underpaid staff had never bothered to remove the tint. The dark glass could help me stay undetected.

I plugged Cy and Soren's address into my phone, donned the itchy wig, and drove over to their place in Koreatown. I felt hot and a little stupid in the disguise, but for all I knew, Cy was the one photographing me, and I couldn't afford to be recognized.

By some miracle, I found a parking spot directly across from the building. It was a busy four-lane street with a suicide lane down the middle. I hunkered down and waited. After a few minutes, my phone rang with a call from a blocked number. I picked up and was relieved to hear Mike Moreland's voice. "Hi Kate, it's Mike. Just got your message."

"Are you somewhere safe?" I asked.

"Yes, knock on wood." Mike listened while I explained about the photographs. "I'm not surprised," he told me. "Jason got a set of those when he threatened to stop making forgeries. Are you still at home?"

"No, I'm out in the field. Why?"

Mike sighed. "Just be careful what you say in your house, all right? Before Jason died, a defense attorney came over to our place. Jason wanted to get his advice about going to the police if Berkland refused to let him quit."

"You think someone was listening?" It seemed I wasn't being paranoid when I refused to talk to Milt in my living room.

"I have no idea, but I haven't been home in a month. Just be careful."

"Mike, I'm worried about your safety. You know the feds are looking into this. They have the resources to protect you."

"Thanks," he said. "But I don't want to risk coming back to LA. I'll call you if something changes."

Good, he'd gotten out of town. "Mike, Aksel Berkland's been missing for about a week. You said before that you thought his partners might try to kill him. Do you have any reason to think that happened?"

"Just speculation, but logically, if he isn't dead, it's only a matter of time. Berkland knows too much; he's a liability. And the guy has a taste for the finer things. I wouldn't be surprised if he got greedy and demanded a bigger cut. This started out as his scheme. It's gotten huge, and he probably wants a payout."

"How huge are we talking about?"

"A friend of mine went to an auction at Hughes a few months back," said Mike. "He told me that a painting supposedly by Jason sold to a shell company registered in Cyprus."

"I remember, Capulous LTD. It's in the chart you gave me."

"That's the one. Anyway, I have an email alert set up for news about Jason. A couple days ago, the *New York Times* did a story on him and the market for his work. Turns out that same painting is now on sale at Sotheby's with a five-million-dollar estimate."

"Jesus," I said. "They built up credibility at Hughes, and now they're moving on to the big leagues."

"Exactly. Jason's not around to cry foul, and his work is so new that no one's really studied it. There's no Martinez expert to say that something doesn't look right. These guys are set to make a fortune."

"Unless you spill the beans," I pointed out. "Or Berkland does, and he's AWOL."

"There's a reason I'm in hiding," said Mike. "And as for Berkland, if you find a new gallery selling paintings by Jason, you'll know he's not coming back."

It made sense: Berkland was expendable. Shady gallerists with money problems are a dime a dozen. "Mike, I'm not going to ask where you are, but can you assure me it's far away?"

He laughed darkly. "I've helped billionaires avoid paying their taxes for years. I know a thing or two about being discreet."

I had a vision of him drinking a frozen daiquiri on some Caribbean beach, palm trees swaying in the breeze. "Well, take care of yourself," I said. "If I learn anything about Jason, how can I reach you? Should I call the firm?"

"You can call my secretary, Wendy Tran. I trust her, and she knows how to get in touch with me."

"Will do," I said. "One more question. Have you heard the name Soren Allinder?"

"Nope," he said. "Doesn't ring a bell."

I hung up the phone and let out a frustrated sigh. The air conditioning was on full blast, but the early afternoon sun was beating down on the car's metal roof. My wig itched and my scalp was starting to sweat. I took a sip of warm, plasticky water from my thermos and turned my attention back to Cy's building.

After twenty minutes of nothing happening, I decided to break up the monotony and call Narek. The little punk hadn't gotten back to me about Margot's phone, which was unlike him.

"Hi, Kate," he said with a yawn.

"Narek, you sound sleepy."

"I just got back from DEFCON."

That explained the radio silence. "How'd your presentation go?"

"My booth was very popular," he said, and I could tell he was beaming.

"Glad to hear it. Any luck on the phone?"

"Sorry, I got sidetracked," he said sheepishly. "But I met a phone guy at DEFCON. I could ask him for pointers."

"That would be great; I'd appreciate it. Let me know how it goes." It occurred to me that Narek might have learned a thing or two about listening devices at his hacker conference. I still needed to sweep my place for bugs, which was going to be a nightmare. My living room walls were covered in 1970s fake-wood paneling. I'd have to give each panel a shake to see if anything was behind it. "Hey, I got another question for you. What do you know about secret recording devices? I'm up to speed on the old-school stuff, but what do you know about modern techniques?"

"Cameras or just voice?" asked Narek.

"Both." I hadn't even thought about a camera. The idea of some criminal beating off to me in the shower gave me the dry heaves.

Narek rattled on about newfangled devices that would make anyone paranoid. He talked about microphones disguised as pens, cameras that looked like phone chargers, watches that lived up to their name. My head spun. In short, if these guys were as sophisticated as I feared, I could spend days combing through my apartment and still miss something. Thank god Amelia would be with her dad this weekend. Whoever was tailing me probably thought I was just a lonely single woman with no dependents. Next weekend, maybe I'd see about renting an RV and take her camping somewhere remote. She'd act like she hated it and beg for TV, but at least she'd get fresh air and sun on her pale skin.

Out of the corner of my eye, I noticed movement coming from Cy's building. I turned and saw a tall, handsome blond man with long hair and a short guy with an upturned nose. They were standing outside the front entrance holding large rectangular objects wrapped in newspaper. The blond sported a busted lip and an enormous black eye. He looked miserable. It was unmistakably Soren. "Narek, I gotta go," I said. "I'll call you back."

I hung up the phone and snapped a picture of the two men. Soren's companion had to be Cy, although he'd aged since his last mug shot. He leaned the rectangular package against the wall and made a phone call. I focused on the wrapped objects—the right size and shape to be canvases.

A large van pulled into the center lane, and an enormous beast of a man stepped out. He opened the back doors to the vehicle and started moving things around. I pulled out my binoculars to get a better look. The big guy started loading the long narrow packages into the van while Cy and Soren disappeared into the building.

I focused the binoculars on his tree-trunk biceps. There was a clumsily inked Madonna and child on one arm with a building behind it topped with two onion domes. I zoomed in on his face. He had powerful features, a broken nose, and the cauliflower ears of a former boxer. I wondered if this guy was responsible for the state of Soren's face.

A few minutes later, Cy and Soren were back with more wrapped canvases. The big guy loaded them into the truck before walking over to where they stood. He said something that looked like a warning to Soren and poked a beefy finger into his chest. Soren shrunk against the railing. The ogre let out a menacing laugh, took Soren's face in one beefy hand, and gave him a few mock-affectionate taps on the cheek. Even from a distance, the message was clear: *Be a good boy and we'll get along.*

Once Cy and Soren went back inside, the big guy climbed into the driver's seat. I saw the brake lights turn on. *Well, here goes nothing*, I thought, starting my engine.

I tried to leave at least one car between me and the van. He was heading downtown, away from Berkland's gallery. Eventually he pulled into an alley in the Arts District. There were fledgling galleries and storage places all over this neighborhood. I remembered Mike's warning: *If you find another gallery selling Martinez fakes, you'll know Berkland isn't coming back.*

I parked about halfway down the block from the alley. This part of the city had a lot less traffic than Koreatown, and it was harder to remain inconspicuous. After half an hour, I watched the van pull back into the street. I turned on my engine and drove slowly past the alley. It was wide enough for two cars and continued through to another street. He'd probably met someone in the alley and passed off the canvases. I'd do a foot tour tomorrow of the Arts District galleries and see if anyone was advertising paintings by Margot or Jason.

It was too quiet. I didn't like following the van under these circumstances. There were no other cars to hide behind, and I was too visible. Hopefully he'd pull onto a busier street soon and I could fall back. I thought about turning around and leaving, but I was finally onto something and I wanted to see where he went. He could lead me to whoever was running the forgery operation—and whoever had been following me. At that point, I'd have to get Luke involved, but if I backed down now, I'd hit a dead end.

Suddenly, the van came to a stop and the driver door swung open. The bruiser got out of the car, positioned his body directly in front of me, and pointed a gun at the windshield.

I shifted into reverse and hit the accelerator. The car flew backward, almost crashing into a parked sedan. I backed up to the intersection and heard the blaring horn and screeching brakes of a car coming from the opposite direction. I ignored the other driver and tore down the street.

The ogre didn't follow me. He didn't fire his gun; there was no need. If they knew it was me, they knew where I lived. And if Mike was right about a bug, they'd know the moment I got home.

32

Present Day—Kate

I DROVE RANDOMLY, MAKING turn after turn. Every few seconds I looked over my shoulder to see if the van was behind me. When I knew I was alone, I pulled into a strip mall and parked. My heart pounded so hard I could feel it in my temples.

What was I supposed to do now? Was it even safe to go home? Maybe he hadn't connected the curly-haired woman following him to the annoying PI who asked a lot of questions. Or maybe he knew exactly who I was and was driving to my place right now with a loaded magazine and a silencer.

I concentrated on inhaling and exhaling, trying to slow my breathing to a normal rate. Panicking wasn't going to help me. I needed to think. Swapping out my car was at least something productive I could do. They'd seen me in the Jetta and photographed me in my own vehicle. I needed something that hadn't been burned yet. I drove over to the rental place. The chick at the front desk stared at me like I was crazy when I asked to trade in my Volkswagen. "You just rented it two hours ago," she said.

"Yes, I know. I was there," I pointed out. I couldn't exactly tell her why I wanted to make the exchange. So I brought up the tinted windows and gave her a brief lesson on the California

Vehicle Code. She rolled her eyes but waved a hand toward the lot and told me to choose a replacement.

I climbed into an anonymous-looking gray Nissan, drove out of the parking lot, and tried to plot my next move. Above all, I needed to rest. I hadn't slept for more than a few hours in days. If I went home, I'd be up all night, jumping every time a floorboard creaked. But if I checked into a hotel, they might be able to track my credit card usage. It would be nice to shut my eyes without worrying about rogue cops and mob assassins.

Too tired to think of other options, I called my friend Jenny and asked to crash for a few nights. Jenny has an active social life and I hate imposing, but I knew she wouldn't turn me down. Her mind immediately went to "guy trouble." I assured her that my love life was still basically monastic and hinted at plumbing problems. I didn't need to scare her with the details of my afternoon.

Jenny and I have known each other since childhood. Our fathers were on the force together, and we used to hang out at LAPD barbecues, playing hide-and-seek or chasing each other with Nerf guns. I grew up and followed in my dad's footsteps, but Jenny never had an interest in police work. She went to beauty school and learned to do hair, like her mom. We don't have a ton in common anymore, but I'm not close to many people, and by now she's more like family.

Before heading to Jenny's, I stopped at my place to pick up essentials but parked two blocks over in case anyone was watching. I didn't want them to see me step out of the new car. It's a strange experience, staking out your own house to make sure no one's watching it. After half an hour of nothing happening, I decided to go inside.

I unlocked my front door, walked straight to the kitchen and grabbed a carving knife, and headed to the bedroom to speed pack. Moving as quickly as I could, I scooped up my laptop and tossed some clothes into a long-neglected gym bag. I spotted Margot's catalog on my nightstand and threw that in as well. Other than the X-Acto project, I hadn't studied her work, and other pieces could offer clues about her past.

Something creaked in the living room. I clutched the knife so hard my knuckles went white and crept over to the doorway. I peered through and scanned the room for signs of an intruder. No one was there. It's an old house. Old houses make noise.

I locked the front door and ran down the stairs to the sidewalk. Before entering the rental car, I looked back at my house wistfully. It was a dive, but for the past two years, this place had been a sanctuary. I'd spent years in a bad marriage, where maintaining the peace meant suppressing my personality. Moving here had given me a chance to just *be* without worrying about treading on someone's nerves. I missed my daughter every minute, but the absence of John, or any other adult, had been a godsend.

This house had seen me at my worst. But it had also given me the safety and privacy to start rebuilding my life. After today, I might never feel safe here again. I needed to get these assholes for myself as much as for the Starlings. Until they were behind bars, I'd be jumping at every bump in the night.

Jenny lives about forty minutes away without traffic, but I took a circuitous route in case anyone was following me. After a while, I started to relax. I hadn't seen Jenny in a couple of months; she runs a mobile beauty parlor for rich Westsiders. That kind of customer expects their stylist to be a walking advertisement for their services, and Jenny more than delivers. She's a natural blond with the same stunning figure she had at eighteen, and many women would kill to look like her. She supplements her income as an Instagram influencer. Basically, companies pay her to post pictures of herself looking good while using their products. Between these two occupations, she was able to buy a two-bedroom condo in Redondo Beach, just a ten-minute walk from the ocean.

Jenny *tsk-tsk*ed as she opened the door and fingered a chunk of my limp, two-toned hair. Her apartment was as Instagram ready as always, with blond wood floors, a 1950s-style home bar, and whiskey-colored leather furniture. Within five minutes of my walking in the door, Jenny had somehow cajoled me into letting her cut and dye my hair. Maybe a different look would make it harder for my new friends to recognize me, at least from a distance. And maybe it would make me feel a little better. Lately, I rarely bothered to look in the mirror. Sometimes I didn't even have the time or energy to wash my hair in the mornings. It would be nice to get pampered and look put together for a change.

It felt good to let go and take a break from thinking about murder and mobsters and forged paintings. Jenny guided my head over her bathroom sink, as she'd done a dozen times when we were teenagers. I half listened while she talked about her new boyfriend, a dentist she fondly described as "ugly but sexy."

When she was done, I barely recognized myself. My dishwater hair was now a rich chocolate brown and lopped off at my chin. Instead of stringy, my thin tresses looked sleek.

I touched the back of my neck and felt my surgical scar, which would now be exposed no matter what I did. Jenny caught my eye in the mirror and shrugged. "People have scars. It's hardly noticeable, and you look good. You just need a little red lipstick." She ran into the bedroom and retrieved an unopened tube. "Keep it," she said. "I was saving it for a client, but I'll pick up another one."

"Thank you," I said. "How much do I owe you?"

Jenny waved me off. "Please, it's on the house. I couldn't have lived with myself if I let you walk out of here with three inches of roots."

I laughed and swiveled my head again from side to side. "Thank Jenny. It's nice to feel like a person again."

We talked while Jenny made dinner. The meal was good despite being vegan and carb-free. I mostly listened while she gossiped about the sex lives of her VIP clients. After a while, Jenny excused herself for bed. She had to be up early. A pop singer needed extensions put in before a shoot and expected Jenny at six sharp.

I retreated to the guest room, curled up on the bed, and called Amelia to say good-night. She told me about the sea monkeys her teacher bought for the classroom until John cut our call short and sent her to brush her teeth.

Feeling dejected, as always after hanging up with Amelia, I picked up Margot's catalog to distract myself. Her work was impressive, but intense for my taste. Unlike Jason's paintings, this stuff was impossible to imagine hanging on my wall.

After flipping past some self-indulgent nudes, I came across several paintings of incarcerated men. This could be her connection to Farabee. I fished my laptop out of my gym bag and started reading about the project. In an old interview, Margot alluded to sneaking a camera into Men's Central Jail. If police had investigated, there had to be a report somewhere. Was there some kind of nonprosecution quid pro quo? I made a mental note to mention it to Luke.

And if Margot was into hidden cameras, maybe she'd used one to record her blackmail victims. It would explain how she was able to secretly capture images of them in the buff. I had assumed Margot waited for her victims to fall asleep and snapped candids. But maybe she had a more sophisticated operation. If the men looked awake in the pictures, it would suggest she used a hidden device.

I flipped through the catalog before realizing that the blackmail pictures wouldn't be in there. The book was a year out of date, and the Venice Biennale hadn't even happened yet. If I wanted to see the photographs, I'd have to go through Garlington. I'd pay him a visit tomorrow.

I didn't really care how Margot pulled off her sordid little prank. But if she had a hidden camera in her apartment, she could have used it for security too. Maybe she activated it when two cops showed up to threaten her. Then there was the actual murder. If someone had come over who made her nervous—a week after Bennett threatened her—she might have started recording. There was a chance that the murder had been caught on tape. But where would her recording device be? I'd have to ask her father.

33

Present Day—Kate

IT WAS LATE morning when I woke up. I'd been passed out for a good ten hours, and I felt a million times better. After showering, I threw on fresh clothes and, for the hell of it, applied the lipstick Jenny had given me. I looked almost pretty: a different person from the ball of tension I'd been eighteen hours ago.

Jenny had told me to help myself to breakfast, but I was already imposing enough. There was a coffee shop down the block from her building. I walked over to the café and enjoyed the cool ocean breeze. It was a beautiful day, and you could hear seagulls calling overhead.

After picking up a coffee for the road, I drove over to Garlington's. This would be my third time pestering the prickly gallerist, and there was a solid chance he'd throw me out. If I were really lucky, maybe he'd be gone for the day and I could try my luck with his charming assistant.

I parked on the street and strolled into the gallery. Anya was at her usual perch. Not recognizing me, she started to smile. But when I pushed my sunglasses up over my ears, every trace of friendliness vanished.

"Hi, Anya," I said.

"What are you doing here? The last time you showed up, Peter screamed at me. You need to leave."

"Tell your boss I just need five minutes."

"No, you have to get out of here."

I reached past her and knocked on the door to the office. A moment later, Garlington emerged and glowered at Anya. "What now?" he barked.

She crossed her arms over her chest and nodded in my direction. He looked up and squinted, trying to place me.

"Kate Myles," I reminded him. "We met the other day. I have a quick follow-up question. If you can give me five minutes, I'll get out of your hair."

He let out an exasperated sigh. "Five." Garlington shot Anya another dirty look, as if to ask, *Why did you let this idiot back into my presence?*

I followed him into his office. "Do you have the images Margot was going to display in the Venice Biennale?" I asked.

"Yes," he said.

"Can I see them?"

"Fine," he said gruffly. "You can look at them, and then you can leave. I'm not giving you copies, so don't ask." Garlington clicked on a folder on his desktop and pulled up a slide show of naked men in compromised positions. Margot was a visible participant in a few of the pictures. She clearly hadn't been hovering over these men with a camera, so she must have set up a hidden device. In most of the photos, the men looked like they were having a good time and engaging with someone, presumably the artist. But there was one exception: a snapshot of a naked, mustachioed man walking out of the bathroom. The picture was taken at a weird angle. Maybe that guy was her first subject and she hadn't figured out the hidden camera system. Or maybe he caught her off guard and she hadn't had time to finish setting up.

Either way, there was something different about this guy. He wasn't trying to connect with Margot. He hadn't even bothered to take off his socks. "She had a concealed camera?" I asked.

"Yes," said Garlington, crossing his arms over his chest.

"For how long?"

"She started experimenting with hidden cameras shortly before the prison project."

"So she didn't make secret recordings of men until after the prison project?"

Garlington was tapping his foot impatiently. "Not that I know of." He looked annoyed.

"Mr. Mustache. Is that the first one she did?"

"Yes," he said, glancing at his watch.

"Is that Captain Farabee of the LAPD?"

"I'm not going to tell you that," he snapped. But his face answered my question. "Ms. Myles, it's been more than five minutes. I need to get back to work."

"No problem," I said. "Have a nice day."

Outside the gallery, I Googled Farabee's name again and found a picture of him from an old press conference. It was him, all right. Margot's knack for capturing resemblances was uncanny.

I was starting to get a sense of how things could have gone down. Farabee investigated Margot for sneaking a camera into the jails and threatened her if she didn't put out. Margot was too scared to say no. But when Farabee was coming out of her bathroom, his clothes still discarded on the floor, she snapped a picture for revenge. She'd patiently waited until the statute of limitations on filming in the jail had expired. By then, she had installed cameras in her apartment, maybe to help her feel safe and make sure this never happened again. Then she directed her rage toward men who hadn't assaulted her but had taken advantage of her, and men who'd hurt others. I'd read in the catalog that her work explored power dynamics and ways to reverse them. She'd certainly done that.

I called Milt from the rental car. "Mr. Starling, do you still have Margot's personal effects here, or did you bring them back to Ohio?" I asked.

"Everything's here, in the apartment," he told me.

I was pretty sure I'd find at least one piece of surveillance equipment. "Can I come over and look through them?"

"Sure, but I'm in Akron today visiting my wife. I fly back tonight. Do you want to see them tomorrow?"

"Perfect." I made a plan to stop by the next day at noon.

It was still early in the afternoon, and I wanted to get in a few hours of surveillance at Cy and Soren's place. If the ogre in the white van showed up, I'd hightail it out of there. But maybe I'd get lucky and catch Soren alone. Given the state of his face yesterday, I wondered if he was an entirely willing participant in the art fraud. Maybe he'd started out like Jason: a struggling painter in need of cash. And now he was in way over his head and scared out of his mind. If Soren was having second thoughts, there was a chance he'd talk to me.

After driving around their block, scanning for white vans, I parked across from Soren's building. My mind turned to the bruiser from yesterday and the barrel of his gun. This was risky, even with a new do and a different car.

As I contemplated whether to turn around, Soren emerged. I watched him walk up the block and get into a beat-up jalopy with peeling paint. Apparently he wasn't making much of a profit from his new vocation. I followed him onto the 101. He was heading toward the Arts District. With any luck, he'd lead me to the place where they dropped off the fakes.

Instead, Soren pulled in front of an art supply store and went inside. I decided to follow him. I walked through the door and was confronted with a strong smell of raw wood, paint, and an assortment of chemicals. It was pleasant in a brain-cell-killing kind of way.

Soren went straight to the oil paint aisle. I grabbed a basket and watched him as I pretended to shop. Biding my time, I picked up a few things Amelia could draw with the next time she came over. Holy crap, art supplies are expensive. Sixteen dollars for colored pencils? No wonder artists are always broke. I sucked it up and threw a pack in my cart. In theory, I could expense it to Milt, but I wasn't sure I'd feel right doing that.

My target got in line for the cash register. It was now or never. I got in line behind him and felt a burst of adrenaline. "Soren Allinder?" I asked, feigning surprise.

He turned and shot me a puzzled look. There was no hint of recognition in his eyes, but he didn't seem annoyed by the interruption.

"Julia West," I said, flashing him my best flirty smile. "I was the year behind you in art school." My stomach clenched. How did I know he'd even gone to art school? Plenty of artists are self-taught.

Soren looked confused but not unfriendly. "Julia, you do look familiar, but I'm having trouble placing you."

"I'm not surprised," I said. "I was pretty shy in my twenties. But I remember *you*. Your work was incredible. You could draw like Michelangelo." I felt myself blush; I'd just blurted out the first artist that popped into my head. I probably sounded like an idiot. Strangely, up close Soren looked familiar too. Maybe it was from staring at his picture on his artist website.

Soren laughed good-naturedly. "Michelangelo? I always thought his women looked like men. All those muscles."

I needed to get the conversation away from art history before I exposed myself as a phony. "Well, one of the greats, anyway. So many people never bothered to learn to draw, but you're the real deal."

Soren lit up. "Thank you. That means a lot."

It was his turn to be rung up. I needed to work fast or he'd nod a polite good-bye, and I would have blown my anonymity for nothing.

"It was nice seeing you, Julia," he said.

Luckily, Soren had a sizable collection of supplies and the sales clerk was moving at a snail's pace. "Hey," I said. He turned back around and faced me. "This is crazy, but I always had a bit of a crush on you in school, and here you are. It almost seems like a sign. Would you like to get a drink with me?"

He looked flattered, but his body language was hesitant. I jumped in again before he could brush me off. "There's a bar across the street with great cocktails. I'm buying. You look like you could use one."

Soren's face darkened, and his left hand instinctively reached up to touch the bruised skin around his eye. As his fingers moved to his cheek, I noticed that he was missing his left pinkie.

"Just one drink," I insisted. "It would really make my day."

The clerk was watching with amusement. I was laying it on thick, but this was my only shot. In my personal life, I tend to be shy and I suck at flirting. If I'm interested in a man, I talk to him like a person, maybe make a couple of jokes, and hope that we have enough in common to sustain the conversation. But I didn't have time for that. And my pride wouldn't be hurt if a dissipated art forger rejected Julia-his-former-classmate.

"Sure," said Soren. "Why not? Honestly, I really could use a drink. It's been a hell of a week. A hell of a year, actually."

The clerk handed him a large plastic bag full of art supplies. The total came to hundreds of dollars.

Soren told me he'd wait for me outside. I watched him walk out the door and then handed the drawing pad back to the clerk. "Sorry—I'm not gonna get this after all." She looked annoyed as she rang me up for the pencils, which would at least make a nice present for Amelia. But a twenty-dollar sketch pad wasn't happening.

I wondered if Soren was going to disappear. I'd come on a little strong, and it wasn't like the guy didn't have enough on his plate. But as I walked out into the hot sun, I saw him leaning against the graffiti-covered wall and smoking a cigarette. He looked sexy with his long blond hair and square shoulders. Ten years ago this guy wouldn't have looked at me twice. But life had dealt him his share of hard knocks, and I was doing my best to project confidence and easy sex.

"I wasn't sure if I'd find you out here," I said teasingly.

He laughed. "What do you mean? An attractive woman compares me to Michelangelo and offers to buy me a cocktail, I'm not going to say no."

I blushed, feeling genuinely flattered. We all need the occasional ego boost. "Well, then I guess it's my lucky day. Follow me."

He tossed his cigarette, and we crossed the street to the hipster bar. I'd been there once on a date with a graphic designer. The evening had been a snooze, but the bar did have great cocktails.

"Let's sit outside," I suggested. I wanted to be far away from other customers in case he felt like opening up.

I led him through the dark, funky bar with its leather booths and tin ceiling to a walled courtyard in the back. Several rustic tables and benches had been set up, and the space was shaded by a series of orange triangular awnings. They looked like big cheery kites against the bright blue sky.

We sat close together on the bench and put the single menu between us. As Soren leaned in to read it, his arm grazed my sleeve. I felt the warmth of him and realized there might be real chemistry here. It could be useful, but I couldn't get distracted. I reminded myself that he defrauded people for a living.

"Do they wait on us, or do we go to the bar?" he asked.

"They come around. I'm actually kind of hungry. Will you split some truffle fries with me?" I asked. "Still my treat." That would give us more time to chat.

"Sure," he said. An adorable waitress in jeans and a vintage baseball T-shirt came over and took our order. I had a gin and tonic, and Soren ordered a Moscow mule.

"So, I can tell that you still paint. I'd love to see your stuff," I said.

"I can show you pictures," Soren offered, pulling out his phone.

I leaned in closer as he flipped through an album of boringly beautiful nudes. I gushed appropriately. "They have soul," I told him.

Soren beamed. "Thank you. I try to look past the model's appearance and capture something of her personality. It's why I only paint people I know."

"You mean if I play my cards right, I might get to sit for you?" It was an obvious invitation, and he picked up on my meaning.

"If you play your cards right," he teased.

"What happened here?" I asked, pointing at the nub that used to be a pinkie. Soren winced and pulled his hand away. "I'm sorry," I backtracked. "It's none of my business."

"No, it's fine," he said. "You just took me by surprise. I was making a wood frame, and I had an accident with the band saw."

Something about his delivery told me he was lying. "Ouch, that's terrible," I said. "When was that?"

"About two months ago," he replied. *Holy shit, they cut off his pinkie.* I willed myself to control my face. "I'm sorry to hear that. At least it's your left hand." What better way to send a message to an artist? *Sorry about your pinkie; next time it'll be your painting hand.*

Soren shrugged. "I was really upset about it at the time. My right hand is dominant, but you know how it is; you really use both hands when you're working. I've gotten used to it, I guess." There was an awkward silence, then the waitress came with our drinks and the truffle fries.

"Thank goodness," I said. "I'm starving." I popped one in my mouth. They were good: hot and buttery.

"What about you?" asked Soren. "Do you still make art?"

I should have rehearsed this answer. "No, I tried for years, but I just couldn't sell anything. Eventually I gave up and went to beauty school, so now I do hair."

"You like it?" he asked.

"Yeah, I still get to be creative, and I make my own hours. How about you, do you have a day job?" I needed to steer the conversation back to Soren. This was turning into a pleasant fake first date, but aside from the mutilated pinkie, I'd learned nothing new.

"Not right now. I taught drawing for a while as an adjunct at UCLA. The former dean liked to hire alumni, but after he retired, they eliminated my position. Things got tight for a while. I even went back to bartending for a bit, but now everything's starting to ease up."

"Glad to hear it," I said, trying not to show my excitement. I'd told Soren we'd met in art school, hoping he'd mention his alma mater to fill in the gap. If Soren went to UCLA, he probably knew Margot and Jason. He was certainly in the right age bracket. Maybe Soren wasn't just a low-level patsy after all. "Hey, by the way, did you know that UCLA alum who killed herself?" I asked. "Margot Starling? She was your year, I think."

Soren turned white as a ghost. He took a long drink of his cocktail and looked off into the distance.

I opened my mouth to walk it back or change the subject but thought better of it. He'd have to say something eventually, and the look on his face told me there was a story here.

"We dated," he said finally. "All through grad school, actually."

Well, there's your provenance. Early Margot Starlings straight from the collection of her art school ex-lover. It was a forger's wet dream. "I'm sorry for bringing it up," I stammered. "Now that you mention it, it's coming back to me. You guys were a beautiful couple."

"Yeah, she was really something," he said wistfully.

"How long were you together?"

"A little over two years. She organized a postgraduate show for a few of us. Somehow Margot convinced Peter Garlington to come check it out. She had a way of making people do things. He was dazzled by her, like everyone else. He literally offered her representation on the spot. We lasted a little while after that, but she got distant, and then one day I found out she was cheating on me. That was the end of it."

"I'm sorry," I said.

He shrugged. "It was a long time ago."

"Your class has had a lot of loss," I pointed out. "Did you hear about Jason Martinez?" Soren's face told me he was quite familiar with Jason's death. "The guy finally makes it and then literally falls off a cliff. Terrible."

"Yup," said Soren. He was avoiding eye contact and staring down at his nails.

"Did you know him well?" I held my breath.

"We were friendly. He was in Margot's postgrad show." Soren downed the last of his drink and started looking around. I could tell he wanted the check. I needed to keep him here for one more round. Lighten the mood and leave the door open for another meeting.

"Soren, can I tell you something?" I asked.

He turned to me and smiled politely. "It's my birthday," I lied. "I was supposed to be going out to dinner with my ex, but I caught him cheating last week. So I know the feeling. Anyway, I saw you in the art store—this handsome, talented guy from art school, and it just brightened my day. So thank you."

He smiled. "Of course. Happy birthday."

I was grossing myself out, but the flattery seemed to be working. Soren was a sensitive person who'd spent fifteen years chasing his dreams and failing. His self-esteem was in the gutter, and a little ego stroking can go a long way. "Will you have one more drink with me, and I promise I won't talk about anything dark?"

Soren scooted a little closer. "Of course," he said. "But since it's your birthday, this round's on me."

I did my best to channel Jenny's casual flirtiness and ease with men. We chatted lightheartedly about movies and books. I realized there was a parallel universe in which I liked this guy, and he laughed easily and seemed to enjoy my company. I didn't press him on anything. My goal was to wrangle an invitation to his apartment to see what I could find out.

Eventually, the waiter brought our check. "Do you realize we've been here for three hours?" asked Soren, his eyes dancing.

Suddenly, I realized where we'd met before. Soren was the hot bohemian I'd seen admiring Jason's work at Bauman & Firth. He must have been studying the source material. Hopefully, Soren wouldn't connect the dots. Julia-the-former-classmate would surely have introduced herself. I plastered on my best casual smile. "I had such a good time talking to you, I lost track of time."

"I did too," he said. "Can I see you again?"

"Absolutely." I wrote my number on a cocktail napkin. "Now you have to call me so I have yours." He called me right then and there. I took my phone out to store the number but saw several texts and quickly jammed it back into my pocket before Soren could catch a glimpse of my screen.

We said good-night and agreed to see each other soon. He flashed me a knowing grin before turning around and heading toward his car. I watched him walk for a moment. He had a nice build, wiry but strong. And piercing blue eyes, almost turquoise. As I started my engine, I had that rush of euphoria that follows a good first date. I was surprised by the intensity of the feeling. But then again, I'd only been on two dates since the divorce, and both had been duds. There was something about the way Soren had looked at me, leaning in and really concentrating on what I was saying. It had awakened parts of me that had gone dormant. "Kate, get a grip," I said out loud. "You're working, and he's a criminal."

I took out my phone to store his number and saw a text from Narek: *It's ready.* True to form, he'd waited until dinnertime to summon me.

34

Present Day—Kate

NAREK HAD MANAGED to crack the phone with help from his DEFCON friend. By the time I picked it up and got back to Jenny's, I was exhausted. Putting on an act for Soren had been emotionally draining, and I needed to recharge my batteries. Jenny informed me that her ugly-but-sexy dentist would be dropping by for a nightcap. I offered to go out for a few hours to give them privacy, but she insisted that I stick around and meet him. I downed a cup of coffee to get up the energy for socializing.

Dr. Phil McKenzie exceeded my expectations. Not my type, but he was a laid-back, interesting man who'd traveled the world, and he was visibly smitten with my friend. Phil showed up with a bottle of rosé, Jenny's favorite, and made a genuine effort to get to know me for her benefit. After learning I was an ex-cop, he regaled me with horrific tales of fixing gunshot victims' shattered teeth. It wasn't exactly great cocktail banter, but he got an A for effort.

The next morning, I turned my attention to Margot's phone. On the day after her murder, she'd received twelve missed calls from Garlington. He'd also sent her a series of increasingly panicked and nasty text messages. My favorite one read, *You stupid selfish cow, if you're not here in fifteen minutes, I will RUIN YOU.* I was starting to understand why Anya quaked in her booties when her boss came within earshot.

There were a few missed calls from the night Margot was killed, all from the same number. She hadn't stored it in her contact list, so I decided to call and see who picked up. Hopefully I'd just get a voice message identifying the culprit and I could simply hang up. If someone did answer, I'd just pretend to be a telemarketer or something.

I couldn't call from Margot's phone, so I typed the number into my cell. Four digits in, it autopopulated with Soren's information. I tried to hit delete but clumsily pressed call instead. To my horror, he picked up.

"How's it going?" he said eagerly.

"Sorry, I think I butt-dialed you," I stammered.

"Damn, I thought you missed me already."

"Since I *do* have you on the phone, do you want to hang out again soon?" I asked. "I'd still love to see your work in person." I bit my lip, waiting to see if he was flattered or weirded out.

"How about dinner tomorrow?"

"Absolutely." What was I doing? This guy might have killed Margot, and here I was scheduling another rendezvous.

"Any food preferences?" asked Soren.

"I'm easy," I said. "Surprise me."

My heart pounded as I hung up. Was it really his number in Margot's call history? I checked again. It was. Why had Soren called Margot hours before she died? From my conversation with him at the bar, I'd gotten the sense they hadn't spoken in years. Maybe he was trying to warn her—or maybe he'd killed her. Too early to tell, but he was certainly involved in whatever went down.

And now I was going on a date with him. When Soren answered the phone, I hadn't had time to plan my response. I suggested another meeting on impulse, which might have been a very stupid, very dangerous mistake. Now I was stuck. If I canceled, I'd never get another shot at him. My gut told me Soren was the key to the whole case.

But there were serious risks, and my gun was still booked in an LAPD evidence vault. Plus I had California's pesky recording laws to deal with. It's illegal for a civilian to record someone without their consent. My court diversion required that I follow the law. This was not the time to play fast and loose with legal technicalities. If I wanted to tape our encounter, I needed Luke.

As usual, he picked up right away. "I need to speak to you," I said. "It's important."

"I can stop by your house tonight," he offered.

"No, I'm not staying there right now. I know who the new forger is. He called Margot on the night of her death. And I have a date with him tomorrow."

"What the hell, Myles! You're just springing this on me?"

"Well, it happened kind of fast. Can we meet?"

"Obviously. Come to my office. When can you be here?"

I winced at the thought of entering LAPD headquarters. "I'll meet you downtown, but I'm not going inside headquarters." By now half the people I used to work with would know about my arrest. I didn't feel like getting stared at or playing twenty questions about my prowling.

We arranged to meet in a café on Broadway. I hung up and walked over to my rental car. Luke should have been thrilled that I'd found the forger. Instead, he sounded like I'd just told him he needed a root canal. Something else must be going on that he wasn't sharing with me. That was his business.

After finding parking, I strolled into the coffee shop and texted Luke to meet me. I ordered myself a cup of dark roast and a maple scone and settled down on an uncomfortable wooden bench in the back of the café. Luke arrived a few minutes later, looking annoyed. He spotted me and came right over.

"What's going on, Myles?" he demanded. "Who's the forger, and what do you mean you're going on a date with him?"

I told him how I surveilled Cy and Soren's apartment and got chased away by the ogre. Luke flinched when I mentioned the gun. I pulled up Soren's artist page and pointed out how his technical skills made him a perfect forger. He wasn't the most creative guy, I realized, as I scrolled past dozens of similar-looking nudes. But he could probably duplicate anything. Luke listened quietly, occasionally sighing or rubbing his temples. I explained how I followed Soren to the art store, invented a character for myself, and convinced him to get a drink with me.

"You shouldn't have done that," said Luke.

"Why not?" I protested. "I learned that he was in a bad financial situation until recently and that Margot was his art school sweetheart. Think about that, Luke. He can forge the work *and* supply the provenance. And he likes doing portraits of women. I'm pretty sure I can convince him to take me back to his place and draw me. Then who knows what I might find out?"

Luke shook his head. "Absolutely not. Myles, this is crazy. You don't even have a gun right now. This guy could have killed Margot, for all you know."

"He doesn't seem like a killer. He tried to call her before she died, but I think he was trying to warn her." I only half believed what I was saying, but I needed Luke to come around.

"Myles, this is too risky. You certainly shouldn't go back to his place—you're unarmed with no backup."

"That's why I need you," I said. I take a lot of dumb risks to solve a case, but being alone with Soren in his apartment was probably a level too far. Having an LAPD officer ready to swoop in as backup changed that calculation. But I needed Luke to think I was going in regardless. He has a protective streak, so it would be better if he felt like he was looking after me rather than using me to bolster a case. "I can be your informant. I'm going to meet Soren with or without your help. But I want to record it, and that's only legal if it's for law enforcement. I don't want to commit another crime and mess up my diversion."

Luke shook his head. "I don't feel comfortable with this level of risk."

"You've put CIs in worse situations," I pointed out.

"That's different," he said.

"You're right, it is different," I countered. "I know how to protect myself, and I'm meeting an art forger—not a hit man—at a crowded restaurant."

Luke sighed and put his face in his hands. "An art forger with mob connections who might have killed a young woman. And you're talking about going back to his apartment."

"I'll be fine. You've wired up CIs and sent them into gang houses dozens of times. Why is this different?"

"Because it's you," he snapped.

He looked embarrassed, and I felt myself turn red. There was a moment of awkward silence as his words hung between us. "I'll be fine," I said finally. "But I'll be a lot safer if you do this with me. Otherwise, it's just me and Soren, and as you pointed out, I don't have my gun. Under the judge's order, I don't even think I can take pepper spray."

Luke winced and looked away. I bit my lip. He seemed to be really struggling.

"I'll be careful," I assured him. "We can come up with a signal in case anything goes wrong. This is our best chance to find out what happened."

"Fine," said Luke. "But just dinner, all right? We'll wire you up and see what he has to say, but you're not going back to his place for art modeling or some shit like that."

"Okay," I said. He'd have no way to stop me if things moved in that direction and I felt like it was safe. But we could deal with that when it happened.

My phone rang, and I looked down at the screen. It was Amelia's school. "I gotta pick up. Give me a second." She'd better not have lice again. "This is Kate Myles," I said.

"Mrs. Myles, we were trying to get hold of Amelia's father, but he's not answering the phone."

"Why, what's the matter?" I asked. "Is she sick?"

"No—something strange happened. A man called claiming to be her father and asked if she was in school today." My blood froze. "He asked for Amelia, but we have two—your daughter and Amelia Cruz. Then when we asked *which* Amelia, he kind of hesitated and said Amelia Myles, and—"

My daughter's last name is McDaniel. "That wasn't Amelia's father," I cut in. "Call the police. I'll be there as soon as I can. You need to pull her out of class and take her to the front office."

I hung up and leaped to my feet. "What's wrong?" asked Luke.

"It's my daughter—someone called her school pretending to be John. I have to go get her."

"I'll take you," he said. "I'll put on my siren and we'll get there faster." I nodded, too upset to speak. We ran back to the station and got in Luke's car. He was probably doing a hundred miles an hour as we flew down the 101, dodging in and out of lanes. I called John and chewed my thumbnail as the phone rang. The asshole didn't answer. After the third missed call, I texted him *Call me ASAP about Amelia*. That did the trick.

I was in the middle of dialing John's number for the fourth time when my phone lit up with his name. "John, someone called the school pretending to be you and asked about Amelia."

"What?"

"They wanted to know if she's in class today. The school's calling the police, and I'm on my way."

"What did you do?" he demanded. His voice verged on hysterical.

"I didn't do anything. I'm an ex-cop and you're an ex-DA, and we've both put away a lot of people who hate us."

"I left the DA's office four years ago, Kate. Don't pin this on me."

"Yeah, and some of your defendants are probably just getting out of prison."

John went silent. I didn't tell him about the last-name mix-up. He'd get his lawyer involved and take away whatever access to Amelia I had left. "John, this is too serious to fight over. I'm going to get her, and I'll call when she's with me."

"Okay," he said quietly. "Can you take her to your place?"

"I don't think that's a good idea. We don't know where this is coming from. I should take her to my mom's house while the police look into it. It's out of the way and the address is hidden." My dad was a smart cop. He'd bought his house through a trust. It would take a substantial amount of digging to link the address to me.

"Fine," said John. "That makes sense. Until we figure out what's going on." He was too scared to argue, which was terrifying.

I hung up the phone and went to work on my thumbnail. I hadn't bitten my nails in years, but in the last ten minutes, I'd reduced it to a stump. How could I have let this happen? John was right, I was a danger to my daughter. First I drive her into a parked car. Now I almost get her kidnapped. This had to be coming from the people who slipped the pictures under my door. The timing was too much of a coincidence. I should have dropped the case when I had the chance. Now Amelia was in danger because I was too stubborn and selfish to admit when I was in over my head.

"You know this isn't your fault," said Luke.

Something inside me broke at the sound of his words. I felt tears welling in my eyes, and I looked out the window so he couldn't see.

"Maybe we should reconsider this operation tomorrow?" he suggested.

I shook my head. "They already know where I live and where my daughter goes to school. We're not gonna be safe until I catch these motherfuckers."

Luke nodded.

"Thank you, by the way." I said. "For doing this."

"Please, Myles, it's your kid."

We were silent the rest of the way. My thoughts turned to Amelia's friends' parents and their safe, crime-free jobs. Michelle's mom worked in tech. Veronica's mother worked in the school library. No risk of their daughters getting kidnapped by Russian mobsters. It was my kid who'd drawn the short straw in the mommy department. When this case was over, I was going back to chasing adulterers and leaving murder to the police.

After what felt like a million years, we pulled in front of the elementary school. I ran inside, and Luke followed after me. Amelia was sitting on the couch by the front office, sucking her thumb and reading a picture book. She frowned as I scooped her into my arms. "What's wrong, baby?" I asked.

"Short hair," she said, scrunching up her nose.

"Sorry," I said, laughing. I'd forgotten that she hadn't seen my new do and that kids often don't like changes. Luke was talking to a young patrol officer from the Van Nuys station. I turned to Edna, the elderly school secretary, who was watching the spectacle. "Did you get the call?" I asked.

"About your daughter? Yes." She was beaming, thrilled to be the center of so much excitement.

"Thank you for being on the ball. Can you tell me what the guy said exactly?"

"Just what I told you on the phone," she replied. "He wanted to know if Amelia Myles was in school today. We don't have an Amelia Myles, so I thought something was wrong and I'd better call you."

"You did the right thing," I told her. "What did the guy sound like?"

She thought about this for a moment. "Nervous. He sounded a bit nervous. Something was funny about him."

"What did his voice sound like?" I asked. Edna looked confused. "Like—how old did he sound? Was his voice high- or low-pitched? Did he have any kind of accent?" I held my breath. I didn't know whether I'd feel better or worse if she told me he had a Russian accent. At least I'd know who I was dealing with.

"No accent that I can recall," she said. "He sounded young—I guess his voice was a bit high. There was nothing that really stood out to me."

"Did he sound familiar?" I asked. "Do you think he's called here before?"

"Oh, I can't say one way or the other. We get so many calls. I might have spoken to him before, but I just don't remember."

Great. He could literally be anyone. "Did he leave a phone number?" I pressed. "Or did he say he'd call back?"

Edna was starting to get flustered. "Well, let's see. I told him we didn't have an Amelia Myles—and then he thanked me and hung up."

Her answer was mildly comforting. Hopefully the caller had taken it to mean that my kid went to another school and wouldn't try this again.

"Mommy, can we go?" asked Amelia, who was starting to look distressed. She had no idea what was going on but could sense that her mother was upset. I needed to calm down and get her out of here. I took a card from the young patrol officer and told him I'd call as soon as I dropped off my daughter. It sounded like Luke had filled him in on a lot of what was going on, and I was grateful for that.

I took Amelia by the hand and led her outside. "Where do you want to go?" asked Luke. "I heard you say you're taking her to your mother's."

"It's all the way in La Verne," I told him. "Let's just go back downtown. I'll take my car. I'm sure you have work to do."

"It's not a problem," he said. "We'll drop her off, and then I'll bring you back to your car."

I tried to protest, but Luke insisted. He pointed out that we could talk about the operation on the way back.

Amelia asked me a million questions about why we were going to Grandma's in the middle of a school day. I've never been good at lying to children. They're smarter than we give them credit for, and it's hard for me to lie with conviction when I'm saying something ridiculous. "Grandma misses you," I told her. "It's a special treat. All your friends have to go to school, but you get to watch cartoons with Grandma." I turned around and looked at her. She wasn't buying it.

"But why today?" pressed Amelia. "It's not her birthday." She'd make a good detective.

"What are you gonna do with your grandma?" Luke chimed in.

"Eat snacks and watch cartoons."

"What's your favorite cartoon?" Luke continued to ask her distracting questions until she seemed to forget that something highly unusual was going on. For a man with no kids, it was impressive.

It suddenly dawned on me that he was talking to her like he would a child victim. It made sense: his primary interactions with kids were through criminal investigations. My mind flashed on a case we'd worked years ago. The only witness had been a little girl who'd hidden in the closet while her stepdad butchered her mom. I'd watched in amazement while he chatted with her about *My Little Pony* for twenty minutes before asking what she'd heard from the closet. I shook my head hard, trying to erase the memory.

"You okay?" asked Luke.

I nodded, still too upset to say anything. I didn't like the idea that my daughter was being handled. But it worked. She was happily chirping away about why music class was her favorite.

"Do you ever have any parent volunteers in your class?" asked Luke.

"Yeah," said Amelia. "Arecely's mom and Jaden's mom."

"Have you seen any new adults in your school?" he asked. "Did any grown-ups you don't know try to talk to you?"

It hadn't occurred to me that whoever was doing this might have gone to the school in person. What was wrong with me? It was like all my investigative instincts went dormant the second my daughter was involved.

"If any strangers do try to talk to you," continued Luke, "you need to walk away and tell the teacher, okay?"

I felt sick. My friend, the detective, was asking my daughter if any strange men had tried to chat her up. This was all my fault. I was a shitty mother. I should have gone back to school and become a paralegal or something.

I felt relief when we pulled up in front of my parents' home.

"That's a cop's house if I ever saw one," said Luke.

I smiled. He was right. It was a pinky-beige 1950s tract home complete with attached garage and ostentatious flagpole. When my dad was alive, he'd taken pride in maintaining the place to perfection. The upkeep was too much for my mother, and the white shutters were starting to chip. But she still kept the lawn watered and mowed to velvety-green perfection. "What can I say? My dad was old-school."

Luke waited in the car, and I walked Amelia to the front door. My mother took one look at my face and told my daughter to run ahead and pick out a Popsicle from the fridge. "What's going on?" she asked.

"Everything's fine. I'll call and explain in a bit. Can Amelia stay here for a few days?"

"Of course," she said.

"Thank you. I'll stop by tonight with a toothbrush and some of her clothes. Everything's okay, but don't tell anyone she's here— especially on social media, all right?"

"What's going on, Kate? You're scaring me."

"Someone called the school and pretended to be John. We don't know who yet. I have to go. My friend drove us here, and he's waiting for me."

I kissed my mom on the cheek and jogged back to Luke's car. As I opened the door, I felt my phone vibrate. I pulled it out of my pocket, eager for any news from Amelia's school. It was Milt Starling. I was supposed to have been at his apartment hours ago.

"Milt, I'm so sorry," I said. "There was an emergency at my daughter's school. Can we do this tomorrow?"

"I wish you'd told me that," he said. "I've been here since noon."

"I know, I completely forgot, I'm sorry. What time works for you tomorrow? I can be there tonight if it's easier for you."

He sighed. "How about ten o'clock tomorrow morning?"

"That's perfect. I'll be there."

"Please call if you can't make it."

I winced. "I'll be there, Milt. I really apologize—it was an emergency and won't happen again."

35

Present Day—Kate

MILT MET ME at the door of his month-to-month apartment. The place was small and depressing, with yellowed linoleum flooring and a water-stained popcorn ceiling. An enormous fan circulated the stale air, exacerbating the smell of mildew. His daughter had left behind a fortune, and he could have easily afforded something more comfortable. But I guess he never expected to stay this long.

The unit was set up like an informal shrine to Margot. Other than the lumpy double bed and the floral couch in the living room, every square inch was covered with her possessions. The closet was filled with Margot's clothes, and the dining room table was piled high with framed photos, sketchbooks, and exotic tchotchkes from her world travels. Milt had laid a small blue tarp on the floor, which was covered with art supplies, even a half-used bottle of paint thinner. On top of the mold, there was a faint smell of turpentine, and I wondered if living here was affecting his health.

I'd spent hours the night before pouring over spy websites, familiarizing myself with all the weird surveillance gadgets available. There were pens with tiny recording devices, phone adapters with hidden cameras, microphones stuffed inside lightbulbs. You

could even buy secret-camera showerheads and toilet paper hold-
ers for the pervert in your life. I'd printed out pictures of the most
popular ones and brought them with me hoping that I'd recognize
something. But nothing seemed to fit the bill.

On the nightstand, I spotted a picture of Margot and Soren.
It had to be at least ten, maybe fifteen years old. Soren looked
healthy and confident. His arm was wrapped around Margot, who
wore paint-splattered jeans and an itty-bitty second-skin tank top.
They must have been the king and queen of campus. Now one of
them was dead and the other was a struggling failure producing
fakes for rent money.

It said a lot that Margot had kept this picture for more than
a decade. I certainly don't have framed photos of my exes. Margot must have really loved Soren—enough that she thought
about him in low moments. It made sense. When you're wading
through the cesspool of dating options in your thirties, it's nice
to look back to a time when your whole world was wrapped up
in someone else.

Soren seemed like a sweet, slightly broken person. And I'd
seen the look of pain in his eyes when I brought up Margot's
death. He clearly still had feelings for her after all these years. I
didn't know why he called her on the night she died. Maybe he
killed her. Or maybe he knew something and was trying to warn
her. It was even possible they'd stayed in touch and the timing
was just a coincidence. Soren was a victim here too. A victim of
whoever killed Margot and Jason, and whoever was messing with
me and my daughter.

. I turned to the dresser and spotted a night-light. It was big—
several inches tall—and ugly. I couldn't see Margot owning a night-
light. It was something purchased by moms, or anal-retentive,
hyperorganized types. Not a free-spirited artist who collected
Oriental rugs and floral sex robes. I picked it up and examined it
more closely. There was a tiny round hole right in the middle. I
turned the light around and found a small USB adapter. Next to
the light was a remote control.

I stuffed the device into my purse and went back to the living room. Milt was sitting at the kitchen table, nursing a cup of coffee. "I found a couple things that I'd like to take with me," I said. "Your daughter had a remote control-activated nightlight. I'm not sure, but I think it might have contained a hidden camera."

"Why would she need a camera?" he asked.

Oh boy, how could I explain this one? "A lot of women have them for security," I told him. "I'm hoping there's footage on here from the night she was killed."

He set down his mug and stared at me in disbelief. "You think that's on there?"

"It's a long shot," I said. "But we want to make sure we leave no stone unturned."

Milt nodded. "Okay. Let me know what you find."

"Will do," I assured him. As I walked toward the front door, I remembered the photograph. "Milt, I saw the picture of your daughter with Soren Allinder. Do you know if Margot stayed in touch with him?"

"I don't think so," he said. "That was a long time ago."

"What can you tell me about their relationship?"

"I think it was strong. I liked him," he told me. "I met him once in her first year of graduate school. They both had pieces in a student show, and we came to see it. He seemed like a nice young man. I wasn't too keen on the idea of her settling down with another artist, but I could tell he loved my daughter."

"Do you know why they broke up?"

"Margot never talked to me about it, but she told her mother that he proposed and she turned him down. We were relieved at the time, but now I wonder what would have happened if they got married. Maybe they'd both be high school art teachers somewhere with a couple of kids."

His eyes were getting shiny with unshed tears. I put an awkward hand on his shoulder. "I'm so sorry, Mr. Starling. I'm going to go take a look at these. I'll let you know if I find anything."

"Please do," he said.

I let myself out and headed back to Jenny's house. It was going to be my last night there. I needed to deal with my problems and stop mooching off her hospitality. But until this meeting with Soren was over, I didn't want to jinx it.

When I got to her place, Jenny was making herself a healthy-looking salad in her gleaming white kitchen. She'd just gotten back from a photo shoot with a pop star at the Los Angeles Arboretum in Arcadia.

"How'd it go?" I asked.

Jenny shrugged. "The client decided she didn't want to come out of her trailer or let anyone else in. So we all just waited around."

I stared at her. "That's so bizarre."

"Not really," said Jenny. "It happens sometimes. I get paid either way. Instead of working, I sat around and chatted with a cute cop who was there for security. The garden's really pretty, by the way. You should take Amelia."

I winced at the reference to my daughter. My maternal guilt was at an all-time high.

"Everything okay?" asked Jenny, picking up on my anxiety.

I sighed. "It's a long story. I don't really want to talk about it. But I have a date tonight—sort of."

Jenny lit up. "That's exciting. With who?"

"It's not a real date; he's a criminal suspect. But I was wondering if you have time to help me out in the makeup department. I need to look like I'm trying to make an impression. As you know, getting gussied up is not my strong suit."

Jenny laughed. "Yes, I'm aware. Sure, it'll be fun. Although I'd rather be doing it for a real date. Whatever happened to that former partner of yours? The cute one?"

"Luke? We've actually been working together. He's a great guy, but way out of my league, and there's too much history."

Jenny rolled her eyes. "You think everyone's out of your league."

I poured myself a glass of water and disappeared into the small guest room. My mind drifted back to Luke, which had been happening a lot lately. Maybe I was wrong about him. He obviously cared about me. Possibly just as a friend, but maybe not. At any rate, I'd have to put these thoughts on ice until the case was over.

Reaching into my purse, I pulled out the night-light. I flipped open a back insert and slid it into my computer's USB port. A folder popped up with a single video file, and I hit play.

Margot must have activated the camera when she heard a knock at the door. I saw her walk across her living room toward the front door, look through the peephole, and drop her glass. She turned around and stared straight at the camera. From the look on her face, whatever was on the other side had shaken her to her core. She opened the door to confront her visitor, and I spit out my water.

36

Six Months Ago—Margot

I PULLED BACK THE security latch and stared at my beautiful
Soren. I hadn't seen him in over a decade, but I dreamt about
him a lot. Sometimes he was standing naked in the ocean. I waded
toward him, but as I reached out to touch his glistening skin, a
wave swallowed him up and pulled him out to sea. I'd never loved
anyone like Soren. And then I threw him away.

"How did you find me?" I heard myself ask.

Soren didn't meet my gaze. Instead, he looked past me into my
apartment. He was jittery, practically bouncing on his heels. "Can
I come in?" he asked.

I opened the door wide, and he strode past me into the living
room. Broken glass crunched under his heels. "I dropped a glass,"
I explained. He didn't seem to hear me.

Soren was fidgeting nervously. The years hadn't been kind to
him. He was thinner and looked malnourished. His once glowing
face had dulled, and his ruddy complexion had turned yellow-
gray. I noticed several small scabs on his cheeks and watched him
absent-mindedly pick at his face. It reminded me of a sculptor I
knew who developed a meth problem. Was that what was going
on? I didn't know why he was here, but from his body language,

I could tell that seeing me again was just a means to an end. I felt very, very sad.

"Have a seat," I said, gesturing toward the table. I could think better if he stopped moving. The jittering was making me nervous. "You want a drink?"

Soren nodded, and I poured us each a glass of Jameson. I caught a whiff of myself and realized that on top of everything, I smelled. It had been a couple days since I showered. "Ice?" I asked. He shook his head. I set the glass in front of him and watched him down it in one gulp. "Thanks, Margot," he said. The coldness in his voice cut me to the quick.

"What are you doing here, Soren?" I asked. "I haven't seen you since you told me off more than a decade ago, and now here you are—at my door unannounced. What's going on?" For years, I'd imagined what I'd say to Soren if I ever saw him again. In my mind, I was at my best. Beautiful, witty, and full of life. In my mind, he was healthy and had carved out a niche for himself in the world. But here I stood, unwashed and drinking with this shell of a man.

"I called," he said. "You didn't pick up."

I heard myself laugh. "That was you?"

He nodded.

"What's going on, Soren? Why are you here?" I repeated.

He looked over at the whiskey bottle. "This is hard to say. Can I have some more?"

I pushed the bottle toward him. He could pour it himself. This was getting more pathetic by the second, and my sadness was quickly turning to anger. "Easy, tiger," I said as he downed his second drink.

"I'm at the end of my rope, Margot. I need money."

The bluntness caught me off guard, and I laughed. He slammed his glass on the table and met my gaze with narrowed eyes that scared me. I'd never seen that expression on his face before, even when I broke his heart. It sent a chill down my spine.

"I lost my job. I'm thirty-nine years old, living in a garage, and I don't even know if I can pay my rent, let alone buy paint.

It doesn't have to be money; just give me a painting. Something I can sell."

I snorted. "What are you on, Soren?"

He glared at me. "That doesn't matter; something to take the edge off. This isn't easy, you know."

"Poor baby," I heard myself say, my voice dripping with contempt. There was a time when I would have given him a kidney, a lung—hell, an eye. But for him to show up here out of the blue, without so much as a *Hi, how are you?* and beg for money like he was entitled to it? I used to be everything to this man. Now, apparently, I was a meal ticket.

Soren glared at me. "Stop it," he growled. "You sit there judging me when everything came so easy for you. You were on the cover of *Artforum* at twenty-seven while the rest of us were down in the trenches. Everything just fell in your lap."

I picked at a hangnail to avoid looking at him.

"Do you hear me, Margot? I'm gonna be out on the street. Just give me one painting—it would change my life."

"Everything I have, I worked for," I said coolly.

"Bullshit," he snapped. "We all worked hard—you just got lucky." Soren got up and walked over to my easel, which was facing away from him. He spun it around and stared at the canvas. "I could make this," he said. "It's no better than the portraits I did of you in grad school. It's not talent, Margot. The art world needs stars, and you were in the right place at the right time. And you weren't afraid to turn on the charm when you needed to. Just give me that painting. You'll never miss it."

He almost spat the words *turn on the charm*, and I read his message loud and clear: I was just a no-talent whore who slept my way to the top. I'd learned to ignore that kind of misogynistic bullshit, but hearing it from a man who had loved me enough to propose, who used to stare at my canvases in wide-eyed amazement and tell me I was brilliant . . . For years, I'd clung to my memory of him as proof that there are good people out there—real artists and lovers who aren't tainted by selfishness and cynicism. He'd destroyed that illusion in ten minutes.

A dam inside me burst, and the anger rushed out. "I'm not going to be lectured in my own home by a beggar looking for a handout. And you're right, Soren. That one isn't my best. It does look like your mediocre art school studies." I walked over to my bar, picked up a metal cocktail stirrer, and drove it into the painting. I pulled down as hard as I could, ripping through the thick canvas. I stared into the Jolly Rancher eyes. There was something exhilarating about destroying your own work, your own image. I raised my hand above my head and brought the stirrer down into the painting again, ripping through the fabric to form a clean, X-shaped hole.

I wrenched my hand back a third time, but Soren caught my wrist. "Get the fuck off me," I said, pulling myself free.

"Stop," he pleaded. "If you don't like it, give it to me. Even with the hole, it's gotta be worth something. Margot, you don't need the money. I read up on your auction figures. You could doodle a picture of your tits on a cocktail napkin and it'd go for six figures."

I winced at his analogy. Soren was never vulgar. He respected women. Who was this person in front of me? I felt like crying, and I was not going to give him the satisfaction of seeing me in tears. "Get out," I said.

Then, to my horror, he literally got down on both knees and begged. "Please, Margot, you owe me this. You broke my heart. You left me high and dry so you could go fly around the world and get famous. I loved you, and you threw me away because I wasn't useful anymore. It's okay. Water under the bridge. But you owe me this. One painting. A drawing even, and I'm out of your life, like you wanted."

I wrenched the bottom of my robe out of his hand, reached down, and lightly smacked his cheek with the back of my hand. Like you'd smack a dog pawing at the remains of your dinner.

"Stop it," I ordered. "Get up. You're pathetic." I walked away toward my bedroom, trying to think of something to say that would be hurtful enough to make him leave. But I doubted I even had the capacity to wound him at this point. Life had drained away any reserve of affection he had for me, and that realization made me feel empty and alone.

I turned and faced him. He was slowly rising to his feet. "I didn't leave you because I'm some money-grubbing succubus. I left because in my heart, I knew you'd end up like this. A penniless loser nursing a mediocre talent who was too stupid to come up with a plan B. If you need money, go get a job at Walmart. I really don't give a shit. But stop begging for leftovers from your art school girlfriend. I'm sorry you're a failure, but you could at least hold on to your dignity. Now get the fuck out."

I turned my back on him and started toward my bedroom. As I gripped the handle, I heard rushed footsteps. I turned and saw him coming toward me, his eyes full of hatred.

37

Present Day—Kate

"WHAT DID YOU want to tell me?" asked Luke. He looked anxious, and I couldn't blame him. No one wants surprise information right before an operation.

"I found a video of Soren in Margot's apartment from the night of the murder," I said. "I think he killed her."

Luke smacked the table. "What do you mean you *think* he killed her? What was on the tape?"

We were sitting across from each other in his office. I'd gotten past my recent humiliation and agreed to meet at the station. I gave him a quick rundown of what I'd seen on the video. "Soren enters and Margot looks surprised. There's no sound, but they're clearly arguing. At one point, he gets on his knees like he's begging. Then she goes into her room and he follows her, but you can't see what happens on the other side. He comes out looking scared and makes a call. Then he just paces the room, checks his phone, and leaves the apartment. The tape cuts out a few minutes after he's gone. It must be on a timer or motion activated or something."

Luke's brow furrowed. I could tell he was trying to decide if he had enough for an arrest warrant.

"There's still too much doubt at this point," I said, answering his unspoken question. "He wasn't in there long enough to both kill her and fake a suicide. When he left, I think he went to let someone in—maybe Cy."

"It's enough to arrest him," said Luke. "I can haul him in and see what he has to say."

"And what if he doesn't talk?" I countered. "He's not stupid. That video alone isn't enough to convict him, let alone implicate anyone else involved. A defense attorney will argue that he was just visiting an old flame. Maybe something he said upset her enough that she killed herself. That's reasonable doubt right there."

Luke opened his mouth to say something, but I cut him off before he could argue. "Besides, the homicide case is officially closed. Let's say you do have enough for an arrest warrant. What then? You're not assigned to the murder investigation, and the warrant would never get approved by management. Bennett would see to that; it's his case. But you can send me in to chat with Soren as part of the forgery investigation. If I happen to find evidence that someone killed Margot, so much the better."

Luke sighed and ran a hand through his shaggy hair. I could tell he wasn't convinced.

"Even if I just ask Soren questions about the roommate relationship, that could help us build a case against Cy," I pressed. "Soren had a busted lip and a shiner when I saw him the other day. I want to know if he got that from Petrov or one of his psycho friends."

He shook his head. "I can't justify sending you to meet a murderer when we already have him on tape—especially looking like that."

I glanced down at my outfit. Jenny had dressed me. I wore a belted red dress that screamed sex, and flats in case I needed to run.

"Don't be a dinosaur, Luke. It's supposed to be a date. Besides, we're meeting in a crowded restaurant, and I won't go back to his place if something feels off."

Luke almost spit out his coffee. "That's not going to happen. You're not going into a killer's apartment with no gun—especially in your little dress when he thinks he's about to get lucky. That's a disaster waiting to happen."

"I'll make sure he knows he's not getting any."

Luke went silent and rubbed his temples. I stayed quiet to give him a chance to think. "I'll go along with the restaurant meet," he said finally. "It's a public place, and I'll be right outside. Get whatever you can and get out. But you're not going home with Soren. It's not happening. Are we clear?"

"Crystal," I said. I'd thought it over, and Luke was right. I didn't think Soren was a significant danger to me. He had no criminal record, and whatever he'd done to Margot was the product of a long and painful history. I wasn't the woman who broke his heart; I was just a random person he was dining with. But Soren's roommate and the bruiser with the gun were a different story. I couldn't risk encountering those guys, especially if there was a chance they'd recognize me.

When the time came, Luke had a female officer wire me up. Soren had suggested a Japanese hole-in-the-wall down the block from his apartment. He was probably hoping to parlay dinner into a nightcap. Luke dropped me off one street over so Soren wouldn't see me climb out of an unmarked van. "Remember," said Luke, "if anything goes wrong, just say, 'Everything's good,' and we'll be in there within a minute."

"Got it."

Luke handed me a small canister of pepper spray. "And take this. It'll fit in your purse."

I turned the pepper spray over in my hands. It was pink and rhinestone encrusted. "A very dignified choice," I said.

Luke shrugged. "I wanted it to look like something a civilian would keep for self-defense."

"Thanks." I reached up to pat him on the shoulder, and he moved in for a hug. Luke is not an emotionally demonstrative person, and I was taken by surprise. He felt good. I didn't want to let go. "See you soon," I said, pulling away.

I walked quickly down the street, toward the restaurant. I'd been there once before, years ago. The food was delicious, but more importantly, the service was slow, and the portions were tiny. I could always order one more thing to extend the conversation.

The place was half-empty, and the bored hostess was playing with her phone to pass the time. After checking me in, she led me past the sushi bar, where beautiful slabs of red tuna and fatty salmon were on display. Soren was seated at a dark booth toward the back of the restaurant. He lit up when he saw me. I felt sick.

When Soren got up to hug me, the chemistry I'd noticed before registered somewhere in my lizard brain. But now I knew he might have strangled a woman and left her hanging from a chain. And I had to act romantically interested—cling to his every word. I felt like one of those crazy women with an inmate fetish who mail their panties to serial killers. Soren kissed my cheek, and I repressed a wave of disgust.

I slid into the opposite side of the booth. The moist patch on my face where he'd kissed me burned.

"How was your day?" he asked.

I plagiarized one of Jenny's stories about a client who wanted her hair bleached three times until it was "Nordic white." The end result was the color of chicken fat and the texture of dead leaves, but the client was happy.

Soren laughed along pleasantly. His inhibitions were starting to lower. I ordered us a bottle of sake and told him I needed a few minutes to decide what to eat.

After the drinks came, I filled his glass and asked him about his childhood. People love talking about themselves, and it seemed like a safe place to start. He told a romantic story of growing up the son of Scandinavian immigrants in Maine. His dad was a fisherman who owned his own boat. I wondered why Soren hadn't just moved back and joined the family business when the art thing didn't work out. But some people are incapable of giving up a dream. Or maybe there had been a dark undercurrent in his childhood that he wasn't sharing. Either way, I didn't have time to dig deeper.

A waiter came and took our order. We selected several rolls to share and ordered another bottle of sake.

I refilled Soren's glass and looked up to find him staring at me. "Wait a minute," he said. "Didn't I see you at Bauman & Firth? Right before the Hamish Gunderson lecture?"

This was dangerous territory. I forced myself to smile. "You caught me," I said. "I recognized you, but I was too shy to strike up a conversation."

"But you did talk to me," he pointed out. "If you remembered me, why didn't you say who you were?"

I sipped my drink slowly, trying to think. I was one bad answer away from blowing my cover. "I was still dating my ex, and I didn't think an extended catch-up session with you would be good for the relationship. Plus I had somewhere to be. But I'm glad I did finally introduce myself." I refilled his glass. Time to change the subject. "Did you do any painting since I last saw you?"

He took the bait. "Yeah, I was surprisingly productive."

"I'd love to see your work in person sometime."

Soren's eyes lit up. He thought I was pushing for an invite. I hadn't meant it that way, but I did want to keep the door open.

"Do you live alone?" I asked.

Soren's face darkened. "No, I have a roommate."

"Have you guys lived together long?"

"About five or six months." So, since right after the murder. Cy could have cleaned up Soren's mess and then forced him to work off the debt. "He's not here now, though. He's out of town for a couple days."

Soren was letting me know we'd have the place to ourselves. Maybe I should finagle an invitation after all. My biggest concern had been running into his psycho roommate, but I felt pretty confident that I could handle Soren on my own. So far, he'd been easy to manipulate with a smile and a few lines of flattery. And if anything happened, Luke was just minutes away.

"Oh yeah? Where is he?" I asked.

Soren shrugged. "In Vegas, taking care of some business."

Half of their shell companies were incorporated in Nevada. It made sense that Cy would have to go there from time to time.

"Did you guys know each other before you became roommates?" I asked.

"Yeah," said Soren. "We met at an art fair and became gym buddies." His back had stiffened, and he was looking down at his hands, which were clasped together tightly. The ease of our prior conversation was gone, but I still had more questions.

I put one hand over his, suppressing a gag reflex. He looked up in surprise. It was the first time I'd initiated physical contact. "Soren, do you guys get along?"

He looked away but didn't move his hand. "He's kind of a volatile guy."

"Did he do this to you?" I asked, reaching up and gently touching his swollen cheek.

Soren grimaced and downed his glass of sake. "We got into it over something. It's hard to explain."

I'll bet.

He sighed deeply and looked at the wall. "Can we talk about something else?" The table was vibrating ever so slightly, and I could tell he was nervously bouncing his leg up and down. I needed to be careful not to push too hard.

"Of course," I said, stroking the side of his hand with my thumb. I sensed a jolt of electricity run through him. This was someone who'd been deprived of physical tenderness for a long time. I looked down at his hands and imagined them wrapped around Margot's neck, snapping her hyoid bone and compressing her carotid artery until she passed out. He suddenly took one of my hands in his, and I panicked. I needed to get out of there.

"I have to run to the restroom," I said, forcing a smile. I slid out of the booth and speed-walked toward the back of the restaurant.

A waiter gave me a funny look as I pushed on a door leading to the kitchen. "Bathroom's by the front entrance," he told me. I smiled and hurried in the other direction. I could barely see where I was going. I just needed a moment alone to steady myself. It was a single-stall bathroom, thank god.

Resting both hands on the sink, I stared at myself in the mirror. My heart was beating a mile a minute. I splashed cold water on my face and then carefully dabbed at the mascara under my eyes, which was starting to run. "You got this," I told myself. I reapplied the lipstick Jenny had given me and took a deep breath.

I could end this quickly. Ask a few more pressing questions, thank Soren for dinner, and get out of here. But I owed it to Milt and Margot to solve this case. Margot had been abused and mistreated for years. Then, to top it off, someone had killed her and hung her from the ceiling like a grotesque Christmas ornament. Even after Margot died, Bennett had deprived her of the proper investigation she deserved. Her family was counting on me to get her justice. Soren's apartment could be an evidentiary gold mine. And this was my chance to get in there without encountering Cy.

Besides, my gut told me that Soren wouldn't hurt me. He was just a lonely, pathetic guy looking for companionship. I'd been in rooms with scarier people dozens of times when I was on the force. Granted, I'd always had my gun, but I'd never had to use it. Soren was attracted to me, which gave things a creepy edge. But how was that any different than being in Vice? When I was a rookie, they had me walking Figueroa Street in stilettos, waiting for johns and pimps to make contact. One of them had even pulled a knife on me. Soren seemed like a puppy dog compared to those psychopaths.

I took a deep breath, opened the door, and walking back to the table. A rainbow array of sushi now lay before us. "This looks awesome!" I said, although I didn't feel like eating.

"Yeah," Soren agreed. "Hey, listen, sorry if I got moody there."

I waved away his concerns. "No worries; I've had bad roommates before. And you're allowed to have moods."

He seemed to relax a little. My stomach was clenched into a ball of nerves, but I forced myself to eat and babble about how delicious everything was. "Tell me what you've been painting," I said. "Another portrait?"

Soren smiled. "Not really. I'm working on something new."

"I saw you were buying gold leaf at the store. I can't pretend I wasn't intrigued."

"Yeah, that's for the new project."

Well, that was something, at least. Almost no one uses the expensive material in this millennium. "Can you tell me about it? I'm dying of curiosity."

Soren refilled his sake glass. "It's in the beginning stage. I'm not ready to talk about it."

I helped myself to another dragon roll. "That's okay. It's cool that you found a way to make it as an artist. Most of us gave up long ago. How does it work? Do you have a gallery? Or a patron?"

"I'm supposed to have a solo show at a gallery called Finials," he said.

I felt a chill run down my spine. They'd found a new place to sell the forgeries, just like Mike had predicted. Aksel Berkland must be dead after all. "That's so cool! Where is Finials?" I repeated the gallery name to make sure it was clear on the wire.

"Downtown," he told me.

"When's your exhibit?"

"Not for a while. After I finish my current project. It's sort of a commission, you know?"

I nodded. His solo show was probably never going to happen. It was most likely just a shallow promise they'd thrown at him to keep up his energy, a sad little carrot that had carried him through the last six months. "Who's the commission for?" I asked.

Soren started to tense up again. "I can't really say. The client is very private."

"Now I'm intrigued," I teased.

He started fidgeting again. Maybe I was pushing too hard. I needed to do something to reel him back in. "Well, I don't know about this new project, but I love your old stuff. Would you ever draw me?"

"Sure," he said with a smile.

"What about tonight?" I imagined Luke ripping off his headset and cursing. He could yell at me later. I'd be fine, and he'd be there to back me up.

"Why not?" Soren wore the broad grin of a man who thinks he's about to get laid for the first time in half a year. He clearly thought the modeling was just a pretext. I started to panic.

"But I need to make something clear," I told him. "I just got out of a relationship, and I want to take things slow."

"Of course," he said, looking deflated.

"I don't feel ready to take my clothes off with anyone yet, even for a drawing." I'm never this direct in my personal life. It felt liberating in an awkward, cringey kind of way.

"Absolutely. I never thought otherwise," lied Soren. He spoke quickly, trying hard to cover up his obvious disappointment.

We finished our meal and left the restaurant. Soren grabbed for my hand as we walked down the street. His long, bony fingers felt powerful and kept bringing me back to Margot's last moments. I saw them curled around her throat. Then I felt the rough stump of his missing pinkie against my palm. I let go of his hand and pretended to scratch an itch on my cheek so it didn't look like a physical rejection.

As his building came into view, I wondered if Luke knew the address. I'd texted it to him, but he might be too mad at me to remember. I needed to get him that information so he could find me if anything went wrong.

"Oh wow," I said, "what's your address? A guy I used to date lives on this block."

"It's that yellow-brick one," said Soren, pointing to his place.

"Three nineteen?"

"Yeah."

"Yup, that's where he lived," I said into the wire. "He was on the second floor."

"Well, I'm on the fourth," said Soren. "So I doubt we'll run into him."

We walked up to the building, and I heard his keys jingle in the lock. My stomach knotted up as it suddenly hit home that I could be making a big mistake.

38

Present Day—Kate

S OREN PRESSED THE elevator button, and I swallowed hard. The doors opened right away, and we stepped inside. I didn't like the feeling of being alone with him in a confined space. He slipped an arm around my waist, and it took every ounce of my self-control not to stick my fingers between the elevator doors, pry them open, and run out of the building.

What if Soren was wrong about Cy's whereabouts? People's plans change. What if it was all a setup? Maybe Soren knew exactly who I was and two goons were waiting for me on the other side of his door. In my mind, I saw Margot swinging from a chain, and my hand involuntarily flew up to my throat. Dr. Greco had said strangulation takes eight to ten minutes. Could Luke get to me in time? What if I survived but ended up brain damaged from oxygen deprivation? This was a terrible idea.

I could hear myself breathing, faster and heavier than normal. It suddenly felt very warm in the elevator. Shit, I couldn't afford to panic right now. Soren was a sensitive guy, and he'd be able to tell. I stared at the slit between the two doors to steady myself and focused on my breathing.

Maybe I should bail while I still could. But that would make him suspicious and could place me in greater danger. Besides, Luke had my back. I had to trust him.

The elevators doors opened onto the fourth floor. Soren was starting to sense my anxiety. I forced a smile to keep up the pretext. "I'm excited to see your stuff," I managed.

Soren's unit was right across from the elevator. I needed to orient Luke in case he had to bail out my reckless ass. "Can you hear the elevator from your place?" I asked, for the benefit of the wire. "You're right across the way."

"Not usually," he told me. "I can from the living room, but I've learned to tune it out."

I followed him inside. The place had the air of a temporary setup, with cheap secondhand furniture and no attempt at decorating. It reeked of oil paint and turpentine. Three easels were set up in the living room. Two displayed finished-looking portraits of a nude woman. Soren had probably put them there for my benefit. The third easel was covered with a large piece of fabric. In the corner was a blue tarp concealing more canvases.

"What can I get you to drink?" asked Soren.

"Just water." I watched as he took a plastic bottle out of the fridge, staring at it the whole time to make sure he didn't slip something inside.

"Thank you," I said as he handed it to me. I went over to the finished paintings. "These are beautiful."

Soren beamed. "They're pictures of my friend Nathalie. I've been painting her for years."

"She's lovely. All that red hair."

I moved over to the third aisle and started to lift the cloth. "Don't!" cried Soren. He reached up and grabbed my hand. I stared up at him in surprise. He quickly let go and looked embarrassed. "Sorry, it's not finished, and I get shy about my work."

"I understand," I said. "I promise I won't judge, though, and I'm sure I'll love it."

He shook his head. "Some other time."

"What about those?" I asked, pointing to the tarp.

"Works in progress. Not for public display."

I walked over to the uncomfortable-looking couch and sat down.

"Let me go get my charcoal," said Soren. "I haven't drawn any-one from life in a while. It's tucked away somewhere in my room."

I smiled and watched him disappear. His room was on the other side of the apartment. If he had to find charcoal, it could take him a couple minutes to get back. I lifted the cloth cover-ing the canvas on the third aisle. There was an instant flash of gold, and I recognized Jason's style. I moved over to the blue tarp and peeked underneath. More fake Martinez paintings. About a half dozen canvases in various sizes were stacked on top of each other. In the very back, I saw a portrait of a woman who looked distinctly like Margot.

"What the hell are you doing?" asked Soren. His tone was ice-cold.

I spun around and saw him glaring at me. His shoulders were tense, and his hands were balled into fists. This was a version of Soren I hadn't encountered yet.

"I'm sorry," I stammered.

"I asked you not to look at those, and then I turn around for a second and find you snooping. What are you doing exactly?"

He was furious, and for the first time, I felt genuinely scared. I needed to appeal to his other side, the one I'd just spent two hours having dinner with. I willed myself to cry. It's an effective tool in undercovers, especially with men who have a sensitive streak.

"I'm sorry," I said, conspicuously wiping my eyes with my forearm. "I just think your work is beautiful, and I got curious. Now I've ruined everything."

Before I knew it, Soren had taken me in his arms. I wanted to push him off and run for the door. "It's okay," he said. "I'm sorry I overreacted. Please don't cry. It's okay. Just ask next time, yeah?"

I nodded, too weirded out to speak. And then I felt his lips brush against my hair. He was comforting me like I was a repentant little girl who got caught with her hand in the cookie jar. This was turning into a freak show. "Can I use your bathroom?" I managed.

"Yeah, it's just down the hall."

I broke away from his embrace, found the bathroom, and locked myself inside. In contrast to the neat living room, the bathroom was gross, with beard shavings in the sink and dark yellow stains on the raised toilet seat. My hands were shaking. I took out my phone and saw a text from Luke. *Good?* It was from a minute ago. I was sure there was more he wanted to say, but he was probably worried that Soren might catch a glimpse of my screen. *Yes,* I typed back. *Half dozen fake Martinez paintings and one fake Starling.* I pressed send and then immediately deleted our message history.

I heard a knock on the bathroom door. "Julia, are you okay?" asked Soren.

"Yeah," I said. "Just give me a second." I flushed the toilet and washed my hands before opening the door. He was right on the other side. Whatever happened to privacy?

"I'm sorry I overreacted," he said again.

I forced myself to smile. "Water under the bridge."

"I was thinking I could draw you reclining on the bed," he suggested.

I'd completely forgotten that I was supposed to model for him. This was getting more demented by the second. What the hell was I even doing? My daughter was hiding at my mother's house after nearly getting kidnapped, and here I was posing for a potential killer. I need to stop acting like an adrenaline-addicted rookie cop with no dependents. But if I didn't find a way to get Cy and company arrested, how did I know they wouldn't kill me anyway? They'd killed Jason and possibly Berkland. There was no reason to think I'd be any different.

"I mean, you could pose with your clothes on," said Soren. "It just might be more comfortable." He must have noticed me looking anxious and thought it was his reference to the bed.

"You're the artist. Whatever you think is best."

I followed him into his room, which was right next to the bathroom. It was a little larger than a standard prison cell. He'd crammed in a twin bed, a tiny desk, and a child-sized dresser. There was one single-paned window with a view of the brick apartment building next door. I felt like I was back in a college dorm. My house was cramped, but it felt huge by comparison. It must be hard fitting your life into this space at Soren's age.

The bed was made, and he looked like he'd straightened up in anticipation of my arrival. "I know it's small . . ." he said self-consciously.

"Oh, Soren, I don't care about that," I assured him. I lay across the twin bed and realized that I didn't know the first thing about posing. That was probably something Julia-the-former-art-student would know how to do. I thought back to watching *Titanic* on repeat with Jenny as a tween. There's a scene where Leonardo DiCaprio draws Kate Winslet. I tried to remember her pose and stuck one arm behind my head dramatically. "How's this?" I asked.

"Perfect," said Soren.

He took out a pad of paper and a stick of charcoal and started sketching.

"So, when are you supposed to finish your special project?" I asked.

Soren put a finger to his lips. "No talking, I have to draw your face." Now I couldn't even probe for info. I flashed on Luke sitting outside in a van while I was being sketched by our prime suspect. Luke was going to kill me—if Soren didn't get there first.

"You have a beautiful neck," said Soren.

Of all the possible compliments from McSqueezy over here. "Thanks," I said.

He put a finger to his mouth again, leaving a small mark of charcoal on his upper lip. "No talking."

I lay there for what seemed like forever. The blood drained from my upper arm, and I could feel my fingers going numb. My neck and lower back throbbed from the lack of motion. How was I going to extricate myself from this ridiculous situation?

There was a sudden jangle of keys in the door, and Soren sat up, ramrod straight. "Oh my god, he's here. He's back early!" Soren looked absolutely terrified. "You need to hide. Can you get in the closet?"

"Excuse me?"

"It's my roommate. He's supposed to be out of town. He's a violent psychopath, okay? I'm not allowed to have visitors. Please, just get in the closet. I'll distract him so you can escape. It's not safe."

Violent psychopath? I'd figured out that Cy was dangerous, but those words still had a terrifying ring. "Okay," I whispered. I hopped off the bed and did as I was told, leaving the closet door open a crack so I could listen.

"Hey, Picasso, get your ass out here!" called another male voice.

"Coming!" stammered Soren. What the hell had I just walked into?

"What's all this girly shit? We're having a Martinez show in a week, and you're behind schedule."

"I'm sorry, Cy, I was just taking a break."

I heard the sound of flesh smacking against flesh. "You can take a break after everything's done. What's with the charcoal? Martinez didn't use it. You're getting sloppy."

"I was just doodling, Cy."

"You don't do that anymore. We cleaned up your mess, remember? We own you."

"I haven't had a break in months," Soren protested.

"You want me to call Dima?" asked Cy.

"Please don't call Dima," Soren begged. He sounded petrified.

"Dima's gonna be mad, and when Dima gets mad, he cuts fingers. You think you can paint with just your toes?"

"I'm sorry, Cy. It won't happen again."

"Damn straight. Now you're gonna get back to painting, and I'm gonna watch you."

"Now?"

"Yes, now."

A white glow emanated from my purse. I pulled out my phone and saw a text from Luke: *WTF is going on?* I called him, which was risky but faster than texting. "Cy came home," I whispered. "I'm hiding in the closet. He's forcing Soren to paint and threatening to cut off his fingers."

"I'm coming in," said Luke. "I'll be there in five minutes."

"Okay," I said. "Fourth floor, across from the elevator."

I heard footsteps approaching and snapped the phone closed. The door to the room swung open, and I watched through the crack as Cy and Soren walked in. "Where's the weed?" asked Cy.

"I'm getting it." Soren's voice had jumped an octave.

"What is this shit?" asked Cy, turning to my portrait. "Was someone here?" He grabbed Soren by the neck and shoved him against the wall. Soren shook his head vigorously. "I was drawing from a photo. I haven't had a woman over in six months, you know that."

Cy let go of him and laughed contemptuously. "You needed a little inspiration to beat your meat? I guess whatever gets those creative juices flowing."

I shuddered. Whatever Soren had done, he didn't deserve this.

Soren retrieved some marijuana from the top shelf of his dresser, rolled a joint, and handed it to Cy, who lit it and inhaled deeply. "All right, now back to work. I'm gonna watch you paint."

They went back into the living room, and I could hear Soren fumbling with the easels while Cy berated him. Through the crack in the door, I noticed Soren's phone plugged into an outlet by the closet. I snatched it off the cord and touched the screen. Surprisingly, it didn't require a password. Soren might be a decent painter, but he was a lousy criminal.

I found a chain of messages between Cy and Soren. Cy had texted that morning that he was going to Vegas on business and would be back in two days. I wondered if his plans had changed or if this was a test that Soren had failed miserably. I kept scrolling until I found an exchange that made my blood turn to ice.

Cy: *Did you call the school yet?*
Soren: *Yes, but this is fucked up.*

Yes, Soren, it is *fucked up.* My sympathy for the pathetic asshole went out the window. Apparently they were the ones who
called my daughter's school. Soren clearly hadn't recognized me.
But there was a solid chance Cy knew what I looked like. I could
only imagine what he might do if he found me cowering in the
closet. Luke better hurry the hell up.

I still needed evidence of what happened to Margot and Jason.
I scrolled through various conversations about forged paintings.
Then I started reading older texts and found a link to an article
about Jason's death that Cy had forwarded to Soren. *Beautiful day
for a hike,* wrote Cy. *Back to work.* It was a clear message: *Don't
fuck with us or you'll end up like your predecessor.*

I needed to get out of here before I got myself killed. I started
to put Soren's phone back when I heard Cy announce, "I gotta
take a shit."

"Okay," said Soren, "I'm gonna get some more blue paint. I
have another tube in my room."

Two sets of footsteps were approaching. I slipped Soren's phone
into my purse. The closet door swung open. "Now's our chance,"
whispered Soren, "you gotta go."

I would have rather waited for Luke, but I couldn't exactly tell
him that. "What about you?"

"I'll be fine. Just go—now."

I tiptoed into the hall, but the floorboards creaked under my
weight. "Who's there?" shouted Cy. I bolted for the door. Leaping
across the hallway, I hit the elevator button a half dozen times. I
could hear the machine slowly grinding upward. Not fast enough. I
reached into my purse and pulled out the pink pepper spray canister, clutching it tightly in my hand.

The elevator arrived, but as I stepped inside, the apartment
door swung open. Cy ran into the hallway, holding a pistol.

As he came toward me, I reached out and sprayed a stream of pepper spray into his eyes. He screamed and took a step back. I got back in the elevator and pressed the close button. My eyes burned from the cloud of pepper spray. It coated my throat as I breathed, setting my lungs on fire.

The doors started to shut, but Cy shoved an arm through and forced his way onto the elevator. The doors closed behind him, and the machine groaned to life.

Cy pointed the gun directly at my face. "Who are you, and what did you hear?"

I had to gamble that he wouldn't shoot me in the elevator. The noise would cause someone to call the police, and their living room was full of forged paintings. But if he could get me back in that apartment, anything was fair game. He reached for the buttons, and I shoved my entire body against his arm, pinning it against the wall.

Out of the corner of my eye, I saw a flash of silver as Cy's arm came down toward my face. I reached up to deflect the blow. White-hot pain radiated through my forearm as I heard the hollow thud of metal on bone. I reached up with my other arm and pepper sprayed him again. In the confined space, I might as well have sprayed us both. He cried out and stumbled back.

The elevator doors finally opened, and I lunged forward. Cy grabbed the fabric of my dress, pulling me back inside.

"Don't move!" shouted Luke. "Drop your weapon."

Cy tried to close the doors, but Luke forced an arm into the elevator. "Drop it," he repeated. Cy did as he was told.

Relief flowed through me as Luke forced Cy's hands behind his back. He walked Cy through the front door to the street, where a backup car was waiting. I followed behind, dabbing at my watery eyes. My throat burned, and my eyes felt like I'd mistaken hot sauce for contact solution. "Take him down to the station and put him in an interview room for me," Luke instructed a young patrol officer.

"What are we booking him for?" asked the officer.

Luke turned to me.

"He hit me with the gun and tried to keep me in the elevator—so you got ADW and attempted false imprisonment, at least," I said.

Luke winced at the mention of the blow. "Where'd he hit you?"

"Aimed for my head, but he got my arm."

"We got a 245(a)(2) and an attempted 236," Luke told the officer.

The patrol officer shoved Cy into the squad car. Cy turned to look at me and glared. I waved and blew him a kiss.

I felt a hand on my shoulder, and I swung around to face Luke. "You were never supposed to go in there!" he yelled. "Do you know how reckless that was?" He was shouting. I'd expected him to be pissed, but not like this.

"Nothing happened," I protested. "Soren said his roommate was out of town, so I thought it would be fine. But you didn't know what I was going to do. None of this comes back on you."

"That's not the point," he shouted. "You could have been killed, and then I'd have that on my conscience the rest of my life. And you lied to me."

"That's not true." My arm was throbbing, my eyes stung, and my throat felt like sandpaper. I didn't have the energy to deal with this. "I didn't plan on going in there until Soren told me he had the place to himself. I figured I could handle him." I felt water collecting again in my eyes, and I reached up to brush it away.

"Oh shit," said Luke awkwardly. He leaned in clumsily to try to hug me, and I realized that he thought I was getting emotional.

I pulled back and laughed. "I'm not crying, I have pepper spray in my eyes."

"Oh," mumbled Luke.

"Dude, I just had my portrait drawn by an overly sensitive murderer and then got pistol-whipped by a drunk mobster. Getting yelled at by you isn't gonna break me." Luke started to tense up. "Listen, I agree that I'm a jerk and I shouldn't have put you in that position."

Luke opened his mouth to speak, but I cut him off before he got the chance. "And I agree that I owe you a very large beer and an opportunity to yell at me to your heart's content. But for now, you have enough for a search warrant for that apartment, and," I said, "I have an idea."

"What's that?" grumbled Luke. Remembering that I was still wearing a wire, I fished my phone out of my purse, pulled up the text message screen, and started typing. My burning eyes strained to see as the letters blurred together. I held up the phone to Luke, who read it quietly. My meaning must have come through despite the typos, because I saw the corners of his mouth curl upward. I quickly deleted the message so no trail was left.

39

Present Day—Kate

L UKE HAD NO problem getting a warrant for the apartment.
Another fraud detective handled the search, freeing him up to
question Cy and Soren. Luke let me watch Soren's interrogation
behind a two-way mirror. It was a highly unusual move to let a
private detective—and an informant—watch the interview. We
got our fair share of side-eye, but Luke knew what he was doing.

Soren made a pitiful sight. His face was still bruised, and he
sat quietly with his cuffed hands resting in front of him on the
table. He had an air of resignation, like he was glad it was all
over. Luke strolled into the interrogation room and took a seat
across the table. He was carrying a water bottle, which he slid over
to Soren. "How's Julia? Did she get away?" asked Soren. I felt a
twinge of guilt. Then I remembered the text about my daughter's
school, and it evaporated.

"She's fine," said Luke. "Now I need to read you something."
He took out his Miranda card. Most cops just read the required
words, eager to move on to the next part of the inquiry. Half the
time they practically spit out the admonitions, an automatic signal
to the perp to shut up. Luke takes his time. He reads each advise-
ment slowly and then explains what it means. The message he

conveys is *I'm fair and reasonable and you can trust me* rather than *I'm trying to trick you into incriminating yourself.*

Soren didn't need much prodding. After six months of holding it in, guilt or fear or pure exhaustion finally bubbled over and the whole story came spilling out.

He'd met Cy at a local art fair. Cy claimed to be a frustrated artist who worked in a frame store, but it was clear in retrospect that he'd been sniffing around for Jason's replacement. Cy and Soren hit it off and started working out together. They became drinking buddies and started doing meth, supplied by Cy.

Then one day over beers, Cy said he might have a commission for Soren. Not for original work, just copying masterpieces, but hey, it was a paycheck, right? Soren had balked at the thought of making reproductions. Then Cy pressed him, asking him if he knew a single artist who made a living selling their own work. That's when Soren name-dropped his ex and everything cracked wide open.

Cy pressed him to ask her for a painting. Soren laughed it off, but Cy brought it up again the following week. This time Soren had just enough alcohol and meth in his system to consider it. And Cy had already looked up her address.

Even in retrospect, Soren didn't fully understand Cy's motives. Maybe he really thought Margot would give him a painting that they could sell for a small fortune. Maybe he wanted an example of her work and signature as a model for future forgeries. Or maybe he planned to kill her all along and threaten to frame Soren if he didn't agree to make fakes.

At any rate, the nagging worked. A drunk and high Soren stumbled over to Margot's place, cap in hand. Margot had laughed at him, belittled him. And with the combination of meth, disappointment, and sexual humiliation, he snapped. Soren strangled Margot until she passed out. In a panic, he called his buddy Cy and asked him what to do. Cy showed up with a two-man cleanup crew and a bag of supplies. Soren knew the other two other men only as Dima and Mischa. He described them in detail, and one sounded identical to the ogre who pulled a gun on me.

The three mobsters had disappeared into Margot's bedroom, according to Soren. A few minutes later, Soren heard her groaning. He tried to enter the room to see what was going on. But Cy pushed him out, lifting up his shirt to show the handle of a pistol.

Margot's death gave them a brand-new contemporary artist to forge. And after cleaning up Soren's mess, they owned him. They had a perfect recipe for making fakes. Soren could paint competent forgeries and supply a thin but plausible provenance as Margot's ex-lover and Jason's grad school friend. Soren's resistance to their scheme had been met with brute force. He raised his shirt to reveal burn scars that I could see from twenty feet away through glass.

At one point, Soren tried to run away, but they found him using a tracker they'd placed on his car. Dima cut off his left pinkie and warned him that next time it'd be his painting hand. They forced him to move in with Cy, who would keep watch over him. That's when Cy told him about his predecessor. He showed him a picture of a terrified Jason standing on the edge of a cliff. Soren got the message.

"Why do you think they went to such extremes?" asked Luke. "It sounds like babysitting you was a full-time job."

Soren shrugged. "Margot and Jason's real work sold for seven figures at auction. We sold the fakes for a fraction of that, but they still probably made millions off the forgeries. And they could transfer money back and forth without getting caught. It was a perfect system."

I'd been surprised at how easy it was for him to crack. But as he spoke, I realized the full horror of his situation. Cy and his crew were never going to let Soren go. He was their cash cow, and he knew too much. If he ever refused to pick up his brush, he'd end up at the bottom of a ravine, like Jason. Confessing must have felt like a way out. If Soren agreed to testify against Cy and company, he'd probably cut a deal for assault, serve a few years in protective custody, and then disappear into witness protection. It would be hard starting over as a penniless felon. But he'd have his freedom, his talent, and his remaining fingers.

I thought about Milt. Soren would get less time in custody than Milt probably wanted, but his arrest would bring some closure to the Starling family. I would explain the nightmare that Soren had gone through and how his prison time would be spent in solitary confinement to protect him from Russian mobsters. Despite everything that Soren had done, including strangling Margot until she passed out, he'd cared about her and never intended for her to die. Hopefully, after he served his time, he could find peace and some semblance of happiness.

The door behind me opened, and I turned around to see Bennett standing behind me. Right on schedule. "What are you doing here?" he snapped.

"Observing," I said. "I went undercover, and I'm watching as a professional courtesy."

"That's against protocol, but I guess the rules don't matter for Delgado's whore," he sneered.

"Actually, I've never been romantically involved with Detective Delgado," I said, more for the benefit of the recording device than Bennett. Fuck him, he could think what he wanted.

"Sure, Myles. Whatever you say. Well, I guess I better get in there. Glad your lover boy could warm him up for me." Bennett turned and reached for the door.

"You know," I said. "I went through Margot's things and found a video of her murder."

Bennett swung around and faced me. "I know—Delgado told me." I suppressed a smile. That was part of the plan, and Luke had delivered. I needed to establish credibility so he'd believe what I was about to say.

"You would have found it too if you'd done a real investigation. But I guess you had every incentive to keep things superficial."

Bennett let out a forced laugh. I was starting to get to him. "Did you pick up some tips on policing during your latest criminal stint?" he asked.

"You know what I haven't told Luke yet?" I continued. "I found a second video from about a week earlier: the last time Margot was scared enough to activate her security system. Can you guess what was on it?" No such tape existed, so far as I could tell, but he didn't need to know that.

Bennett's face blanched, and he stared at me with a look of pure hatred. It was enough to confirm what I already knew, but I needed him to admit it on tape. "Two cops start banging on her door, just like the neighbor said. Then Margot lets them in—an Asian cop and an ugly white guy with a cartoon tiger tattoo. Any idea who that could be?" I asked in mock ignorance. Bennett just stared at me. "Wanna know what happens next?"

"Are you threatening me?" he asked. It wasn't quite a confession, but it helped.

I smiled at him. "No, Bennett, I'm filling you in on the investigation—isn't that what you're here for? What do you think happens next?"

Bennett stepped forward until he was inches from my face. I could smell his cheap aftershave. "Listen to me, you dumb bitch. You're going to delete that, do you understand?" Now I had him on tape telling me to destroy evidence. But since there was no second video, I needed him to be more explicit about what happened that night.

"The tape shows you entering Margot's apartment—uninvited—and then hitting her. You didn't have to do that, Bennett. She was already scared."

"The bitch wouldn't listen. Something you should relate to." That was him acknowledging the assault. But it wasn't enough. I wanted Farabee.

"It didn't work, you know. She was still going to expose Captain Farabee and what he did to her. Last I heard, they're still going to out him as a sex offender at the Venice Biennale."

"It'll be the word of a crazy dead bitch over a respected police captain. No one would believe her even if she was alive—the girl carved herself up." He shook his head in disgust. "These days you sleep with a girl, and she calls it rape just to fuck with you. But no one's gonna believe an unstable freak like that."

I hadn't known what happened between Margot and Farabee, but I'd suspected as much. Whatever he did to her had been the catalyst for her restitution project. It had caused years of pain and trauma that she'd worked out in her own unconventional way, including with an X-Acto knife. There aren't too many things that can hurt someone like that.

With Margot dead, I doubted they'd be able to prove sexual assault. But it should be enough to start an investigation and lead them to her snapshots. Even if Farabee had had consensual sex with Margot when he was supposed to be investigating her for a crime, that should be enough to end his career.

"I've seen the picture of Farabee in flagrante," I told him. "Her dealer still has it on his computer. It ain't pretty."

"Listen to me," snapped Bennett. His index finger was pointed at my face, inches from my skin. The closeness was disorienting. I took a step back toward the wall, and he moved closer in my direction. "You're going to delete that recording and shut your mouth, or you'll have to watch your back every minute of the day. You know how easy it is to get into that shitty little house of yours?"

"Yes," I said. "I learned that the other day when you showed up at my door and grabbed me by the throat."

Bennett backed me up against the wall. My arms swung against the plaster, and I felt a searing pain where my right fore-arm had connected with Cy's gun. The pain and surprise caused me to cry out. "Get away from me!" I shouted.

His sweaty hand gripped my shoulder, hard. Normally I can take care of myself, but with the agony in my forearm, my defenses were down. I reached past him and banged on the two-way window as hard as I could. Pain radiated through my arm, and I felt a wave of nausea.

"Calm down," hissed Bennett. "I need to make sure I'm getting through to you. You need to drop this right now or you're gonna have all of RHD on your back." The door swung open, but not before Bennett had dropped his hands to his side.

"What's going on?" asked Luke.

"Thanks for your help, Delgado," said Bennett with forced calm. "I'll take it from here."

"Didn't you get the message?" asked Luke. "You're off the case. The FBI is involved now, and the Money Laundering Task Force is stepping in."

"What the fuck are you talking about?" asked Bennett. He looked down through the glass for the first time, where Gus Vargas had laid a six-pack in front of Soren, who was nodding and circling one of the faces.

"Soren is cooperating in a racketeering case. You can go talk to Lieutenant Sanchez if you want it more official. His office is down the hall. But you're off the case."

"This is bullshit," said Bennett. "No one said anything to me."

"We've been a little busy," replied Luke. "And it appears that you might have a conflict of interest, so it's better if you don't have any more involvement in the investigation." Luke turned to me. "Did you guys have a nice chat?"

"We did," I said. "Very informative."

Bennett looked back and forth between us. His eyes showed genuine fear as he started to realize he'd been set up. "People are going to hear about this," he said.

Luke smiled at him. "Yes, Bennett, they will."

Unsure what else to do, Bennett turned and walked out the door. As soon as he was gone, Luke removed the recorder from an empty Styrofoam coffee cup and switched it off.

"Did he talk?" asked Luke.

I nodded. "Tacit admissions to hitting and threatening Margot. He threatened me and ordered me to destroy evidence and even used the word *rape* in connection with Farabee. You got him on assault and a couple counts of witness dissuasion. He's done. And I think there's enough for IA to start looking into Farabee."

"Fantastic," said Luke. "Are you okay?" My hair had gotten tousled in the struggle with Bennett, and a lock had made its way into my eyes. Luke reached over and tucked it behind my ear. I looked up, and our eyes met. Neither of us said anything for several seconds.

"Yeah," I said. "I'm fine. I need to get my arm checked out, though."

Luke's hand dropped down and rested on my upper arm. I felt my pulse quicken. "I can have someone from patrol drive you to the hospital," he offered.

I shook my head. "I'd rather go on my own steam."

"I'd take you myself, but I gotta get back in there."

I nodded. "Don't worry about it."

"And I'll call you tomorrow about Bennett after I've listened to that recording."

"Sounds good."

"Myles," said Luke. "When all this is over . . ." We looked at each other silently, his eyes registering a hunger that I hadn't noticed before.

He didn't finish his sentence, and he didn't have to. I knew what he meant. We couldn't start anything now. I was a witness. If some defense attorney asked, he needed to be able to testify under penalty of perjury that our relationship was strictly professional. "Yeah," I said, my heart pounding. "When all this is over."

EPILOGUE

"P ASS THE BLUE," said Amelia, pointing to the fabric marker by my elbow.

My mother clucked disapprovingly. "Say please," she scolded. Amelia rolled her eyes but complied. I handed my daughter the marker, and she began the thankless task of coloring in blue sky on a stretch of white cloth surrounding two stick-figure princesses and a shaggy dog. Next to her, my mother was carefully drawing an impressively neat bouquet of pink and red tulips.

T-shirt making had seemed like a fun thing we could do together and a fitting end to my recent exploration of the art world. With my forearm still in a cast, my own participation was limited to left-handed squiggles and lopsided hearts and stars. Not that I could have done much better with my right hand. It didn't matter: this masterpiece would be confined to the pajama drawer and never see the light of day.

"Why don't you add some white clouds?" I suggested. "So you don't have to color as much." The cheap blue marker was already starting to run low, leaving faded streaks on the cotton. Amelia looked confused.

"Let me show you, honey," said my mother. She took the marker from my daughter and drew in the outline of several big, fluffy clouds. "Just color in around them. You'll have less to do." My daughter gave a satisfied nod and went to work scribbling in areas surrounding the loopy shapes.

The timer went off on my phone, and I noticed the tantalizing aroma of freshly baked cookies. They were premixed—the kind where you pull little clumps from a smushy tube of dough and slap them on a pan. It wasn't exactly Martha Stewart material, but I think I deserve some props for one-handed baking. I put on an oven mitt shaped like a bear claw and pulled the pan out of the oven. My daughter squealed and clapped her hands in anticipation.

"Not yet," I cautioned. "They have to cool." Ignoring my own advice, I broke a little piece off a funky-looking one, gave it a perfunctory blow, and popped it in my mouth, immediately scorching the tip of my tongue with molten chocolate.

I ran my wounded tongue along my palate and sat back down at my mother's kitchen table. This would be my second week staying with her, and claustrophobia was starting to set in. I'd met with Angela's friend, the family law attorney. She thought I had an excellent shot at joint custody. The problem was, I had no money in my bank account, and John would never agree to share Amelia without a fight. Jenny had suggested that I move in with my mother for now and list my place on Airbnb. It turns out you can actually make money renting out a one-bedroom shack with no central air in Los Angeles. The plan was to do this for six months. By then, my diversion would be almost complete, and I'd have enough money to fight John in court. Just five and a half months to go . . .

In addition to no privacy, living with my mother came with a whole set of rules. Her requirements included a decree that couches must be covered in protective plastic, a specific guide to loading the washing machine, and a prohibition on alcohol in the house. This last rule was left over from my dad's retirement years, when beer drinking in front of the TV had gotten excessive. I couldn't complain; this was her house. And frankly, that last rule was probably for my own good. If I was ever going to get Amelia back, I needed to truly get it together.

My life was pretty much on pause, but that wasn't necessarily a bad thing. It gave me time to regroup and plan for the future. I let my mind wander forward to next year. If things went according to plan, I'd be living in my house with my daughter. Cy and Dima's trial would be over, and maybe Luke would be back in the picture. He'd been calling once a week or so to check up on me. Of course, six months is a long time, and Luke's always been popular with the ladies. I guess we'll see what happens.

I walked back over to the stove, scooped several cookies onto a little plate, and brought them over to the table. Amelia immediately grabbed the top one and bit into it, leaving a healthy chocolate smear on her chin. My mother dipped a napkin in her water glass and tried to wipe Amelia's chin, but she squirmed out of reach. I smiled, surveying the scene. Things were definitely in flux, but for the first time in quite a while, I felt confident that they were getting better.

ACKNOWLEDGMENTS

I'D LIKE TO thank:

Ben Leroy and the team at Crooked Lane for taking a chance on an unknown writer from the slush pile. Sara J. Henry for making WMTE a better book, and Rachel Keith for detailed and thoughtful copyedits.

Freddie and Nicole for instilling in me an early obsession with art and books. Mike, for teaching me the value of hard work and always putting his children first.

DW for letting me carve out a space to paint and write, for reading an obscene number of drafts, for spending countless hours toddler wrangling while I worked on this book, and for many, many other things. Zelda for regular snuggles and for not eating the baby. Christina for providing wonderful care to OW.

My art and art history professors at Penn for teaching me to think and write critically about art.

The brilliant Jess Righthand for early feedback and Annie Hogsett for generous advice about the book world.